Cynthia Rosi was born [...] the age of twenty, she moved to London and she has lived in the UK ever since. Having worked as a journalist for newspapers and magazines, Cynthia turned to writing fiction. *Motherhunt* is her first novel.

Cynthia lives in Bedfordshire with her husband, Paolo, and two young children.

Motherhunt

Cynthia Rosi

HEADLINE

First published in 1998
by HEADLINE BOOK PUBLISHING

First published in paperback in 1998
by HEADLINE BOOK PUBLISHING

10 9 8 7 6 5 4 3 2 1

ISBN 0 7472 5911 9

Printed and bound in Great Britain by
Mackays of Chatham PLC, Chatham, Kent

HEADLINE BOOK PUBLISHING
A division of Hodder Headline PLC
338 Euston Road
London NW1 3BH

Thank you to Paolo, Kelly King, Stephanie Cabot, Clare Foss, Rhian Lewis, Timothy Sagosz and Joan Deitch for support and advice; to Charlotte and Bill for the gift of imagination; to Nonno and Grandma Gaynor for giving me the time to write; and to my Women Writers Network friends, especially Sally Jayne, Mary Querida and Laura.

A portion of the author's income from this book
is donated towards the American Indian Trust, Bristol,
a registered charitable foundation based in the UK. It
promotes Native American culture and information from
a Native perspective through the development of arts,
crafts, languages, music and dance. For further information
about the AIT, contact its president, Carlisle Antonio,
on 0117 942 6437.

Prologue

Patrick's dreams plagued him.

In his dreams he was a boy, ten years ago when his family had lived in London. His mother, alive, rushed ahead of him, her legs in jeans scissoring along, the rubber soles of her tennis shoes making sucking sounds against the pavement slabs. He tried to keep up, but his short legs made him stumble. 'Mommy, stop!' he screamed, but she didn't listen. She hurried away until, like a cartoon, she fell under the horizon and disappeared.

He sat down on the strange pavements of a strange city, lost and crying, while English strangers walked by. Far away he heard her calling, as if they were playing hide-and-seek: 'Come find me! You have to find me!'

At the sound of her voice he turned back into his young-man self.

Then he'd be in their Victorian house in north London trying to scramble out of the loo window, his bulky shoulders stuck, trying to wriggle and push himself through, trying to catch his mother leaving through the garden gate, her back always turned towards him, even her smell slipping away from him.

Patrick wanted to understand his dreams. He had to make them stop.

1

* * *

Kitsy went to make a cup of tea. In the kitchen she checked the back door locks, the window locks, and the lock on the toilet window. If the young man on her doorstep didn't go away by the time she'd drunk her tea, she'd call the police.

She left the tea on the kitchen breakfast bar, went back to the sitting room and stood behind the net curtains so that he couldn't see her. It began to rain. The young man didn't step forward under the eaves. The rain clung to his black hair in bright, dainty droplets. Then it hit harder, faster, bigger until runnels channelled over either side of his straight, high-bridged nose, until four streams of water coursed over his wide lips, clung to his hard-cut chin and joined in a river down his throat, down each muscle standing out in his neck.

He closed his eyes so that the water running off his hair, water no longer contained by the dam of his long black brows, wouldn't pool into his eyes.

Kitsy watched his T-shirt turn from white to transparent, his jeans from blue to indigo. They stuck to his thighs. His shirt pasted against his chest: tanned, and hairless, hard and looped with muscle. Kitsy watched.

She wondered if he slept there, standing up.

She felt cornered. Cornered and scared. She crept into the kitchen, past the windows, and took the butcher's knife out of the block, laying it on the breakfast bar. Feeling both ridiculous and afraid, she grabbed the yellow kitchen curtains, one edge in each fist, and yanked them shut. In the shadow of her fabric shield Kitsy climbed onto a barstool, hitched the stool sideways, and like an old biddy peeped out at the garden gate. She hadn't touched her tea going grey and cold.

Finally she decided she had to move for Lucy's sake. The baby would wake up from her nap soon. That the young man might trap Lucy indoors made Kitsy angry. She strode through her house to the front room and pulled back the nets.

The young man had gone.

Kitsy took out a pen and a piece of paper from the sideboard to write down his description in case she had to tell the police.

Patrick didn't expect it would be easy. But he had to try to introduce himself to the woman living in his mother's London house. He'd fucked up, felt like a fuck-up standing there getting wet. Take it slow – that would be the key. But first to find a place to sleep.

Patrick remembered his mom taking him to a park near here. Playing soccer on the giant lawn. Thick cedar trees. A stately home, its outbuildings in ruins. He would need to keep his little money for food. Shelter had to be free.

Maybe now his dreams would end.

CHAPTER 1

Iktome Interferes

The cuts along the tip of each finger on his left hand were like paper-cuts but thicker. Knife-cuts, and the knife razor-sharp: a hunting knife, a Bowie longer than his hand meant for skinning bear and deer, for slitting brown pelts from red flesh. On the other side of the knife was a bottle opener and a serrated edge for scaling fish.

In a house little more than a shack, Patrick sat in a steel chair with a cracked plastic seat. He played with the knife, stropping it on his arm, up and down in slow beats. In the summer after graduation from West Seattle High he swigged at a bottle of Jim Beam and let the slow warmth spread through his stomach on its way to his head.

The cuts on his fingertips were beginning to close up. Drying blood made red spiderwebs of his hands. There was blood on the yellow plastic tabletop, blood drying into orange smeared into yellow.

Patrick remembered how he and Jimmy McPherson would hide in the bushes, take out their penknives and cut their index fingers to mix their blood. Jimmy said because Patrick was half-Sioux Indian it really did make them blood brothers, that it wouldn't have counted if they'd both been Irish like Jimmy was.

Now Patrick turned his forearm over and started stropping from his wrist to his elbow. He played with the knife, felt its power over him, tempted that power. At first he stropped slowly. Confident. He was equal to the knife. They were old collaborators. His power was the knife's power; he drew power from the steel, from the leather hilt, from the slip and smell of his bright blood. With the knife he was more than Patrick.

He made the first cut high up, at his elbow. By the time he finished the rungs of this ladder, he would be at his wrist. The point of the knife would reach deeper until he could twist out Patrick with that point, like shucking an oyster, releasing the jelly of his soul from its shell.

Shallow. No sting. He thought it would sting, but it didn't. Everything in the room was at an incredibly numb distance, and he was at a numb distance too, as if he watched himself make these incisions from a place near the ceiling. The blood showed its bright eyes at the opening of skin. 'Hey! Let's party!' it called. The droplet became a trickle of warm that slid to the table.

He could hear Charlene batting a tennis ball against the house. If he stood up he could look out the window over the sink and see the top of her head, shiny straight dark hair, and the tennis racket, wooden, loosely strung, see its head rise and swoosh, rise and swoosh.

Louder than the whop of the ball was a throbbing roaring in his ears, a throbbing which had been building up to this aching crescendo since yesterday. He'd felt it in his chest, squeezing. He'd felt it behind his eyes, and as a tight pain in his throat. He felt so incredibly alone and so huge with his aloneness, his aching emptiness, that it was difficult to move through life any more, push against the Jello of things he had to do every day: eat, brush his teeth, get in and out of bed. It engulfed him, sent everything to the distance. Now it had swallowed up his anger, and he had to make it stop before everything in his grey soul got sucked down a hole, the oyster sliding down a night-black throat.

He'd hunted out the knife and the whiskey and sat down.

Patrick didn't feel part of his sister. He saw himself as a car battery. First, the spark plugs had been disconnected, one by one, and then the alternator cable, and then the positive and negative battery cables themselves so that he sat there, alone, and powerless over being alone, and powerless to release his power, to make things move.

Now his questions would go away. He didn't have to worry about whether he would ever be a normal guy.

Charlene called to herself: 'Miss Mary Mack all dressed in black with silver buttons up and down her back,' and at each 'ack' the ball thumped against the aluminium siding.

Patrick made a second cut. He began to think about his mother, his slender, short, black-haired mother always smelling of sage. Now his heart-aching dreams of her would stop. Now he would find her, tell her how he won the Cross Country Championship for her. He should have been more organised about this, should have gone around collecting family gossip. She'd want to catch up. He'd want to give her a present.

The third cut. A small, quick movement caught the corner of his eye. A spider, a house spider, fat with ants and potato bugs from a winter spent in the woodpile, its legs spread two inches at least, walked across the kitchen floor.

'Fuck off,' said Patrick.

The spider didn't move. Didn't twitch a leg or scuttle into a hole. It stood and stared at Patrick, at his silver and red blade, at his bloody arm. Patrick stamped at it with his foot. The spider moved out of reach.

'If you listen quiet enough you can hear them speak,' his mom would say when spiders came up through the drains into the tub. 'Iktome is a troublemaker with a sense of humour. That's why it's bad luck to kill his kids. It's better to catch them on a piece of paper and throw them outside. Then they're out of your way and can't cause any trouble.'

His mother had said those things when he was small, almost too small to remember – certainly other kids wouldn't have. When he got older and could read thick books with no pictures, he borrowed *Indian Myths and Legends* from the school library, kept it in his locker and read it during rainy-day recess. How Ikto and his friend Coyote were always trying to fool the *winchinchala*, the pretty girls. How their wives were always trying to stop them.

For Patrick, although these stories weren't spoken, were encrusted into a book, even so they were more believable somehow than the Bible, more immediate and lifelike, so that when he saw a spider, instead of stamping on it like the other boys, he'd get down on his stomach, eyeball to eyeball.

Once, when his father had Patrick cornered in the bedroom, had raised his open hand to clobber him, a spider scuttled between them and climbed his father's jeans. Patrick watched its eight legs crawl the vertical up to his father's knee. His father followed Patrick's stare and yelled: 'Jesus God, get off me!'

The spider scurried up the Reverend Frank's thigh and he backed up, hopping, shaking his leg to knock it off. He jumped around the room too afraid to brush it off with his hand. Patrick ran out the door and into the yard, went to Jimmy Mac's house for dinner and got Jimmy's mom to take him home.

The next day, his father bought a flea bomb at the pet store to fumigate the house. It didn't work. The spiders lived there. They came back.

The slapping of the ball against the house stopped.

Silence. Patrick could hear the blood running through his body, coursing through his head.

'Trick!' shouted Charlene, excited. 'Trick, c'mere a sec! Look what I found!'

Annoyance. Patrick's whole being was annoyance. They wouldn't give him any peace. Not even twenty minutes of peace.

Charlene burst through the screen door, the aluminium banging behind her. 'I found three silver dimes in the bushes!' she yelled as she ran to show him three muddy coins. 'Oh my God! What've you done to yourself?'

'Get away from me, Charlene!' Patrick pointed the knife at her, swiped it in her general direction to scare her. She backed out of his reach. The coins fell, hit the floor in little tinkles.

Charlene ran into the living room and down the hallway. Patrick heard her dash into one of the bedrooms and the house fell quiet.

The fourth cut. Deeper this time. The other cuts were only scratches, surface wounds. Getting closer. Patrick held his arm over the coins, let the thin stream of blood cover them. He felt sleepy, triumphant. He watched the spider, stared it down. What power did the spider hold over him? None. The spider, Charlene, his father the Reverend – they were all nothing. He had the courage. He had the fight.

Charlene crept back down the hall, crouched next to the kitchen doorframe, used the wall as protection. She had to pee. Her heart banged against her chest so hard she was sure he could hear it. She poked the tip of a pellet gun into the kitchen and followed behind.

'Put down the knife, Trick,' said Charlene, 'or I'll shoot.' She felt so scared she could barely get the words out. If she hadn't heard them so many times on TV she wouldn't have been able to speak.

'That's dumb,' he said. 'Think about it.'

Charlene wasn't expecting an argument. She thought the gun would speak for itself. Patrick would put the knife down when he saw the gun. She wouldn't have to pull the trigger. She said: 'I don't see what's so dumb.'

'That's what's wrong with you. You don't think about stuff. I'm sitting here with a knife and you come along with this geeky little gun. Like I'm really scared, Charlene.'

Patrick brought the knife up to his arm. He placed its edge on the spot, the spot for the final cut. He'd have to go in deep now, to cut the vein. This was it. This one was for keeps.

The spider moved first. It ran as Charlene came out holding the gunbarrel like a baseball bat, swinging it at her brother. She smashed the side of his face with the butt, knocking him out of his chair, sending the knife skittering across the kitchen floor, a single red squiggle tracking its way.

'Goddamn you bitch!' yelled Patrick from the floor, holding his stinging face, his knees into his chest.

Charlene ran around the table and picked up the knife. She went to the knife drawer and scooped out all the kitchen knives as well. She ran into their room and pulled their bunkbeds from the wall and dumped all the weapons behind them. She stopped in the bathroom, gathering up a washcloth, some Bandaids and rubbing alcohol.

In the kitchen, Patrick sat up and leaned against a cupboard, his head thumping, his left arm aching. He felt weak. His little sister had stopped him. That little bitch! That nothing little bitch of a sister of his stopped him by bashing him over the head. Fucking who needs them anyway?

'Get the fuck away from me! Just get the fuck away!' he shouted at her when she came into the doorway, her arms full. Charlene sat crosslegged in the door, her long, brown-black hair a curtain over her face. She stood the bottle of rubbing alcohol on the floor, laid out the Bandaids in a row, folded the washcloth, everything as neat as a doctor's bag. 'Here,' she said, shaking back her hair and holding out a Bandaid in her hand. 'This is the biggest one.'

Patrick took it. He peeled off the plastic strips and stuck it on his arm over the last cut. The first cuts had begun to dry now, like the cuts on his fingertips. But the last cut still bled.

'Not like that, silly,' his sister said. She walked on her knees over to him, the bottle of rubbing alcohol in one hand and the washcloth in the other. She peeled back the strip, dabbed some alcohol onto the cloth, and cleaned the cut. He sucked in his breath. For the first time it stung, stung like hell. The sting sent away the numbness, called back his anger, called him to be Patrick again. Charlene pinched the two edges of the wound together as best she could and stuck the Bandaid down again.

Charlene felt afraid to say anything in case whatever she said set him off, sent him running through the house looking for his knife, or he might beat her up or lock himself in the bathroom with the razors.

'When's the Reverend home?' said Patrick. Since he was twelve he'd refused to call their father 'Dad'.

'Bible Study then Youth Club. Not until late.'

'What's for dinner?'

'Macaroni and cheese.'

'Let's have spaghetti.'

'OK.'

Patrick watched his sister take care of him, then wring out the washcloth in the sink and mop up the table, the chair, the floor, the blood over the coins. Charlene was drowned in her busyness. What would their father say when he got home? The mess had to be gone, and a long-sleeved shirt hunted out for Patrick's arm, a story made up about the red bruise on his cheek, the Jim Beam bottle hid, the kitchen sprayed with Glade.

'Do you remember Mom?' he said.

'Not much.'

'I keep having nightmares. She says she wants me to find her . . . but maybe . . . maybe it means find *out* what happened to her? I mean, she died over there and we came straight back home . . .' As Patrick said the words, he felt sure he was right.

'She just died.'

'Nobody *just dies*, Charlene. They have to die *of* something. Even if it was only a heart attack. Maybe she wants to be honoured by making me find out.'

Charlene shrugged. She wanted to say the right words, but didn't know what they were. 'Dad said she just died.'

'Dad said, Dad said. Like you believe everything the Reverend says? What's he ever done for us? We live in a shitty place on *food stamps*, for Godsake! If it wasn't for the money we get from the government 'cos Mom was Indian he wouldn't have a fucking cent!'

'So what are you going to do?'

'Go there.' Patrick didn't know why he hadn't thought of it before.

'What do you mean? To London?'

Patrick nodded.

'Where will you get the money?'

'I'll get it,' he said.

CHAPTER 2

Liars and Hypocrites

While his son was at home trying to kill himself, Frank
Hunter had just finished giving an after-lunch Bible Study
class at a church in the Admiral district. At the moment
Charlene pointed the pellet gun at her brother and told
him, 'Put down the knife, Trick or I'll shoot', Frank and
Bud Foster were folding up grey metal chairs and standing
them in a row at the back of the hall. They were clearing
up before Youth Club met at 3 p.m., a bunch of ram-
bunctious sophomores, juniors and seniors from West
Seattle High. It was the last day they would meet before
summer recess and Frank planned to talk to the kids about
their Contracts With Jesus, especially the ones going to
college next year.

Even though he'd aged, even though some of the years
had got him down, still Frank kept his battered Robert-
Redford looks, a thick thatch of blond hair, almost false for
a man with his wrinkles, the deep lines carved around his
mouth, his cheekbones cut higher by a slight slackening of
skin. Today he wore a white shirt with short sleeves, a navy
tie with thin white stripes done up tight to his throat, so
tight, like his view of the world, everything sifted through
the Bible verses he'd memorised. Frank wore jeans and

Nikes too because he wanted to be cool to the kids, show them he understood the rap. While he was with 'his' kids, Frank quoted verses as if they were solid objects, as if they were a string of beads, a gold cross he wore on a gold chain under his shirt. Genesis 1, verse 2. 2 Corinthians 12, verse 7. Gotcha.

'How's your kids?' said Bud.

It took Frank a moment to realise Bud referred to Charlene and Patrick. 'Yeah, they're fine, just fine. Charlene – I'm hoping she'll come this afternoon to sit in. I think she'll do a Contract.'

'Does she have a boyfriend?'

'She's coming up to that age. I want her to pledge her heart to Jesus before it's too late.'

'The ring comes off on her wedding day.'

'That's right. Until then their hearts and their bodies stay pure.'

'That's the theory anyway,' joked Bud.

Frank put down the chair he was carrying and stared at Bud. 'That's the *fact*,' he said.

At last week's potluck dinner, Bud had taken his plate of fried drumsticks and potato salad over to a corner of the hall at the base of a huge wooden pillar, a shaven and polished tree that held up the roof. He leaned against the trunk while he gnawed at the chicken and balanced his paper plate on a palm, a buffet-eating expert.

'You never see his kids here, you know,' said a voice. Bud looked around for the owner, his ears pricking up to over-hear gossip. On the other side of the pillar stood a tall potted plant, at least as tall as Bud, and between its thousands of tiny leaves he could see scraps of an electric-blue satin dress stretched over a battleship ass.

'I hear the son's completely wild,' responded a woman he couldn't see.

'Bad blood,' said Battleship Butt. 'You know about his wife, where she came from, don't you?'

'Mmm. With his looks he could've had his pick as well,' said the voice.

'You're telling me! You know, Becky was in his little girl's Sunday School class, and Becky goes: "There's always something weird about Charlene. It's almost like she was *foreign*".'

The voices, their whispering hisses, stopped suddenly. Bud glanced up from jabbing at his potato salad with a plastic teaspoon and saw Frank making the rounds of the room, smiling, shaking hands.

Now Frank said: 'Thanks for clearing up. Help yourself to a buttermilk crueller on your way out. There's still a bunch left in the doughnut box from Bible Study.'

Frank went into the church's kitchen and pulled out a pillbox of what he called 'heart tablets' from his jeans pocket. He popped in a Prozac and swigged some cold coffee. After Alice died he'd realised with a punch, *I'm a widower now. She's gone.* He thought he'd be able to shake it. He'd thought there were enough distractions. He began to sink, get lower and lower until he wondered if Frank was there any more. Who was inside of him running the show? First it was Valium, and now Prozac, better than Valium but still not a cure. Only church was a cure. Only when he was fielding the questions the teenagers bounced at him, telling them the scripture, talking about the Lord Jesus, only that was a cure. But it didn't last long enough.

Frank wanted to get rid of Bud now, get him out the door. Debbie – a bleach-blonde, long-haired girl with a porcelain doll's face that he'd been working with at Youth Group – had asked him after the last meeting if she could come today to talk privately with him. At the last session, Debbie confessed she'd been going to parties. He got her to tell the group about the drinking, but most of all he wanted to know about the sex which Frank called 'messing up'. He liked to talk to the kids about it, put them in their circle to rap about it. He always went home from those sessions feeling high, like he was a channel for the Word of God. High on the sex-talk, high on all those wondering eyes. High on the dripping words, the words flowing out of him, the words they strained to understand.

'Mr Hunter?' a girl's voice called. 'Are you here?'

Frank's heartbeat ground up a gear at the sound of Debbie's voice. He came out of the kitchen. Bud had gone. Now it was only him: Frank and Debbie.

Steady Frank, he told himself. *Take it easy now.*

'I'm cleaning up from the Bible Study,' he said. 'Do you want to talk in here or go in the church?'

Debbie walked over to him, her heels clacking against the tiles, her miniskirt swishing against her sheer pantyhose, a little cotton summer top clinging to her chest. She held a math book and a folder scribbled with blue Bic *Debbie* again and again where she had practised her signature, the 'i' dotted with a circle and a smiley face.

'Here's fine I guess,' she said.

The smile she gave him, and then stroking the hair back from her temple with her right hand, Frank swore that was a come-fuck-me gesture. He could swear on a Bible that Debbie wanted him.

Frank fetched two of the chairs that Bud had just finished putting away, and picked his Bible up off a table.

Debbie sat on the metal seat and crossed her legs. He could see right back up to the top of her thigh, all the way up that smoothness, that young leg. He wanted to stare at it, how he wanted to stare! But he couldn't have more than little stolen glimpses, little pieces of that thigh.

16

'How did it go last night?' said Frank. 'You were supposed to go to a party.'

'I did.' Debbie bowed her head, dropped her hair over her face. Then she swung it back, swished it over her shoulder and faced him with that little button nose, that red mouth. 'But I remembered what you said. And I didn't drink. And I didn't mess up.'

'Great! Wonderful!'

'I think I want to save myself. I think I want to do the Contract With Jesus.'

'That's terrific! But you have to be sure. This is a commitment to the Lord you're making. You don't want to mess up on Him.' Frank smiled.

'I know. I think I can do it.'

'You would have to put away your carnal urges. Get thee behind me, Satan! Those urges are the work of the Devil.'

'I know. But it doesn't help – it doesn't stop me *feeling* them! And then when I'm out with my friends and we're having fun. I *want* to have fun! These are the best days of my life and I don't want to waste them.'

'Dedicating yourself to the Lord is not a *waste*, Debbie. The Lord is fun! Loving the Lord is the best thing you can do for yourself.'

Debbie uncrossed her legs and bent forward. In his peripheral vision Frank could see the top of her breasts. He wanted to stare at those breasts. He wanted to lick them, all the salt off them. Just the breasts, nothing else. Well, maybe something else. Maybe something else salty . . .

'That's why I think if I dedicated my life to Jesus, at least I could do something different.'

'Look, why don't I give you an application form anyway. Think about it carefully. Pray about it. I'm sure Jesus will show you the right path. Now the other kids'll be here soon, so why don't we go in the church?'

Debbie stood up. So did Frank. 'Thanks, Mr Hunter,' she said, and put her arms around him in a hug.

All his kids gave him hugs at the end of their talks. That was one thing Frank always believed in. Long hugs.

'You're welcome, Debbie,' he said, and gathered her into his arms. He held her as long as he dared, rocked her even. Pressed her breasts against his shirt, met her thighs with his thighs. Until he felt himself begin to rise. Then he separated himself from her and bent to fold the chairs, holding his Bible over himself, to cover up the lump. And all the while his blood sang: 'She wants me, she wants me, she wants me,' and he felt desperate to be in that hug again, that miniskirt a nudge away from flapping up, that body a small effort away from bliss.

There had been a brief time, once, another Debbie, a hidden corner of the hall at midnight, the unzip of his fly, the pushing up of her skirt and pushing aside her panties. Oh yes, these Debbies came now and again, every few years. Something in him sang with something in them. And before that, in another country, there was Elizabeth and the promise of what they were going to do together. Nearly nine months of happiness, seeing himself reflected in her eyes. Ten years ago when the church had offered him a nine-month sabbatical, gave him the opportunity to preach fire to the apathetic English and raised the money for him to go, he had no idea that Elizabeth existed over there, waiting for him. Now, he ached for her. Instead, he had to settle for hugs from Debbies, for stopping before he ever started, until she stopped fighting it. Until that something in her rec-ognised *him* and rewarded him, and then went on to a boyfriend or off to college. She would use distance to fend away disgust, the part of her that drew her to him, to his looks, his power, his gift.

If only I could get back to Elizabeth, he thought. *Everything would come good for me again. It would be like it was supposed to be before things got in the way.*

CHAPTER 3

Independence

'He sent you to do his dirty work, did he?' Kitsy asked Peter as he stood on the step of her north London home in jeans and workboots. This friend of her husband held a roll of black plastic binliners in his hand. Kitsy thought: *If you think I'm going to let you roll in here and take whatever Michael wants, you little wanker, you can bloody well think again.*

She said: 'A bit of a wimp, isn't he? Man doesn't even have the guts to face his own wife. What am I going to do, buy a gun and shoot him?'

Kitsy patted Lucy's back and held her close, resting her cheek on the top of Lucy's head, feeling the warmth of the six-month-old baby, the comforting warmth, and her pink smell of sweet milk and baby lotion, and somehow of bubblegum.

'I don't want to get into it with you, Kitsy,' said Peter. 'I'm just here to do a job.'

'A job! Listen to you! What's he doing – *paying* you to come here?'

'He needs his clothes.'

'Who cares? Who's thinking about what *I* need? Hmm? You? Michael? Has it slipped your tiny minds that Michael's left me?'

21

Peter looked down at the binbags and twisted the roll in his hands, scoring the plastic with a thumbnail. He looked back up at Kitsy. 'Maybe I should come back another time.'

'The only person with a right to come in this house hasn't got the bollocks to do it. If Michael wants his suits he'll have to come and get them himself.'

Kitsy slammed the door on him, hoping that she'd smash Peter's fingers, listening to the *whack* of wood forced into a metal doorframe echo around the hallway. Peter and Sarah, mutual friends? Like shit.

Lucy began to fuss and cry at the violence of the sound. 'Now now,' whispered Kitsy, 'don't cry, sweetie. Don't cry,' but the baby's fussing turned into a wail, and then an out-and-out scream which swallowed up the house so that Kitsy couldn't think for herself or cry for her betrayal, her loneliness, her utter lostness of how to begin to take care of Lucy and herself.

Before, when Lucy had cried she had known what the cry was for, what she had to do to make the baby stop. But for the past three days, sometimes when Lucy started to cry Kitsy stared at her and walked out of the room, leaving Lucy on her back shaking her wee fists at the lightbulb and screaming until her screams became great shuddering breaths and coughs. Meanwhile, Kitsy would be sitting on the toilet lid fully dressed, waiting until she couldn't hear the crying any more, planning her next move: change Lucy, go to the DSS to find out what happened once her savings ran out, go to Tesco, and somewhere along the line get some food down her throat or her milk would dry up and bang would go Lucy's best comforter, and Kitsy's comfort too.

That night when Lucy woke for her early-morning feed Kitsy took her into the big bed, hemming her in with a line of pillows. It felt secure to have warmth beside her, to wake in the night searching for her daughter and find her sleeping, breathing without a noise. It almost made her believe they were better off without Michael, that he was an accessory, not really a core member of the family. In the big bed Kitsy and Lucy were a unit, mother and daughter united. But she couldn't fool herself that Lucy took Michael's place, that this demanding, insistent, screaming baby ever took the place of a fully-giving and loving man.

'We always want what we can't have,' Kitsy said. The night ate her words and Lucy slept on, sucking and smiling in her sleep.

Kitsy began to cry. Thoughts crashed around her head: how was she going to live? Everything that she'd worked for so that one day she and Michael could have their dream home would dribble away until she had nothing and the State took Michael's place as breadwinner. That after sacrificing her body to give Michael a child he had walked out, that he sent Peter instead of facing her himself and giving them that chance to make up, that he didn't care about his little girl, never called to ask after Lucy. *Why did he go? What was wrong with me that he left us?* The perpetual question spun around Kitsy's head. The answers presented themselves, neatly queued up, ready to give their perpetual replies. *The house was a mess*, whispered the middle-aged one. *You should have made sure he always got his tea on time. You never gave him any pudding!* it sulked.

RIDICULOUS! Kitsy yelled at it. But another voice popped up, the one from the lady in the red basque with the little nipples and a whip, the lady she found in the porn magazine that he used to keep rolled up behind the toilet cistern, the lady that scared Kitsy the most. *You didn't give him what he wanted any more. No imagination*, she tsked. *How's a man supposed to survive with you lying there like something on a butcher's slab? With your insides all stretched out of proportion so that he'd have more fun with a greased chicken?*

SHUT UP! yelled Kitsy. *Michael's not like that!*

He's gone, isn't he? Porn Queen pouted as she flounced away, her labia rubbing against themselves as she walked, underscoring her point.

Now it was the turn of sensible shoes and pebble glasses. She always came to Kitsy's defence, but never before the others had whispered their lies.

Michael's always had a problem with intimacy, she lectured from her prim, tight lips. *Responsibility scares him. He's a little Peter Pan, wants to be always eighteen. He doesn't realise he's nearly thirty. The power of your womb frightens him. The vulnerability of Lucy frightens him.*

BUT HOW COULD HE DO THIS TO MEEEEE?! Kitsy wailed inside. *He promised to love and to cherish until death do us part in front of all those people and then after a little teeny tiny fight he walks out! What did I do WRONG?*

Another persona walked out from the shadows. She wore Doc Marten boots and a red bandana. A silver chain ran from her nose to her ear. When she spoke she was all strength and contempt. *Get with the programme, Kitsy,* she snarled. *Stop being so fucking sad. If he wants to piss back off to his mates, let him go. You don't want a wimp like him poking around the house. Go get yourself a real man.*

The argument finished with no new answers. Instead she felt light-headed, cleaned out, and hungry. Careful not to wake Lucy, she walked downstairs to the kitchen, passing the door to the spare bedroom. As she went by, Kitsy placed her hand on the door and hesitated, stopping, imagining the door was warm with its own glow. That door always drew her to touch it as she walked by; that room seemed to have its own presence. Some great event had happened there which left an imprint, a kind of spirit.

At last she shook herself and went into the kitchen to

make a bacon and egg sandwich, spreading the bread thick with butter and tomato sauce.

Flat stomachs – that's what turned Michael on. Tight, flat stomachs with pink bellybuttons winking between a Levi waistband and a crop-top. He hadn't paid any attention to them before Kitsy gave birth but now, after seeing how ugly a woman's abdomen could be, how distended and distorted . . .

Discos had changed. Clothes had changed. But the girls didn't: they only got younger. Firmer.

Leaning against Stringfellow's bar with a Campari in his hand, watching Sarah and Peter hopping on the dance floor with the grace and style of drowning wasps, Michael ogled, but ogled with a difference: from the height of his experience, from the comfortable knowledge that he could go back to his marriage with little changing, from the security of ten years between himself and almost everybody else in the place. He oozed the honey of confidence in this dancing hive. His face, his suit said: good job, company car. Come to me.

And she did.

He escaped with her, wondering if Sarah and Peter would think he had gone too far. In a black cab on the way back to her flat they snogged and Michael felt for her stomach, laid his hand flat along the taut skin circling her bellybutton and kept it there while he drank her mouth.

The girl thought how gentlemanly it was that he didn't grope her tits in front of the cabbie. She wondered if this man could smell garlic on her breath; she'd eaten spaghetti vongole for lunch not thinking she would be coming out tonight.

She let him into her house and took him into the kitchen for cups of tea and Digestives while her housemates straggled in. She introduced him to them, checking for their approval, before she led him by the hand up a spiral staircase and into her attic room.

CHAPTER 4

The Gift-givers

What Patrick knew about his mother's culture he learned mostly from library books, from spending time in the 900 section, from watching *Dances with Wolves*. Most people knew about the Lakota Sioux now: Book your ticket on the Sacred Medicine Wheel! Learn the Mysteries of the Sacred Pipe and Sweat Ceremonies! He'd seen these ads on the supermarket bulletin boards, in the free newspapers that piled up on their front doorstep. Here was Patrick, half-Lakota, and he had to read about his people from the *Time* series of books on the Wild West and listen to their language on a Kevin Costner videotape. He felt half of himself was missing: fold in half and tear along the dotted line. Patrick belonged to America by birthright, but in this way he was in the same boat as all the Svensons and Olafsons in his school, wondering about his heritage, this half of himself that had disappeared.

When he was in gradeschool, the Seattle School District ran a programme called Indian Heritage. Every Friday, Patrick (who never told his father about this) and six others would leave their classes and go into the library for special studies. They'd make bracelets out of plastic pony beads and listen to legends from a round little Makah lady the school brought in. But Patrick never felt comfortable with these northwestern tribes, these fish-eaters, with their stylised red-and-black carvings of ravens and whales and their rectangular longhouses. He wanted to know about *his* people, the pagan people his father wouldn't let him call or visit, people unobtainably three states away on the Great Plains – see, even that was great about them – where the books said in bad winters you could piss outside and it would freeze like glass before it shattered on the ground.

Four years after his mother had suddenly died and his father stole them so abruptly from England, pulled them out of school and yanked them back to Seattle where they stayed in a motel on Fauntleroy Avenue until he found a crackerbox house to rent, it became Patrick's dream to run away to the Dakotas. At twelve he became obsessed with going to Pine Ridge or Wounded Knee or Winner – any of the names in the books. He made up his mind to run away, to take a Greyhound bus to Winner and find his Aunt Dotty, who by Lakota tradition (he'd read) would be *his* mother now. He began to save parts of school lunch in a plastic bag under his bed, putting in a little bit of bread or spice cake, some tidbit each day. But the bread went hard and the powdered sugar on the cake darkened.

He felt disappointed when after a week he saw it was inedible. He didn't want to throw away the shrivelled, hard bits of food and so he buried them under the apple tree, bag and all.

Still, that wasn't going to stop him. One day during lunchtime recess he walked out of the playground, trying to be calm even though his heart jogged, thinking of himself as invisible so as not to attract attention. As he disappeared around the end of the block he ran to California Avenue, all his socks, undershorts, his extra pair of jeans and his favourite grey Seahawks sweatshirt bouncing in his daypack.

He hid behind a fat lady at the bus stop, praying his father wouldn't drive by. When the downtown bus came, he felt as if he'd never been on a bus before; it felt like his first, exciting ride all over again. He tried to lose himself by staring at the driver's black hands and pink palms, one hand on the steering wheel, the other covering the fare box, noticed how those hands were ringless. He saw acutely the dirt and tiny pebbles stuck between the ridges of the black plastic floor mats, Metro's orange seats with brown stripes, today more orange and brown than on any other day.

Patrick got off at Pine Street feeling big, expanded, adult. He pulled open the glass door of the Greyhound bus depot with manful might, strode up to the Plexiglas ticket window and stood on tiptoe. 'I'd like a ticket to Winner, please,' he said to the man whose head only he could see, one of those white men who combed his thin, brown hair from the side of his head up and over his baldness, flattening it into place with Dippity Do. 'That's in South Dakota,' Patrick added, feeling knowledgeable.

'Bus don't go straight to Winner, kid,' said the man after fiddling around with his computer for a moment. 'Gotta change a few times before you get there. Take a seat. I'll see if I can fix you up.'

Patrick wandered over to the candy machine. A buck for a pack of Jujubees! No way! He could feel the wad of his father's money press against his leg. *Better wait to find out how much the ticket cost before I get any.*

Patrick didn't like any of the people in the bus station. He took a seat alone on a hard plastic bench screwed to the floor. A man came and sat in the seat next to him. Patrick froze, feeling his real size – small, undeveloped, but able to run fast.

'Would you like to make some money?' said the man.

Patrick looked at the ticket window, fear beginning to

trickle into his mind. The ticket man's head was bent over a book. He didn't look up.

'No,' said Patrick, even though it was a lie. The man made him wary and a little bit scared. 'No,' he said again, and shook his head to emphasise the point.

The man put his arm around the back of the bench. Revolted, Patrick scooted forward so that not even his pack touched the man's forearm: pink, sprinkled with brown freckles, but over that, blond hair going grey. The man moved closer and a whiff of him made Patrick queasy: his unwashed teeth, black at the tops where they met the gums and heavy with yellow gunk. His hair was grey and blond again, and unwashed so that it smelled too. The man wore a nylon jacket, green, and stained with oil and coffee, with little rips on the sleeve where the stuffing came out in wisps, like fluffy white hairs.

Almost too frightened to move, Patrick decided he had to get the Jujubees. He got up, desperate and trapped. Although Patrick walked quickly, the man followed him to the machine. The frightened little boy looked around at the other people in the bus depot, hoping to see a refuge, someone he could run to and trust. Near the coffee machine a few girls in short ski jackets and hotpants and orange nylons with high-heeled cowboy boots stood talking to a pimp with nappy hair and a gold tooth. He stared at them, hoping they could read his mind and see how much he needed their help.

Near the ticket window, two ladies sat holding brown paper bags and their purses on their laps, a suitcase apiece at their feet. One had white hair peppered with black. The other had bright chestnut hair, and skinny eyebrows pencilled in the crayon colour Burnt Sienna. She'd lipsticked a browney-red over her mouth, and smeared peach foundation onto her skin. Her make-up seemed like a rubber

Halloween mask, like if he could find the join on her neck, Patrick could peel the whole thing off. Unsure but desperate, Patrick walked over to sit as close as he dared to the grey-haired one. He hoped they would pretend to own him, as if they were his grandmothers.

Flora Eickelburger and Mary Barnes looked at each other, then looked at Patrick.

'Where's your mother?' said Flora.

'She's dead,' said Patrick, trying to be matter-of-fact. 'I'm meeting my father at the other end.'

'Oh, you poor little thing!' said Mary, raising her pencilled eyebrows.

'I can handle myself,' said Patrick, trying to fake back his cockiness.

'You stay next to us,' said Flora. 'Would you like a snow-ball?'

'Yes, please,' he said, feeling grateful.

She dug into her paper bag and came up with a package of cookies. She broke the plastic wrapping and handed a cookie to Patrick.

He bit into the cookie, following the thin, pink meridian stripes, one bite per stripe, making it last, until the cookie base crumbled in half and he had to shove the rest in his mouth.

The ticket man came out of his booth. He shambled over to Patrick.

'Ticket to Winner, seventy-five dollars.'

'One way?' said Patrick, shocked. He tipped his head back to get a better look at the man's face.

'One way,' confirmed the man, his face hard and unyielding.

'How far will fifty bucks take me?'

'Not far enough. Forget about running away from home and go back to your mom and dad.'

Patrick felt like an agate on the beach, picked up and held to the sun between someone's thumb and forefinger, that this old man had seen right through him, and in front of the cookie ladies too.

Patrick's voice rode up with each word. 'I'm not running away!'

'Suit yourself,' said the ticket man and walked away.

Patrick sat with the cookie ladies for another hour. Feeding his anger and sorrow and desperation, he ate most of their snowballs and a package of Grandma's Molasses. He heard all about the trip they were taking to Reno, and how Mrs Eickelburger had a grandson Patrick's age living in Burien, how he was crazy about skateboarding. Patrick stayed with them until their bus came, and helped load on their cases and the paper bags into the big, aluminium locker under the bus. He wanted to climb in and surprise them in Reno, but the bus driver closed the hatch.

Patrick felt sad waving goodbye to Mrs Eickelburger and Mrs Barnes as the bus pulled out from under the station awnings and turned into the road. His last memory of them was Flora's hand, her great sapphire and diamond ring making arcs of blue from the bus window.

Stepping behind the bus as it pulled out, Patrick followed it, what the heck, down the road. He shuffled slowly now, kicking a stone, then a Coke can, then the thick glass neck of a green bottle. He watched the sidewalk, its regimental lines sectioning each piece into two, like Graham Crackers, feeling tears balloon in his throat, keeping them down to be manly. Once he bumped into a telephone pole and stained a knee of his jeans black with creosote. He walked to Pike Place market, then down to the Ye Olde Curiosity Shoppe and followed the Alaskan Way Viaduct to the West Seattle Bridge, then up SW Delaware, up and up to Fauntleroy Avenue until he was on his block, thirsty, hungry for dinner, his feet hot and tingling.

When he spotted his house – well, the house his father rented, its dirty white aluminium siding, its extreme square-ness, as if it had been made of four great sheets of plywood, glued together at the edges – he felt deflated as a flat basketball. But at the same time he knew something in him had changed. He could have made the trip. The only thing that had stopped him was money.

The main door to the house, a hollow wooden thing, a poor-person's door that said to the outside world, What is there in here to steal? had been left open. Patrick walked in and went to the kitchen for a drink. On the table was a nearly-empty vodka bottle. When he spotted that bottle, the fear edging at his mind descended, expanded, filled him with its fog. Patrick forgot about his drink of water and walked as softly as he knew to his room.

His father waited for him, sitting on the lower bunkbed, wearing nothing but jeans, his belt in his hand, his crewcut hair standing to attention. His chest was white with thick blond hair across his pectorals, down his stomach, spreading onto his back, thick hair on his arms past his wrists, like a long shirt.

Patrick felt the fifty dollars he'd taken from his father's wallet press against the cotton lining of one pocket. Upset and frightened, he looked around the room for a place to stash it. Before he could take even one step, before he could take off his knapsack, his father was on him, laying into Patrick with the belt, striking out as if it were a whip, the heavy brass buckle swinging like a stone at the end of a rope. It smacked Patrick across the chest, and then when the boy yelled and ducked, his father aimed for the face. The metal cut into Patrick's cheek. He pressed his hand to the warm wet blood to staunch the pain and doubled over screaming. Frank hauled Patrick up by his back beltloop and lashed him.

Then he picked up a black leather Bible from the bed, threw it under Patrick's face, and said: 'Leviticus 2. Don't come out until you've got it memorised.'

Fucked if I'm going to goddamn memorise anything, Patrick thought in his twelve-year-old brain. Fear fossilised into stubbornness. Desperation became dignity.

Patrick stayed in his room. He smelled Rice-a-roni and it made the juices slosh in his stomach. He heard Charlene cooking, setting the table. He heard them eating, stabbed with aloneness, with his father's rejection and hatred. By the time he heard them clearing the table, his anger curdled as Charlene rinsed the remains of the rice down the sink.

Charlene didn't come in until nine, and she came in empty-handed. His little sister whispered frightened to Patrick: 'He wouldn't let me bring anything. He says if I talk to you I'll get whupped.'

'*Charlene!*' shouted the Reverend from the hall. '*What did I tell you?!*'

They heard him banging at the front door with a hammer, and then at the back.

In the morning, Charlene got up and went to school. Patrick heard his father go out. As soon as the Pontiac left the driveway, Patrick went to the front door dressed in briefs and a holey white T-shirt. He tried to open it. It caught short. Through a small crack Patrick could see that his father had nailed two hasps to the door and doorframe, and shut his son in with a bicycle lock.

The same at the back.

Patrick went to the bathroom, looked at himself in the mirror, touched his cheek messy with dried blood, purple with bruising. Patrick began to be numb with a hate of his own. He didn't wash the wound. He took a pee, went to the kitchen, made himself toast, and sat in front of the TV in his underpants. He turned it on. Nothing. He went around to the back. His father had cut the cord. No plug. Only a brown cord with bare wires hanging out of it.

Patrick stayed in the house Thursday, Friday and on the weekend. Periodically his father would stand in the doorway of his room and say: 'You got it memorised yet?' and Patrick's answer in anger would be to turn and face the wall, silent in his loathing.

On Monday, the swelling had gone down, although Patrick still hadn't washed his face. His father held out a wet washcloth and threatened to pin him to the floor and wash the blood off for him. As Patrick took the cold cloth, Frank said he had to go back to school. 'But when you get home, go straight to your room. You're not coming out until you memorise Leviticus.'

Patrick hadn't touched the Bible, would never read Leviticus again. Never in the rest of his life.

And so, at twelve, he took to his room in the evenings when his father got home. Sometimes he'd crawl out the window and play touch football a few blocks up with Jimmy and a bunch of boys.

They fought over Patrick because he always played angry.

At bedtime on the day he tried to kill himself, Patrick sat in his bunk under Charlene and thought about what he'd nearly done. If Charlene hadn't come in, he'd have been dead by now. The thought that he'd nearly wiped out his life frightened him. He almost couldn't remember the numbness that had put him in that chair, with that knife, with that bottle of whiskey.

Except that morning he'd woken up with the white worm of depression turning in his gut. Lying on his back, Patrick had come out of sleep fuzzy and murky, full of unremembered nightmares, his pillow damp, his body slightly sticky against the sheet pulled up over a child's mattress. He stretched and his heels fell off the bed's foot, his head banged up against the painted wall. The twentieth day of summer vacation, only this was vacation for ever. No next year, no next grade.

Until last week he'd had a job lined up with Mersey's selling men's fashions, his first major break into retail. Then the manager called to say they were having a slow summer and wouldn't need him. When he put down the phone Patrick had wanted to cry. All year he'd thought about this first summer of freedom, that he'd finally *do* . . . but what? What *was* he supposed to do now?

It was as if the answer teased him, called him, danced away, slightly off the scale of his mental map, refused to present itself full-on. He felt like an abysmal, total failure. He'd been around the stores looking for a replacement job: full, full, full. Come back at Christmas, one lady said. *I'll be dead by Christmas*, he'd thought. Everyone had a place except Patrick. Even stoner Sandra who'd skipped sixth period the first half of the year to smoke dope in Lincoln Park had become a waitress on a cruise ship to Hawaii. His life felt loose, unstructured, full of holes like a sweater knit on a roller-coaster.

The one person he really wanted to see, to talk to, to ask, had been gone. Patrick felt his mother, cast in shadow by the Reverend's refusal to discuss her, was the only one with answers. He knew she was alive someplace in spirit, a safe place. And so, he'd wanted to go there too.

Scared about what he'd nearly done, Patrick said a prayer before he went to sleep: *Mom, wherever you are, I need your help now. I've almost done a terrible thing. Show me what there is for me here. Help me know what I'm supposed to do.*

At 1 a.m. he woke into the night, as if someone had

shaken his shoulders, rapped their knuckles on his head. He woke straight out of a dream – London again, at the house. He'd been with a silent blonde woman and they were holding hands across a table. Patrick knew deeply and completely: *she will help me.*

His eyes focused in the dark, picking out the shadows of his blanket by the yellow-greyness of a streetlight. As he came back to reality his conscious mind filled itself with the certainty of one thought; he had to go back to the London house.

He had to find out why his mother died, or next time he'd find himself locked in the bathroom with a razor. And if he died, Charlene wouldn't be able to manage. She'd never hold things together alone.

Maybe there were people in London who had known his mother and didn't mind talking about her. In his mother there was also himself, and the Lakota heritage he drew down from her. He felt that if he knew about his heritage and his mother, losing a piddly-assed job at Mersey's wouldn't mean shit.

Patrick decided: *I'm not going to let money stand in my way again.* He dressed quietly in the dark, unlocked his bedroom window so he could get back in later, crept to the kitchen and slipped out of the back door.

When Patrick had turned fifteen, Frank had told his son to get a job. Bill and Fred, the brothers who owned the House of Appliances on California Avenue, hired Patrick and paid him five dollars an hour to lug around microwaves and refrigerators. That's how Patrick knew that Bill and Fred always left keys in the delivery van with the logic that no one was going to steal a fluorescent green truck with *House of Appliances* written on the side in pink letters five feet high.

Now he walked to the store in the balmy warmth of a

summer night, all quietness and stealth. He strolled through the alleyways in his Iron Maiden T-shirt, his black sweats, black high-tops and gardening gloves, holding a can of molasses in a big paper bag, and a penlight tied into the strings in his sweats. He crunched against broken glass and gravel, hiding behind trees when he heard voices or cars coming.

When he arrived at the parking lot behind the store, sure enough the *House of Appliances* truck glowed green and pink in the streetlight waiting for Patrick to move it. The engine ground and coughed, caught and roared, settling down to a steady thud-thud-thud, its V-8 engine as loud as a small seaplane. The heavy noise brought home the danger and risk of what he was about to do. This first journey into crime made Patrick's blood race. He felt scared and wished there was some legal, less risky way to get fast money.

I'm gonna do it. I'm gonna do it, he repeated to himself, trying to get over the adrenalin. *What the hell – I own this country anyway. It belonged to my people first. I've got a goddamn right to this stuff.* Su casa es mi casa *kinda thing.*

His slippery right palm on the stick, Patrick shoved the truck in gear and drove to the rear entrance of the store, lights off. He sidled the truck up next to the concrete wall, coaxing the wheels over blackberry vines. A beer bottle popped under his tyres. Patrick jumped in the seat at the sound, jerked the wheel, scraping the truck's siding against the wall with a screech. He pumped his arm in quick circles to wind down the window and stuck his head out of the cab, squinting toward the roof. Gunning the engine too loud and too hard, he drove the truck three feet on and cut it. Sluggishly the truck leapfrogged forward as Patrick let the clutch out too quick.

With shaky legs Patrick climbed onto the hood, up on top of the cab, stood up level with the john window. He took the can of molasses from the paper bag, pried open the lid with a stick, and with unsteady hands glugged the sticky black mess over the window. He smeared it around with the stick, plastered on the paper bag, and punched the window's four corners with his fist. Glass stuck to the paper like chunks of hard taffy. Patrick dropped the mess into the blackberries and cleared away glass from the sill, his hands protected by the gardening gloves. He tipped his body into the john and wriggled in, grabbing the top of the stall wall for support, glad he was finally out of the streetlight. Relieved.

Now he could let his eyes adjust to the dark, to the static smell of the place along with the other, sharp ammonia-urine scent, let those smells conjure for him the memory of how it was all laid out.

He stood on the toilet seat and reached with both hands above his head. His fingertips touched the Styrofoam ceiling and he stretched out the whole length of his body and pushed. The Styrofoam bent, then the whole square popped into the crawlspace. Patrick put one hand either side of the square and swung his body up, feet first, into the little hole. He turned over onto his front, untied the little penlight from his sweats and switched it on. By the bouncing dim light he stuck the Styrofoam square back in place.

For the first time since he started out from the house, since he had dressed for this, Patrick felt safe. He was cosy, snug up here in this dark place he'd been once before when the air conditioning broke down. It was hot, a dry warmth of the sun's heat beating on the roof, trapped in the attic and all the heat coming up from the store. The dark fitted around him like a powerful shield, a cloak that made him invisible. Here he felt natural, at home, able to move and think. He was aware of his total body and the way it hummed, tuned, ready to spring, twist, turn, bend, tackle. His eyes sucked in light, felt so aware, so alive to light and in key with his ears that he felt he could breathe through his eyes in the same way the men in the legends he'd read had breathed through their eyes, inhaling through them in little puffs.

I should have remembered to bring a dustmask, he thought. *All this fibreglass insulation. Damn.*

Spreading his weight as much as he could, not wanting to punch holes in the ceiling, to fall through on top of some fridge-freezer or 22-inch television, he crawled forward using his knees and elbows. The office was along the same wall as the john; he hoped it was going to be easy.

Patrick followed the ceiling beams, trying to keep away from the mattress of fibreglass. The journey was short, messy, sweaty. He'd only been up there two minutes and already he could feel the fibreglass itch as it worked its way down the back of his neck, into his scalp, into the sweaty hairs at his crotch and the wet small of his back. His throat itched with the urge to cough.

Finally he was over what he thought was the office. Patrick pried up a Styrofoam board and flashed his penlight down. Yes – there were the brothers' desk and swivel chair, brown impotent little sentries he knew smelled of Bill and Fred's stale sweat.

Feeling unsure and daring and worried, he sat on the edge of the hole and jumped.

'Geronimo!' he whispered to himself. His ankles crumpled with an intense heat and searing pain when they hit the floor. With his knees around his ears he held his ankles, rocking, rocking, feeling like they'd been caught in snapped steel traps. For the first time the frenzy of fear threatened to overwhelm him, to block out logical sense.

'Ohfuckohfuckohfuckohfuckohfuck!' he moaned. When the pain eased off, he crawled across the floor under the desk. He lifted up a flap of carpet and looked down into a hole, an empty concrete hole.

The floorsafe! Where the fuck had they put the floorsafe!

Panicking, Patrick scooted around the floor lifting up the carpet trying to find the new hiding place, but there was nothing. Solid concrete. No safe.

Outside, two doors slammed.

I must have set off some alarm. I have to get out.

With the penlight gripped in his teeth he stood on the desk and jumped for the hole in the ceiling. He felt amazed when his hands caught on either side, bending the aluminium struts which held the Styrofoam blocks in place, and he swung with the momentum of the jump. He could feel the aluminium cracking in his fists and his father's eyes on the back of his head, those hateful brown eyes like a trout's. *You can't do anything right*, the Reverend's voice said. *You can't even be a low-down criminal.*

Patrick tucked in his knees and flung his feet up into the heat of the crawlspace. As he thrust his body over, the Styrofoam board crushed under his stomach. Patrick's hopes sank. Desperately fumbling, he straightened the aluminium struts, fitting the warped Styrofoam board back into place as best he could. Feeling like crying, he crawled to the wall and pressed his back against it.

C'mon guys, please don't find me. I ain't done nothin' like this before. I'm only here 'cos I need money. Please don't find me. I'll get another job or find the money somehow else. Pleeeeze.

Trying to listen, trying to hear them, his heart pounded too loud. He held his breath to get it to slow down. He wondered how long it would take them to discover his body if he had a heart attack and died. He tried to breathe the hot attic air through his eyes.

Getting down on his stomach, Patrick put his penlight between his teeth but didn't dare turn it on. In the dry-sauna heat he crawled blind, shutting his eyes, feeling his way with his hands, keeping his head low. His sweat bottoms snagged on a nail and ripped through to the skin, gashing his thigh. The pain stung up to his groin. He wanted to cry out, to break down screaming. Instead he took a deep breath and crawled on, wriggling along on his stomach until one hand fell into nothing, black nothing.

Patrick switched the penlight on and threw the thin beam in front of him. There was a drop – a three-foot drop. *Yes! The break between the stores!* He'd found his safe place, his place to curl up and think about how he was going to get out.

Turning around and dropping down, feet first, onto the dimestore's ceiling, he crouched there and listened, not so scared now, his heart not pounding out all other sound. The warmth made him relax, feel sleepy. He yawned.

Listening to the silence of the stores in the hot cocoon of the attic, safe now in its quilt of blackness, Patrick fell into a kind of waking sleep – that is, the kind of sleep where you think you are awake, where you see everything in your dreaming mind, the kind of sleep that is pure virtual reality.

He saw two points of light zoom into the attic from a hole in the eaves, a hole he knew was there but could not see. Like two fireflies or two sparklers they looped-the-loop, buzzed his head, zoomed around his legs. The points of light smelled like electricity, like that pop of electricity when a fuse bursts, and they hummed as they went, although it seemed to Patrick they were laughing, giggling away to themselves.

Patrick watched, curious. The two light-points chased each other in a furious circle, then took off in a straight line and zipped to the far wall all the length of the store. They stopped immediately dead at the wall, then split off and in wide arcs looped back to where Patrick sat.

They circled the toes of Patrick's high tops, spiralling up

42

his instep, his ankle, his knees, until Patrick felt as if he was being encased in a slinky of light. He should have been afraid, but something in him made him more amused, more curious than frightened, almost wanting to join in. They hula-hooped in opposite directions around his waist, up his ribcage, tickling enough to make him think: 'Hey, guys, calm down!' Then they ringed his armpits and shoulders and tumbled down over the elbows, his wrists, his hands clasped loosely in front of him. The lights disappeared into his palms and he felt them nestled there like eagle plumes, soft and slightly warm. Suddenly, he knew they were gone, and he felt the loss of their going, that the giggly electric presences had quit the room. Instead he held something hard and cold and scratchy pressed between his hands.

He fell into a deep sleep.

He woke to the yak of bickering crows. Chinks in the roof let in tiny pieces of light. Looking toward the centre he noticed an 'L' of light in the ceiling – two sides of a square.

Patrick stood up. Like a tightrope artist he walked along the beams until he was directly under a trapdoor to the roof. He reached up, shot back the bolt and pushed it open. His eyes hurt, dazzled by the light so that he doubled over to sneeze.

'Uuuuussshaaa!'

Something where he had been sitting caught his eye. A sparkle. Patrick pointed his penlight at it: something tiny that glittered white with darts of red like a prism. He walked back along the path of the beams, stooped to pick it up. A diamond – a sapphire and diamond ring.

'Thank-you thank-you thank-you!' he said and grinned, and then laughed, happy, excited. He did a little dance on a beam, wiggling his hips and holding the ring above his head, both fists in the air punching at the ceiling.

Patrick stuck the ring on his right little finger, hoisted

himself out of the trapdoor, and sat blinking on the roof. Pink fibreglass filaments covered his black sweats. Dirt tattooed the fingertip cuts aching and healing, white cob-webs caught by a little breeze floating in his nearly-black hair.

He spat on the sapphire and buffed it on his T-shirt, smiling at the big square-cut rock set on either hip with chunky diamonds. The ring tugged at a memory in him that wouldn't materialise. He stared at his ticket out and felt the amazement that comes with being blessed by great luck.

Crouching low, Patrick ran along the rooftops to a cedar tree. He grabbed a branch, swung down into the alley and ran hard and fast and happy for home, scolded by swooping crows.

Charlene sat cross-legged on the top bunk of their beds, thin in her K-mart pyjamas, her fine dark hair matted and mussed.

'Is there a clean towel anywhere?' said Patrick. 'I've gotta get this crap outta my hair.'

Charlene jumped down, opened a drawer and handed him a threadbare brown towel. 'What's that?' she said, pointing to his hand.

'Oh, that. Nothing much.' He turned the ring over and showed her the stone. He grinned at her.

'You robbed a little old lady,' she accused, her mouth open in disbelief.

'No! I *found* it!' He was too excited to feel angry.

Charlene looked at him in awe. 'You found it? Where?'

'I'm not telling you!'

'Well, if you ask me, you mugged a poor old lady.'

'What poor old lady would be wandering the streets at one in the morning? Think about it, soup for brains.' Patrick grinned at her again, and snapped at her thigh with his towel.

Charlene squealed and scampered back up into her bunk and hid under the covers. She peeped out at him.

'You better not let Dad see that.'

Patrick tugged open the warped bedroom door, checked the hallway was clear, and tiptoed into the bathroom. He bolted himself in and pulled off his shoes and stripped naked. He stood in front of the mirror, looking at his body, and then turned over his left arm. He peeled off Charlene's Bandaids, grubby now. The cuts were red, like lips, but puckered white around the edges from sweating.

Yesterday seemed to him ridiculous, like it didn't happen, like he'd seen himself acting on TV, acting out a suicide. With the sapphire ring on his finger the black depression that had draped itself over him seemed distant too.

I've taken action, he told himself. *I've stepped onto the path.*

He ran the shower warm, then turned it up, bit by bit, until it was as hot as he could bear. He soaped himself down and then turned off the hot and turned on the freezing cold, sloughing yesterday off his skin.

Patrick was out of the house before the Reverend woke up, getting on a bus to downtown Seattle to pawn the ring. He knew a couple of pawnshops on First Avenue. Then he'd go straight over to a travel agent on Fifth to buy his ticket.

The pawnshop smelled of gungrease and sweat, of stale clothes and mildewing cotton. High on the walls were mouldy heads of hunting trophies: deer and elk, grizzly and brownbear, a yellowing polar bear's head, a whole raccoon. Patrick had to ring a buzzer to get in. All five people in the store turned and stared.

Patrick stopped at a derringer case, waiting for two men at the counter to go. He liked the stubby silver guns, fat, small enough to palm – they almost looked like toys, like the gunbarrel was so short they wouldn't be able to get the bullet out.

Cool. Be cool, he thought, feeling nervous. *You found it. It's not stolen. Nobody will be looking for it. Bet he'll try to rip me off. Give me jackshit for it. Look at that little ponytail on his bald-headed ass. He's gonna try to rip me off for sure.*

The men at the counter left the store. Patrick walked up to the owner and laid down the ring. The owner raised his eyebrows and showed the sapphire to the light. It was so clear it looked like an ice-cube in water, the diamonds like little iced lakes on either side. Patrick wanted to suck on the stone. He sucked on his teeth instead.

'Six hundred dollars,' said the store-owner, squinting at the diamonds through a jeweller's glass.

'Six hundred? My mother got it valued at two-and-a-half grand!'

'Your mother?'

Patrick looked him in the eyes. 'She's dead.' By now he could say it without his stomach lurching up to his heart for comfort.

'So you're selling off the family jewels?'

'Not all of them,' he said, trying to make a little joke. He steadied himself, putting his hands on the display case. 'I'll take fifteen hundred for it.'

'Not from me you won't. I'll give you seven fifty.'

'I need at least twelve hundred,' he said, trying not to let the desperation get into his voice. What if it wasn't enough? It *had* to be. The ring was a gift!

'Stones aren't the investment people think they are. They're ten-a-penny these days.'

'But this is a good one!' He tried again, consciously lowering his voice, being cool. 'A grand or I'm walking out that door and selling it to someone who appreciates it.'

With a key the owner unlocked his display case, slid

back the glass and slipped in the ring.

For a moment Patrick thought: *The guy's fucking stealing my ring*! And his stomach rumbled with panic. But then the owner rang open the cash register and counted out ten one-hundred dollar bills into Patrick's palm.

Triumphant, Patrick crunched the money in his fist like a handful of dry leaves, stuffing it into the pocket of his jeans. The owner buzzed him out of the door and it clacked shut behind him.

After he bought the ticket, Patrick took the bus back home. With all that money in his pocket, temptation told him to take a cab or go into Olympus and buy their most expensive pair of Nikes. Instead, he sat at the back of the bus holding the ticket on his lap, flipping through the red carbon-paper pages, reading every word as if baggage and check-in details could tell him what he'd find in London.

He stared out the window and tried to remember what it was like. Suddenly, he felt like he was a little boy again, eight years old and getting up at night. He didn't know if it was a dream or a memory, but he stood at the top of the stairs and saw his father at the bottom. The Reverend had been painting, and there were splashes of red on his arms. Patrick felt himself go chill, felt his little-boy fear.

Dreams can't hurt me now, he told himself. But the image had opened a small door. He felt that something about that house pulled him, an immediate feeling, as if the house was in his head instead of thousands of miles away. Fingering the ticket, he knew it would make him crazy if he ignored the house's call any longer.

It was in London the evil had begun.

'Where's the Reverend?' Patrick whispered to Charlene, standing on the front porch and poking his head into the living room.

'It's all right,' she said, sitting on the hairy old sofa reading *Love on Mystery Island*. On the front cover, a stern fair man towered over a dark-haired woman in a low-cut red dress with huge, half-exposed breasts. 'He's got Christian Youth this afternoon.'

'And he's not making you go?' said Patrick as he walked in and plumped himself down in a chocolate-brown arm-chair. It tilted forward where one castor was missing.

Charlene shook her head. Turned a page. 'Nuh-uh. I got cramps.'

'How long's he been gone?'

'Couple of hours.'

Patrick stood. Charlene looked up from her book. 'Where are you going?' she said.

'To get my passport out of his box.'

'He'll kill you if he finds out!'

'Like I really care. I got my ticket!' He waved it at her, letting it flap around like a little flag, or a wad of notes. Charlene's eyes opened wide. 'I leave tomorrow.'

Patrick walked down the hall, past the bathroom and the bedroom he shared with Charlene to the far bedroom, his father's room. He stood at the door, hesitating. The last time he'd been in there he'd been fourteen, playing hide-and-seek with the kids next door. His father caught him and beat him with a belt so that he felt nauseous and dizzy and couldn't eat dinner even if he'd been allowed to. That hiding had taught him so well that he didn't feel curious about the room, although sometimes when he hated his father most he imagined dead bodies underneath the bed or stuffed into the clothes closet. Still. He knew that what he wanted was in the room. He had to get it.

Patrick put his hand on the doorknob and twisted. The door swung into the room, easily, not sticking like his bedroom door. Somehow he'd expected to fight with the door, expected that things would be blocking it – dirty shirts, dirty underwear, empty vodka bottles.

The room smelled closed. It smelled of carpet underlay and ground-in cornchips. The brown shag carpet was matted and dusty with white specks as if someone had scattered miniscule bits of paper and seashell and stomped around with hiking boots. On the bed a yellow drip-dry coverlet crumpled back to show sweat-stained sheets; on an upturned milkcrate next to his bed Frank had laid a Bible.

Charlene stood at Patrick's elbow and looked in: He wanted to say to her, 'Stand guard.' Instead he stepped into the room and looked around. Getting down on his hands and knees, he pulled a dusty white shirtbox from under the bed and lifted the lid. On top was a *Hustler* and two *Penthouse* magazines. Patrick put them on the floor. Instead of being shocked, he felt cynical – almost 'of course'.

'*Oh my God,*' whispered Charlene.

At the bottom of the box were the family's four passports. He flicked each one open and handed one to Charlene. 'Here, this is yours. Keep it someplace safe.'

Charlene rolled up the leg of her jeans and stuck it in her sock, one of Patrick's old white gymsocks with a hole in the heel which she'd sewn together with red thread, so that the puckered seam poked out of the top of her tennis shoe. Patrick rifled through the papers, mostly letters in envelopes, some bills, trying to be as quick as possible. He looked for addresses, London addresses. He took those letters, his own passport and his mother's passport, and tucked them into the waistband of his jeans, flopping over his sweat-top. Then he put the magazines back in the box, stuck on the lid. Feeling relieved, he shoved the whole thing back under the bed.

Patrick and Charlene retreated into their room, breathing normally again in their place of uneasy peace.

They both heard the front door open and looked at each other. Patrick saw fear in his little sister's face and felt some of it jump to him, like the shock of a nine-volt battery tipped to his tongue. He lifted the carpet and put under it the letters and passport with his ticket and most of the leftover money. Charlene stuffed her passport under the covers of her top bunkbed, pushing it down to the foot.

'Don't worry,' said Patrick, trying to soothe her, feeling guilty that he might get her into trouble. 'There's no way he's gonna know.'

A shout came from the front room. 'Charlene!'

She looked at Patrick, afraid, almost accusing, then called, 'Coming, Daddy,' and went out.

He heard his father through the thin wall, yelling: 'What's this sinful trash you're reading? This is the work of the Devil – Satan's work! The lust of the flesh! Arise, O Lord, in Thine anger, lift up Thyself because of the rage of mine enemies and awake for me to judgement that Thou has commanded! Psalm eight, six! Let not sin therefore reign in your mortal body that ye should obey it in the lusts thereof! Romans six, twelve!'

'But Daddy . . .'

'No buts, Charlene. Your sin must be *punished*!'

'No!' Charlene screamed, and cried: 'But God commendeth His love toward us that while we were yet sinners, Christ died for us! No, Daddy! NO!'

Charlene's footsteps pounded up the hall. She shoved open the bedroom door and shut it fast behind her. Patrick heard the lurch of his father's feet, heavy, slow. Charlene tugged impossibly at the bunkbeds, trying to shove them in front of the door.

'Help me!' she pleaded, sobbing, tugging at the post. 'Help me!'

But Patrick didn't move. It was as if his father's footsteps were coming to *him*.

Charlene gave up on the bunkbeds and ran behind her brother. She pulled Patrick's sweat-top from his back and hid her head under it. She put her arms around his waist and pressed her face and her hair against her brother's soft skin. She clutched him, tighter than she would clutch him in a hug, or if she were riding behind him on a motorcycle going a hundred miles an hour. He could feel her shake, her skinny arms around his waist, the tightness of his shirt where it pulled taut against his stomach and chest and made them stand out in distinct outlines, all tense.

His father shoved open the door and stood in it, leaning against the frame, *Love on Mystery Island* in one hand.

'You,' he accused, and swung his arm. 'Get out of the way. Your sister needs to be punished.'

'I got a job today, Dad,' said Patrick, trying to distract him.

'Get the garsh darn it outta the way, I told you!' His father heaved his arm back and threw the book at Patrick who ducked, taking Charlene with him. The book sailed past his head and thumped against the wall, falling, its pages chattering.

'I . . . said . . . I . . . got . . . a . . . job . . . today,' Patrick repeated, louder, slower, emphasising each word, standing upright with his Charlene limpet, angry and strong.

'You? What kind of job could *you* get? You get fired from everything you touch.'

'A good job.' Patrick dug in his pocket and took out a twenty-dollar bill. 'Here, take this. They paid me an advance today.'

'An advance? Is this it?'

'An advance.' Patrick hoped his father would fall for it, a desperate hope. He needed to be believed. He smiled at the

51

Reverend. 'They gave me the money 'cos it's out of state – California. I'll be working at the airport as a baggage-handler.'

'No.' His father narrowed his eyes.

'What do you mean, no? I'll be making two thousand bucks a month, Dad! I'll send you five hundred home every month.'

'Five hundred?' The eyebrows lifted.

'Sure. Five hundred.'

Patrick's father wadded up the money in his hand, wadded it into a ball the size of the pellets of paper Patrick used to throw at the teachers at school. He held it there in a fist. Charlene began to loosen her grip on Patrick's waist, to lean against him, to enjoy the warmth coming off his body, the feeling of hugging her brother, a person she loved. She never got this close to him any more, not since he was about twelve, because they had to share a room together and didn't allow themselves.

'I'll deal with you later, young lady. In the meantime, fix some dinner,' said their father, and wheeled from his spot at the doorjamb. He disappeared into his own room, slamming the door behind him. They heard him thud onto the bed.

'It's OK, Charlene,' whispered Patrick, and pried her hands apart, away from his waist. It hurt him that she was so needy, that he couldn't protect her, or even get his father to love them in the way he should. But maybe after London he'd be bringing home something that would help them both.

Charlene ducked out from under his shirt, blinking in the light, her fine hair all fuzzy and full of static. She picked up *Love on Mystery Island* and hid it under the mattress of her top bunk. She climbed up and sat cross-legged and put a pillow in her lap. She stared at Patrick as he pulled out his big purple backpack and began stuffing it with T-shirts, socks, jeans, underwear. Then he pulled a black leather jacket off its hanger and crammed it on top.

'You're taking Jimmy Mac's jacket?' said Charlene. 'You never wear it.'

'Well, I might want to *start* wearing it, nosey.'

Jimmy Mac's mother gave the biker's jacket to Patrick when Jimmy died. Even though Patrick and Jimmy didn't hang together much in the last few years. Still, after Jimmy got shot she'd come to the door holding that heavy black slice of leather, sewn and stitched, running with bright chrome zippers on the sleeve, slashed with zippers over the chest. Mrs Mac handed it over to Patrick and he'd taken it without saying much. Fact is, he thought the jacket was a reproach, that Mrs Mac meant Patrick should've looked after his best friend from kindergarten a little bit better.

Patrick had tried, but Jimmy wanted to hang with the gangs.

Charlene didn't want to watch her brother leaving. 'Guess I'd better go make dinner,' she said.

'Trick?' Charlene's voice came out into the night. A streetlight shone into their window and created half-shadows of the bedposts, of Patrick's bag packed on the floor.

'Hmm?'

'Are you asleep?'

'No – otherwise I wouldn't say "hmm".'

'Oh, good. Do you mind if we have a prayer?'

'A what?'

'A prayer, for your safe journey. Not like Dad's prayers – one of Mom's prayers. That kind.'

Patrick rubbed his eyes. He curled upright, keeping his back bent so he didn't hit his head on the springs of Charlene's bunk. 'You need the stuff for that.'

'I got the stuff – I saved it. When I see a cigarette butt in the alley I pick it up and peel out the tobacco. I stole a couple of Dad's cigarettes too, so there's enough. And last time I went to the beach I found some feathers. I know they're not eagle feathers or nothin', but you can't get those because they're endangered. And I've got a couple of shells too, and some dried sage I bought at Safeway.'

'OK.' Patrick got up and opened the window, slowly, so his father wouldn't hear. Charlene got out of bed and dug underneath her mattress. She pulled out a baking tray, a box of matches and a little leather pouch which she'd sewed together herself in blanket stitches. She went to the chest of drawers, opened her sock drawer and drew out the feathers and the shells and the box of sage.

Charlene crushed a sage leaf between her fingers and put it on the baking tray. She placed a feather on top of it, crushed another leaf, and put it on the feather. She did the same for the shell.

'Oh no! I forgot something!' Charlene opened their door, stealthily, and went to the kitchen. Patrick dug his fingers in the tobacco pouch. He laid the tobacco out in four piles, one in each corner of the baking tray.

'If the Reverend caught us doing this he'd kill us,' Patrick said, smiling at Charlene when she came back holding three plastic cereal bowls.

'She'd love it,' said Charlene. She felt so excited she was almost giggling. She laid out the bowls in front of the tray. One held frozen corn, the other a piece of hamburger from the fridge, and the last one some blackberries.

'Hold on a sec!' Patrick rummaged around in their closet, under his pile of rotting old tennis shoes, and came up with a package of smoking papers. He took one out and waved it at Charlene. 'Look – we can even have a little smoke.'

Charlene smiled. Patrick rolled the cigarette with the last of the tobacco from the pouch. He licked it shut and held it up to Charlene's face. She opened her mouth and took it between her lips.

'It's not exactly a pipe, is it?' he said. 'You present.'

'It'll do,' said Charlene as Patrick struck a match for her. She sucked in the smoke and blew it out. 'All my relations,' she began.

'All my relations,' he echoed.

She sucked in again and blew, making her mouth into an 'O', sending four times into the room the sound of the wind. 'To the West wind, help us. To the North wind, help us. To the East wind, help us. To the South wind, help us. Grandmother, help us. Grandfather, help us. We are nothing. We are your children, needing everything from you. Without you, we cannot survive.'

Charlene took another puff. 'We have prepared this altar for you. We know we haven't used the right things, but it honours you. Please help Trick in London find out what happened to our mother. Please make sure his airplane flies there safe.'

Charlene handed the cigarette to Patrick. Already it was half-burnt down. Patrick took it, and as he did so, looking at Charlene, he remembered his mother. She'd done this once with them, in secret. She had told them never to tell their father. It was ten years ago but they both still remembered. The smell of tobacco and sage brought back his mother so that it was as if she sat there next to Charlene, watching her son and daughter.

Patrick sucked in. 'Grandfather, Grandmother without you we are nothing. You made the winged people, you made the fish people, you made red, black, yellow and white. Protect Char while I am away. Make her safe from the Reverend until I get back. Please give her enough to eat and help her to know what to say to him and when to say it so that she doesn't get hit.'

As he said the words, he knew their power. The power of the old words hummed through him. The words carried his mother with them, and her mother, and all the People. The words had power.

Patrick sucked the cigarette again, then handed it to Charlene who smoked it down. When it was almost finished, she put it in the first pile of tobacco.

They burned the tobacco piles one by one, and at the end burned some sage too. When it was all finished Charlene picked up the hamburger and divided it in half. She gave half to her brother, and ate the rest. They did the same with the blackberries and the frozen corn, sucking on it to make it thaw, crunching on its raw sweetness.

'All my relations,' said Patrick.

'All my relations. I bet we'll dream tonight.'

'I hope not,' said Patrick.

'You've been having nightmares.'

'I hear her screaming. She's in this little room, and then . . .'

He fell into silence. Neither of them wanted to think about it. But he was going to go and confront her death. He was going to challenge the dream.

Patrick got up with the dawn, a pink, August dawn smelling of cut lawns and the salty bay which paints blue the western edge of Seattle. He caught a bus downtown and transferred to an airporter taking him to SeaTac.

Within three hours he had boarded a British Airways flight. Nine hours later he touched down on the tarmac at London Heathrow.

CHAPTER 5

Sleeping in the Dream Room

One Saturday morning (Michael still hadn't come for his suits) Kitsy stared into the front garden through the kitchen window, her eyes fixed on the black bin. A brown banana skin hung over its lip. White plastic nappies propped open the lid.

Would Michael come back? Not knowing spread over her mind in a thick layer of white. It straddled her like the wide legs of a rodeo cowboy; it rode her thoughts, pressed heavy against her so that it felt as if someone squeezed her, tried to make her smaller.

Kitsy had used every china plate in the house. They piled up on the worktop in rickety heaps with metal cutlery handles sticking out, leaning like cartoons of stacked plates. All she needed to do was pull on one fork and the whole heap would tumble down. Kitsy played tower-of-blocks with herself – slide in a mug, a little saucer, balance a spoon. How many dishes could she eat from and stack, waiting for her hands to wash up? Could she empty the plate cupboard? The cutlery drawer? Until finally the only clean utensil was a wooden mixing spoon?

'Fuck fuck fuck,' she said to herself. 'You sad fucking woman you.'

She went to the hall mirror and looked at herself, honestly, not one of those preening suck-in-the-tummy glances, but an open look at who she was now. She saw a plumpish, middle-class woman dressed in nice clothes from Principles that matched and co-ordinated in pastel colours, and she thought: *This is who Michael walked out on, and I don't much like her either.*

She pulled her long blonde hair up from one side, swept it tight to her face and thought, *I might be more attractive bald.* But bald was blasé – no, make it half-bald and the other half cornrows. Then she had a wicked idea, so wicked that it made her laugh to herself. She held her left hand up to her face, that fat diamond engagement ring.

That would be just the trick, she thought. *Saw off the diamond, make it into a stud, and stick it right through my nose.*

Later that morning, she went to have her nose pierced in Camden Town. Now maybe her mum wouldn't say it was 'pert'. Kitsy hated that. As if she still looked like the imitation Hayley Mills her mum had dressed her up to resemble when she was a kid. She wasn't afraid of the pain – no pain could compare to the orange waves of fire that had brought Lucy into the world. That's why she didn't flinch when the man put the gold tack to her nostril, its one sharp tooth scratching into her. He pushed and she stiffened at that small, specific pain, like a pulled milktooth, like a breaking hymen. It went to the middle of her head and dispersed. That jab woke her up, marked the starting point for the changes she had to make, to shed the plumpish woman, to become small, hard, glittering-eyed – a woman who said before any words were spoken: 'I don't take no shit from nobody.'

When Kitsy got home she put Lucy in her backpack and spent the rest of the day dusting, polishing and scrubbing until the house smelled of Pledge and Mr Sheen and lemon multi-surface cream cleaner, and tried not to touch her nose, which itched.

Every time Kitsy passed the door to the junk room she felt a warm place in her reach out to whatever power lay behind it. Something tugged her towards that room until finally she found herself tidying in there too, putting on an electric fire to get rid of the cold, unused smell, polishing the mahogany desk, changing the sheets on the guest bed. As she worked, stuffing a bin bag with old papers, Christmas decorations that wouldn't see another year and a plastic champagne bucket, Kitsy felt conscious of another woman's presence. It wasn't a feeling of being watched, but more an awareness.

Now, the memory of something she'd heard once (and dismissed – she hadn't wanted to think about it) that a woman had been murdered in this house, made her stare down at the blue carpet. She wondered if there had been blood drops there, but it was blank with the emptiness of blue. She stopped polishing the purplish wood to listen.

Finally Kitsy sat on the bed holding a Pledge-soaked rag which was criss-crossed with black lines of dust and stunk of cheap rose scent. She thought about what to make for dinner, Lucy would want something to eat soon. She looked around the tidy room – warm, the bed ready for a guest, the desk shining – and it seemed welcoming.

The early evening sunlight through the window made a square of carpet golden-blue. She took off the baby's back-pack and her shoes and moved her bare feet into that patch of warm sun; its breath of warmth forced her eyelids to shut halfway. Holding Lucy to her chest, Kitsy pulled the bed's feather pillow into the sunny spot and slid from the bed onto the carpet. Curling up into a tight ball, making her body as little as possible to fit into the light, snuggling Lucy close into her chest, the child's little feet resting on her knees, she closed her eyes and snoozed, descending into her unconscious mind like a spider reeling down from the ceiling to the floor. There she stayed and rested until, like warm air rising, her mind opened itself out.

She found herself up high in the corner of a small room, sitting on the picture rail over the doorframe and facing a large wooden cross on the far wall. An arrow flew through the door. Kitsy looked out through the door below her, back to where the arrow had come from, into a green field with tall golden grass and a few bushy trees. In the distance she heard a man and a woman arguing. She smelled violence, its discordance of sweat and urine, fear and ignorance, fear and wilfulness. She tried to move away but they entered the room through a door under the arrow-split cross.

The man's voice grew louder and louder until the woman's voice was submerged, until her mouth was yawing and her tongue flickering but no force, no sound came out. And then, as if she didn't exist, she became translucent, then transparent, then invisible so that Kitsy had a sense that the woman was still there, but that nobody could see her.

This ended.

Kitsy found herself floating in a bed of whipped cream at the ankles of a man floating with her, with her tongue licking his shin, licking the light salty sweat from his leg in long strokes. White rice-paper covered his face, his arms, his torso, so that they were a tracing of a dark outline. She saw only his legs fully and their fine, almost downy, black hair. She reached her arms up over her head and stretched until she could sneak her spread fingers under the thin paper's edge, brushing over the man's long curly hairs and to his warm stomach. She knew from his heat that this was not Michael and she enjoyed it, unworried, because Michael had gone and she must take her passion where she could find it.

This stopped.

Kitsy floated up through grey, floated up to Lucy moving and fussing. Kitsy felt a small dance of guilt go off in her stomach like a string of poppers: for feeling sexual about someone besides Michael; for feeling sexual with a baby sleeping next to her. She got up with Lucy to make the dinner, feeling now like a balloon on a string, pulled down.

The next day, Kitsy's mother came to visit. Her first words were: 'What on earth have you done to your face?'

Flo stood on the doorstep, staring at her daughter through a mask of make-up. Her four miniature poodles yapped and bounced up and down like epileptic marionettes. Her hair looked as if it had been in a gale, sticking away from her face in stiff blonde wisps. She carried a coat on her arm and over her shoulder a huge Tardis of a leather handbag.

Always her mother gave an impression of extreme disarray, carrying with her a cloud of debris like a personal whirlwind. But Kitsy wasn't taken in. Flo always had a Point To Make. She drove that point home with the accuracy of a sledgehammer.

Kitsy tried to be unconcerned, to remember her new resolve. Nothing was going to shake that, not even – especially not – this purple Sta-prest-trousered woman with fake pearls the size of 50p pieces clipped to her ears. She tried to think of a comeback – *What on earth have you done to your own face?* but ended up stepping backwards down the hall to let in the force that was her mother.

'Haven't you done enough already without that *graffiti* in your nose?' said Flo as she went into the sitting room and clicked the poodles off their leads one by one. Each had a diamanté-studded, leather-with-felt-backing collar. Each one was shampooed, curly white fur with pink skin. Each one flew around the room in crazy directions so that as Flo sat down on the settee with a plump, Kitsy ran to scoop up

Lucy from the floor, to keep her daughter from the little, sharp, curious teeth.

'Me, done enough?' said Kitsy when she'd got Lucy squirming in her arms.

'Michael's gone. You'd better watch out or they'll come and take Lucy away. Look at the *state* of you! You used to look like that Ulrika off the telly and now you look like nothing at all!'

Kitsy glanced down at herself, past Lucy's chubby, kicking legs. She wore a man's second-hand shirt, a pair of old jeans with a hole in the left knee and black lace-up boots.

'Mum, I do not look like that bimbo! My nose is crooked for a start, and so are my teeth. And I've got green eyes and she's got blue. I do *not* look like Ulrika for Chrissakes!'

'No need to get your knickers in a twist,' Flo huffed. 'It was meant as a *compliment*. Anyway, you'd never pass for her in the state you're in now.'

'What do you mean?' Kitsy's defences went up another notch. 'What's so bad about this? Maybe I'm sick of you saying I look like her!'

'You used to be so nice. Where's your make-up? Don't you have any of those pretty leggings Michael paid for? The lavender ones?'

Kitsy had bagged all her High Street clothes into black binliners and taken them to Oxfam – *especially* the lavender ones. They were so middle-class, so wanting to look *nice*, as if she belonged to some women's lunch set, or aspired to. Now all the jeans and T-shirts she had left were old and worn and pre-Michael. Except a suit. She kept a suit back for emergencies.

Besides, Kitsy wanted to return to her mother's previous topic. 'Why will they take Lucy away?'

'Oh,' said Flo, waving her hand in a generic gesture that

covered all reasons, gave all justifications. She opened her handbag and took out four rubber bones, a squeaky mouse, and a sandwich bag of chocolate dog buttons. The dogs gathered around her ankles and sat obediently, mouths open and slobbering, while she placed a chocolate button on each pink tongue. She threw the rubber bones onto the carpet and the poodles fought and snarled and headed off to different corners wagging their heads.

Kitsy stared at the dogs. *They are so typical of her,* she thought. *The minute she can't dress me up in frilly frocks and bows she goes out and starts collecting yap dogs. And every once in a while she throws them a bone as well.*

She was so glad she no longer had to live with Mum and Dad in their musty terraced house in Hornsey. How claustrophobic she'd felt growing up – her hair, her clothes always full of smoke and old heat; the double glazing sealing everything in. When she was thirteen and fed up, she got a ladder out of the shed one day, leaned it against the house, and climbed onto the roof. She'd wondered at the cloud-pictures in the summer sky, enjoying the breeze, the smell of hot tiles, of being away from the car-exhaust fumes which smelled to her like frustration itself: grey and peppery and poisonous. She'd also done it so that her mother would take her seriously, look her in the eye and listen to her. But all she got was a yelling-at from Mum followed by a talking-to by her normally silent Dad. You'd think she'd remember what he'd said, considering he was so quiet most of the time, as if by not talking he'd lessen the pollution of chatter her mother spewed out. She could see his face, trying to be stern with her, and underneath that a genuine concern for her safety. But his words? Nothing remained of them.

Then Flo took out a cigarette and a gold-cased lighter with a gothic 'F' stamped on it. She snapped the lighter open. With one corner of her mouth clamped down on the cigarette she said, 'Fathers still get custody, you know. Nowadays more than ever.'

'Don't smoke in my house,' said Kitsy as Flo touched the flame to the tobacco.

Flo drew the smoke down into her lungs, exhaled. 'No?' she said.

'No!' Kitsy snatched the cigarette out of her mother's hand and put it in a mug of cold tea on the side table. The cigarette went out with a small swish. 'It's bad for Lucy,' she said. She felt her jeans squeeze her around the middle, felt the loose skin and fat of her stomach flopping over the waistband. Felt as if she should be wearing different clothes. She touched a finger to her nose, gave the stud a tug, made it hurt. Made herself remember.

'Well,' said Flo, putting the lighter away slowly, settling back, changing tack, squeezing the squeaky mouse in her hand so it wheezed. 'What are you going to do with yourself now?'

'I'm going to do something I've always wanted to do, but never had the guts to,' said Kitsy. She sat down on the floor and held Lucy in her lap. Lucy pointed at a poodle worrying a table leg with his teeth. 'I'm going to become a tattoo artist.'

Flo's eyebrows shot up. She leaned forward. Her hands fiddled with the catch on her bag. Out came the cigarettes. Out came the gold-cased lighter.

'I said no smoking,' Kitsy reminded her. 'Mum, put those away!'

Flo put the bag down, but held the packet of Silk Cut and the lighter in her lap. She didn't say anything, trying her big weapon: get Kitsy nervous, get her to talk, to appease.

But this time Kitsy held onto Lucy, put her mouth and nose to the baby's hair, breathed in that softness, that smell like hay.

'You had so much with Michael,' Flo started in, a little edge of a whine in her voice. 'Are you sure you've done enough to get him back? Michael is your only hope, Kitsy.'

'My hope?'

'Of making something of yourself. What is this tattoo rubbish? What kind of thing is that for a mother with a little daughter to be doing? Look at you! You're twenty-eight years old and you've gone to hell. You used to wear *nice* clothes, take care of yourself. You had that membership to the David Lloyd Sports Centre. I suppose that's gone now! You had BUPA – you had the *best* of *everything*! But now? You won't make *nothing* of yourself. Even if you went back to work, you'd still never earn as much as Michael. Did you really try, Kitsy? Did you really *try*? For Lucy's sake? For God's sake, Kitsy, stop acting like a proper little madam!'

'You and your little fur monsters can get out now, Mum,' said Kitsy, as if she were telling her mother that her toast was ready.

Flo looked at her daughter. She picked up her cigarettes, and her lighter, and her handbag. She picked up the four doggie leads and the squeaky mouse. She stood up.

'I don't want to see you until you can apologise,' said Kitsy, still sitting on the floor.

'And I don't want to see you until you can talk some sense!' said Flo and walked into the hall. 'Yeats! Burnsie! Shelley! Pope! Come *here*! At *once*!' she shouted. The poodles and their bright-coloured rubber bones fell in behind her. She snapped the leads onto their diamanté collars and jerked them along as she headed for the door, stepping stiffly, her back upright.

Kitsy didn't turn around to watch her mother go out, to watch her leading that bouquet of poodles. She cuddled Lucy tight until the baby pushed herself away, and then read *Postman Pat* to Lucy over and over on automatic pilot, until she couldn't stand her thoughts any longer, or the tears beginning to spill into the book.

After Kitsy signed up for a course on Elements of Body Art, she unplugged the telephones.

She had come to dislike telephones. For a while, every time the telephone rang it sent a jolt through her system. She had been afraid to pick it up in case it was Michael, or her mother. But the call never was from Michael or Flo. In silent agreement they boycotted Kitsy, and every time she put the phone down from somebody else it set her to worrying, feeling sad that those two important people hadn't called, and sometimes she cried.

So in the end, she made it impossible for them to call her. She took the fear away from the telephone. She gave everyone her next-door neighbour Barbara's number, even the DSS.

Then she went around the house pulling all the white plugs out of all the white sockets (except for the modem on the computer), wrapping the telephone wires around the telephone bodies, and left them bound and helpless on a little shelf.

CHAPTER 6

Walking the Harder Path

It all gave Patrick a feeling of triumph: the hubbub of the baggage hall, figuring out from black and green television sets hung in the air which carousel would spit out his purple backpack, picking up the pack and leaving through Nothing To Declare.

He felt himself expanding, growing stronger. As if the fact of getting on that plane and coming to London, of getting out of Seattle and away from all those people who knew him only as a little boy, of leaving for a new land on a mission of his own was a metamorphosis in itself. He had emerged from the cocoon of the plane hardened, able to fight, to plan for himself.

Wearing Jimmy Mac's jacket, Patrick changed a hundred-dollar bill at one of the bank windows in the huge white arrivals hall. It made sixty-five pounds. With the independent feeling of foreign money in his pocket he followed signs to the Underground. He remembered the tube journeys with his mother and how he had liked them – the trains going clackety-clack, roaring through black tunnels and screeching to a stop at the next station with a terrific squeal of steel wheels locked on steel track. In Seattle, bendy buses were as exotic as you got.

A train pulled up; its doors swished open. Patrick stepped up into it, feeling as if he were stepping onto a magic carpet. The doors hissed and clattered shut. Patrick stood, not holding onto a steel pole but bracing his feet against the wooden runners in the floor, balancing with the weight of his pack, testing himself, his strength and balance. As if these things could matter, as if being able to stand up when the train came to a jolting halt meant he'd passed a kind of test. At King's Cross he got off and looked at the signs, half-ladders of black lines with names on each rung. He wanted the black line to Finchley Central. Patrick waited on a ledge overlooking the rails, stared at a dirty grey mouse skittering along tracks. Forty-five minutes later the train thumped out of a tunnel and into suburbia, whisking by the backs of red-brick houses with garden fences made out of thin wooden slats woven like paper Easter baskets, washing flapping behind them to the rhythm of the train's clack-clack.

He came from the open-air platform and walked up to the heat of the street and took off his black leather jacket. Being here felt like being transported onto a movie set, as if all the people scurrying by, shoulders bent, looking un-focused at the ground, past all their red-brick stuck-together houses and shops – as if all these people were put here solely for his pleasure.

A car burped by, blowing a white cloud of fumes in his face. That smell he remembered. That smell, blacker, more pungent and acrid than the car fumes at home, made him eight years old and standing next to his mother, ready to cross the street to the papershop. The car smells here belonged to this place; they would be as foreign to Seattle as the brick houses with tall windows crammed shoulder-to-shoulder with no front lawns, everything brick or pavement, red or grey. Patrick tried to follow the thought of his mother: her thin, soft hand, the feel of his head leaning against her hip, the smell of her skirt: cotton and sage, woman's sweat.

Patrick felt he should be walking too, had the urge to fall in. He walked slowly along the street looking in windows, past a papershop, past a Japanese general store and a Japanese restaurant and a Japanese estate agent. At the end of the block he looked for a streetsign. He found it, screwed high up in the red-brick wall of the end building, a sign with scalloped ends, a curlicue finish and thick, black letters – *Lichfield Grove* – almost illegible through dirt.

In this street his mother died.

Even numbers on the south side, odd numbers on the north. He walked up the north side, looking for the number he knew. When he found it he stood in front of the house and stared.

The house in his dreams: red-brick with a black-and-white tiled path leading up to a black front door with inset stained glass, and stained-glass panels on either side. The front of the house curved out in a semi-circle into the front yard. A low, flintstone garden wall kept rubbish from blowing onto the grass. A little wooden gate with a little wrought-iron latch painted black and rusty in patches where the paint had peeled, kept stray dogs out and children in.

Patrick remembered it all, except the pink rose-bushes.

It had all been so easy – the flight, taking the subway up here, finding the house – that it wasn't until now that the weariness, the drip-drip wearing of the journey, the nine-hour flight and eight-hour time difference between Seattle and London began to catch up. It wasn't until he had arrived home.

Patrick propped his backpack up against the wall under a little white box that held empty milk bottles, walked through the gate, up the path and rang the bell.

Nothing happened.

He waited. How many times had he waited on a doorstep for someone to answer? Collecting money for his paper route. Ringing the door two or three times, then standing, listening, until he could hear a person on the other side of the door move around thinking it was safe, that he was gone. Trying to cheat a kid out of his paper money. With the worst customers he'd bang on the door and shout: 'I know you're in there!'

He rang the doorbell again.

This time he heard an inner door open, and footsteps. They stopped, hesitated at the door. He knew someone was watching him, trying to decide. The door opened and crunched against a chain. A woman with long blonde hair pulled back into a pony-tail and a huge diamond stud in her nose squinted at him through a four-inch gap.

'Um, I used to live here,' said Patrick. 'I wonder if I could look at your house?'

'My house?' said Kitsy.

'Yeah.'

'Who are you?'

'Pat. Patrick Hunter. My parents used to live here when I was a kid. I've come all the way from America to see the house again.'

'No,' she said, and shut the door.

Patrick stood, thinking: *I've fucked up, I've fucked up. She's the one and I've fucked up*.

He wanted to be on the other side of the door, within those cradling walls. So close, so close to his mother again. He tried to remember the face of the woman in his dream, the one who'd held his hands across a table. The two weren't an exact match, except for the hair. His dream-lady was heavier, less angular. But it didn't matter. He *knew*.

Patrick stood on the step, staring at the black door into the stained glass. On sunny days, he remembered, it lit up with flights of blue birds. He'd sit at the foot of the staircase and watch them flock over their pond, its green grasses waving in a permanent breeze, an orange semi-circular sun setting behind them. Some birds had settled on brown rocks, some dipped their yellow beaks, wide-open toward the pond, catching insects, others with skinny black legs outstretched waited to land, forever hovering.

As Patrick stood, staring into glass black with the shadow of late-afternoon, he could make out the colours enough to remember he was a little boy again, sitting on that bottom step with his arms wrapped around his shins and his chin resting on a kneecap, staring into the glass which danced blue, yellow, orange, brown and black on his face, shifting stainless imprints onto his white church-school shirt. He sat on the bottom step concentrating, to fill the world with those birds and their pond and a perfect semi-circle of orange sun so that he couldn't think that he'd never see his mother again, so that he'd banish that thought from any corner of his mind, so that he couldn't cry.

It began to rain.

Patrick was aware that the woman watched him from behind her curtains at the window. He didn't care. Something had opened in him. It spilled out gold-bright and writhing and reaching for healing.

The rain clung to Patrick's black hair in bright, dainty droplets. Then it hit harder, faster, bigger until runnels channelled over either side of his straight, high-bridged nose, until four streams of water coursed over his wide lips, clung to his hard-cut chin and joined in a river down his throat, down each muscle standing out in his neck.

The rain didn't bother him. Patrick knew the rain, this June rain with its coolness. He could walk in it barefooted and never catch cold. He could lie in the grass naked and let it wash over him without being afraid, and when it was done pick up a shirt and dry off his body.

It wasn't the rain that drove Patrick from Kitsy's doorstep. It was the end of his memory of the stained glass, an inability to go over it again, to concentrate on it any more. The woman wouldn't let him in yet. Time to move on.

Patrick picked up his pack from under the milk bottles. He shouldered it and walked to the low gate, let himself out. Instead of walking right toward the station and the stores, he turned left to look for a little park which he remembered, holding in mind his need to find a camp, a place to sleep.

Halfway up the road he turned right into a dead end. At the bottom of the dead end was a huge field, the size of two football fields. He stopped, disoriented, until two children on bicycles came out of an alleyway on the right, driven from their play by the afternoon drizzle. Patrick walked down the alley and found an entrance to the park on his left.

It seemed to be a big park. He walked around it twice, and then took all the faint children's paths to their forts in the bushes. Although the park gave the impression of seclusion, it would actually be a difficult place to hide in. The undergrowth had been stripped away, and the lower branches of trees and bushes clipped out. A man couldn't hide in them unless he climbed up and hid in the greenery at the top.

But that was the trees and bushes. It didn't take into account a huge, stone-walled area which looked as if it had been stables three-quarters of a century ago. Every entrance, every window, was bricked up or nailed shut with plywood. That wouldn't stop Patrick. There were chunks missing out of that sandy wall. Straight up for twenty feet, and swing down through trees on the other side.

Patrick glanced left, right, behind his back, looking for people.

He started up the wall, fighting to stay on it against the weight of the pack which pulled him backwards. Fingers, toes, boost up, fingers again – like this he crawled to the top. He lifted his body with his arms, bringing his feet up into a tuck under his bottom. He balanced there choosing a branch of an oak tree. He sprung, grabbing at branches as he flew and fell, a rush of adrenaline making his body feel taut, powerful, beautifully alive. He caught a branch and swung, hanging, for a moment before dropping the rest of the way into tall grass and weeds.

Behind him came the sound of soft clapping.

It was an old man with grey whiskers and a deeply-lined face, wearing an old knitted brown waistcoat which hung to his thighs over a shirt dotted with the round, crusty brown holes of cigarette burns.

'Whoja fink you are, effing Rambo or sommink?' said the man. The only word Patrick understood was 'Rambo'. He walked over to the bushes to pick up his backpack.

'Ain't ya ever heard of a gate, son?' continued the little man.

'Gate?' said Patrick, trying to get past the man's thick East-end accent, picking up a few words in each sentence.

'Shh! Keep shturm!' hissed the man. 'D'ya want 'em to hear ya?'

'Who?'

'The rangers is who! That'll be two quid, a fiver if you're spending the night, seven if you want the suite.'

'Forget it,' said Patrick.

'This is my gaff and anyone who dosses here pays.'

'Your what? This is a park. Nobody pays.' Patrick couldn't believe it. Here he thought he'd found a quiet, secluded place to camp, somewhere to roll out his sleeping bag and make plans. Already it was crowded.

'Ya ain't from around 'ere,' said the little old man, cocking his head at Patrick like a crow.

'Two points,' said Patrick.

'You're American, ain't ya?'

'Uh-huh.'

'Then you can afford to sleep somewheres posh.'

'Look,' said Patrick, beginning to get annoyed. 'Go away and leave me alone.'

'You've got to pay at Ronnie's place,' said the little old man, and he beetled off to a blue tarpaulin stretched between two bushes and fixed at the back with posts.

The old man's camp was at the far end of the walled enclosure. Although grass and weeds grew as high as Patrick's waist, there was a neatness about the place. Little paths had been cut into the weeds with a machete or small scythe. A few fruit trees looked compact and tidy, as if they'd been pruned. The old man busied himself over a patch of earth, digging at a few rows of plants with a miniature pitchfork, stabbing at them and surreptitiously glancing at Patrick, as if he expected the boy to sneak up and bash him over the head.

At the opposite end to the old man were remains of stables and outbuildings, some with roofs on them, some with only jagged fingers of walls. Patrick wondered why this guy Ronnie hadn't camped in there, under shelter.

Patrick took off his pack and leaned it against an oak tree. He tramped through weeds and grass to the ruined walls, gathering stones as he went. He picked up a few bricks, stacking them in the cradle of his arms, and hauled them back to the tree. In a patch of dirt he set them in a circle. From his pack he took a newspaper, separated out some sheets and scrunched them up into little balls. He crouched and put these inside the circle, gathered a few sticks from

74

around himself and laid them on the newspaper in the shape of a little tepee.

He took out his lighter and knelt over the firepit, touching flame to paper. When he looked up it was into a pair of paint-splashed leather workboots. The old man again.

'Go away,' said Patrick. 'I'm busy.'

'You can't light fires before dark,' said the old man, agitated.

'Why not?' said Patrick, not bothering to look up, but watching his fire spread over the paper, lick up the small sticks. He took a larger stick and placed it on top, balancing it on the burning paper.

'The rangers will see it.'

The rangers again. Still, he had a point. This was the middle of the city. Someone might see the smoke.

'I'll think about it,' said Patrick. He sat back from the little campfire. The big stick wasn't catching. It needed drying out with the lighter. The newspaper had almost burned down, and the little sticks were orange and black twiglets. Patrick decided to leave the fire, to listen to the old man's sense. He sat back, leaning against the pack, and took out the bundle of his mother's letters from his pocket. He'd read them briefly on the plane. Now he wanted to read them again, before darkness fell, to look for guidance on how to begin.

He weighed the first envelope in his hand. It was warm from his pocket, from being close to his body. It felt thick, as if the letter inside was worth reading. A small envelope, a small rectangle of nothing paper. Bright white. On the front, a stamp with the Queen's head. The address, *Lichfield Grove*. Postmarked *Harrow*. No return address.

The letter was to Patrick's mother, Alice, from vicar John Abernathy of Harrow-on-the-Hill. Patrick lifted the envelope's flap. He opened envelopes the way she had taught him – the same way she opened them, and had opened this one. It's the slowest, most difficult way of opening envelopes, to slide your thumbnail under the edge and follow the line of licked glue along its wide 'v', bringing the flap free as if it had never been stuck down. Seeing the envelope opened like that reminded Patrick of how she was, how she always said, 'Never flinch from the harder path; just because it's harder, don't take the easy path. You won't learn to be a man on the easy path.'

The envelope, the way it had been carefully unsealed along the harder path made Patrick think: *Mom, it would have been nice to be given a choice between the two.*

He lifted the letter out, leaving the envelope a white husk against the blue jeans of his lap, and gazed at the white sheet of paper with grey lines – its ruffled edge torn from a letter-pad. He unfolded it, this letter that had come through her death, saved, a souvenir.

The writing, spidery, close, backward-slanting, said:

My Dearest Alice,
I write to thank you for your most generous hospitality on Friday night. It isn't often one gets the chance to sample real American food, and cooked by such a fine hostess.

The conversation we had over coffee lingered with me far into the night and held such sway over my mind that I arose this morning at once to change my sermon. No doubt it will be lost on some of Harrow's great and good, but it certainly bears the stamp of your influence.

I must say that whilst I agree, and indeed it is a basic tenet of theology that God is all-encompassing, omnipotent, I cannot begin to bring into my philosophy the doctrine of pantheism, your notion that there is life and spirit in everything, even the dumb rocks! God created man to have dominion over the earth. I also find your argument of

continual fleshly sacrifice deeply unsettling; it reminds me
too much of the priests of old who practised flagellation. I
am glad that the church no longer encourages us to use a
cat o'nine tails to reach a spiritual pinnacle. Did not Jesus
sacrifice Himself on the cross that all may live? That is all
the healing we require. In Christ we have no need for witch
doctors.

Patrick pictured John Abernathy in his mind: short, a big
belly, dressed in tight tweed trousers and a tight brown
sweater, a trimmed beard and a bald scalp. Hair on his face
that should have been on his head. The man would wear
half-glasses that he let slide down his nose, and then he'd
look over them at people and squint, pursing his lips. He
read on:

I am sure you are grateful that Patrick and Charlene
have been baptised into Jesus, that there will be no need for
them to make flesh sacrifices in the way the Red Indians
did. I think we can all be happy that that is now stamped
out, and that thanks to the unselfish work of missionaries
like your husband, your people have been brought gently
into Christ's way.

Yours in Christ,
John.

Patrick re-folded the letter and slid it back into its envelope.
It made him so angry that he wanted to burn it, pick up
one of those smouldering twigs and hold its orange ember
against the paper until a flame licked up and ate the paper
into ash. 'Red Indians' – who the fuck said that any more?
It ranked right up there with 'savages'. And 'your people
have been brought gently into Christ's way'. Gently, sure,

if you call killing most of them off gentle.

Feelings that Patrick had kept repressed since his mother's death, feelings that he couldn't have if he were to survive in his father's house with Bible readings before breakfast, lunch and dinner, feelings for another culture which had rooted itself deeper inside him than his father's Anglo-American family tree began to poke out, like sticks buried in the mud at the bottom of a drying pond.

In the back garden in London his mother had finally taught them some things, Charlene and Patrick taken outside when their father was away. Weekdays sitting in warm grass breathing, listening to stories, learning. Sundays sitting in a row on a cold wooden bench, Charlene in white tights and black patent leather shoes, a pink dress and a little white hat. Patrick zipped into trousers that pulled at his crotch, his neck sealed with a tie, lines of water on a comb like croplines slicked into his hair. Their mother listening to his father's sermon with her eyes closed.

He remembered that she had started when he was five because the year was a shrunken green apple. The memories of each year before his mother's death were preserved, as if they had been sealed in amber, by associating them with a symbol, an event. At five years old he'd found a shrunken green apple in the back yard, taken it inside, and she showed him how to stick toothpicks in it for arms and legs, and cloves for the eyes, nose and a mouth. At six, he'd noticed the man's head on an American penny, and she'd told him that was Lincoln, a President, and showed him a penny from Canada with the Queen on it. He never did understand exactly why America didn't have a Queen. Seven was a straight ash stick that he'd found in the alley and stripped the bark off with a penknife, and she'd helped carve one end into an eagle's head for him. The stick got thrown away when they moved. He'd gone to fish it out from under his bed, but it wasn't there, and no one had seen it. Eight was her death. Memories were the only parts of her that he had, and he kept these clips of little scenes in his mind, back to the time when he had been in diapers in a sling against her chest while she sung and did housework. That's how far back his memory went.

He could remember words of lullabies, snatches of her language. Little tunes. He wondered, Would I understand if that old man over there started talking to me in Lakota? Would I know what he said? And he saw in front of him his mother standing over him in her jeans with her black hair parted in the middle, holding a piece of sage, saying. 'This is for driving away evil. If you need to bring good spirits, then you burn sweetgrass. Sage and sweetgrass together purify.'

Patrick never spoke about her, not because he was ashamed, but because letting air into that part of his mind might dirty her memory. He had to keep it clean. Keep it holy. Hide the memory of her and what she tried to teach him until he could get away and understand it.

Well, here I am, he said to himself.

A word came into his mind: *wasichu*. He could hear his mother shout it at his father, an accusation, a curse. His father must have known its meaning. And another word: *tunka*. He said it to himself then, '*Tunka*.' He spoke it into the air of the early summer evening, and the word itself seemed mysterious and holy, a thumping, deep and solid foundation of a word. '*Tunka!*' he said again, and felt his place in this strong, tall, young-man's body, leaning against a wall in a crumbling stables in a park, and felt himself to be at the centre.

Tomorrow, start with John Abernathy, he thought. *Let's see where that goes*.

That deciding thought brought with it sleep, the urge to

yawn, fill up with good air, good air for sleep. He was more tired than he'd thought. Patrick unzipped his pack and pulled out a red sleeping bag and a roll of black plastic sacks. He flung out his sleeping bag so it unfurled like a red tongue, then cracked open a black plastic rubbish bag, ballooned it out with a thwack. He stuffed the pack into the sleeping bag, then both into the sack so that when dew fell, the black-green plastic would keep him dry. He tucked his passport into his underpants and wriggled himself feet first into the rubbish bag sausage.

Patrick snuggled down, settled his body against the hard ground, his hands under his head clapped together like praying hands on top of Jimmy's jacket, folded up so the zippers wouldn't press traintracks into his cheek. He wished he had someone with him to share his sleeping bag, Becky or Jolene maybe – girls he'd slept with at parties, made out with in friends' cars. Warm willing arms, soft bodies, bright mouths.

Patrick looked up at the oak, at the first darkening of the sky from light blue, the colour of ice, of a hole in the snow, richening to a darker blue and the blink of a plane-light circling. He watched that light until it went and another one took its place. The stars winked open, one, add another, and the amber clouds driven by a high wind moved on to reveal more. He watched this symphony of points of silver light come out for him, watched the branches, and leaves of the oak tree fade to dark green, to black, so that he could no longer see the tree but sense the branches by the spaces where there were no stars.

He was surprised. *This is London: I thought there would be no stars, too much light.* He picked out the constellations, always Orion first, low, then Gemini and Cancer, and knew: *I am here, this world is me.*

Some hooting, in the distance, something calling, like a

ferryboat in fog took him back to a thick grey Seattle morning and hoots loud like breath blown over a wine jug, a jug with a fat round-bottom belly. He was riding an orange schoolbus along the shoreline road on Alki Point, the Sound churned the light green of scratched jade, waves breaking on shore, the whipped edge of jade-green water. On that day he imagined himself as a little statue of jade hovering over the water and then breaking its surface, sinking. He concentrated hard on the picture, felt himself to be stone, stone with no cold, stone with no pain. And for a moment he *was* a jade statue wrapped in the clouds of fog, not feeling the pain from the bruises on his arm – his father's finger-prints – or the welts on his bottom – his father's beltprints.

The ferry's foghorn broke his concentration and he thought: *Out there, with the ferry, the water could be a different colour, red maybe, or pink, thick like Pepto-Bismol. Who knows.*

The fog was thick and he stared into it, trying to see the ferry-lights. He thought he saw a string of lights – there! – like a necklace of white Christmas-tree lights, maybe his mother's spirit lights, maybe his mother on the ferry, her hands stretched above her head to the sky at the front of the boat like a figurehead, praying; at the head of the Vashon ferry she was coming for him wreathed in points of light.

He wished it were true, but his mother swirled into fog, joined the clouds.

He saw commuters on the ferry's car deck staring over the edge at the fog, white clouds swimming by, breaststroke. They shook their heads to themselves, and zipped up their jackets, headed inside to foam-filled pink bench seats and nasty coffee. The ferry chug-a-lugged to the West Seattle dock and the passengers faintly wondered, but not in a way that's really thinking about it in case it came true, will the Captain hit the pier? But in his white cabin at the top of the ship with voices on a crackling radio trying to guide him in, the Captain shut off his ears, let the fog drift around his boat, steered by feeling, and docked with a grunt.

Patrick fell asleep listening to his heart beat *tunka, tunka, tunka*, thumping quietly like a ferryboat engine in the night.

He woke up, ears first: ears open and eyes closed. Voices. He knew where he was, coming up from sleep. He had never left this space, remained aware that he was under the oak tree in a red sleeping bag on the ground in a park in London. Above the voices he heard the pop of a fire; he could see with his mind's eye the spit of spark cracking into the night. He opened his eyes to the dark, but with the shadowiness of a million streetlights and half a moon.

'Did he pay?' said the first voice.

'Nah,' said Ronnie.

'Then he ain't staying.'

'He can pay tomorrow.'

'This ain't for free. Not for every Tom Dick and Harry, this.'

'He's all right. You should have seen him! Like Tarzan he was, swinging on that tree. Didn't know whether to laugh or what.'

Patrick went back to sleep.

Patrick woke in that moment of silence between darkness and grey dawn. He woke and listened, not afraid, not afraid of the silence and somewhere the rhythmic clatter of a train. He had an urgent need to piss, a pressing need, full up. He turned over to climb out of his bag but stopped, listening, feeling this silence too important to break even with the rustle of skin on nylon, this dark silence of no birds.

He lay down again (putting his urge back) to listen for the dawn break. Then, the first trill, the first birdcall above him in his oak tree, and that alarm, that whistle, high-pitched goes on, a singing, goes on with little spaces where the bird breathes and forces air into the dawn and wakes up another bird. A web of birdsong, a web of trilling, and it was a colour to Patrick, the colour orange, of kumquats and mangoes, forcing open the dawn, a dim light. The birdsong bubbled until three, five birds joined in and Patrick knew: *It's here, I'm OK to start my day.*

He climbed out of the bag, walked quietly to the wall and pissed into weeds making a little cloud of steam in the cold morning air. He went back to his sleeping bag and stuffed it into the pack. The garbage sack he hung out on a bush to dry off the dew, so that he could use it again tonight.

Patrick found a stick, took his penknife from the pack and whittled one end to a sharp point. He skewered a five-pound note onto the stick for Ronnie to find when he woke up, and stuck the bottom end of the twig into the earth, making a little pole, the money a stiff green flag at the top. Then Patrick shouldered his pack, climbed the oak tree, and dropped over the wall.

CHAPTER 7

Like a Red Leaf in a Fast River

Patrick walked down to the tube station, past two ticket windows, their black shades pulled over them like sleeping eyes, and skittered downstairs to the platform. A man pulled up the shutters of a blue newsstand, like a mouth snapping open, bundles of papers stacked near the door; he shuffled a bundle to the front of the stand, crouched, severed the plastic string with a knife and a pop, as it slashed up past his head. Patrick stared at the map, its spaghetti of red and yellow and brown, ciphering how to get to Harrow-on-the-Hill. Full of his route he plonked himself down on a bench of grey wooden slats, huddling into himself and the heavy leather jacket, hunched into his pack, keeping its warmth against his back.

Patrick didn't know where he was going, but it didn't bother him. He was following feeling. He was opening himself up, trying to let himself be like a leaf in a river, letting the water carry him to the place he should be, this little red leaf.

The train rattled into the station, swaying with the stateliness of an old elephant, a graffitied litter that bore him to King's Cross. On the way he stared at the Underground maps and the familiar station names – Piccadilly, Tottenham Court Road, Seven Sisters, Charing Cross . . . names he'd heard in songs or read in books. It felt like this whole city had been erected for his privilege as a visitor. At King's Cross he changed to the Metropolitan line and rumbled back out to the suburbs.

At Harrow-on-the-Hill a woman in a yellow sari, her black hair plaited down her back and tied with a red tassel at her waist, swept the pavement outside her shop. Black hair like his mother's black hair. He felt an affinity with this woman he'd never met before. It propelled him to ask her: 'Is there a church near here?' The woman tucked the top of the broom under her chin and pointed down the street. 'Walk that way for about five minutes.'

Patrick came to the woman's church. He pulled at the door handle, wrought iron, worn with the pulls of hundreds of hands, pitted by rust, rough and unfriendly in his palm. The door slowly came open – heavy, reluctant. Patrick was surprised that the church would be open so early, and on a Tuesday. His tennis shoes scraped against the stone flags in a square portico lined with brown wooden benches, a little portico finished with white plaster. The threshold was a long, dusty piece of stone, dipped in the middle like it had been worn away with water. He swung open the glass inner door and took off his pack and sat in the back pew, as if he waited for organ music.

The light of the morning poled in, no longer that first grey light: this was the strong promise of a blue day. Petals of the rose window in front of him exclaimed red and blue and yellow. A red velvet cloth trimmed with a white fringe was laid out over the altar. Behind it, two purple cloths strung on fishing line from the ceiling hung straight as plumblines, yelling *CHRIST IS RISEN!* and *LOVE THY NEIGHBOUR!* in wobbly yellow appliqué.

Even though old stone laid on the floor, the pews dipped, bumworn, and the stained glass spoke silent stories to people long-dead, the church still had a living air about it. He could hear his father up there, preaching.

The Reverend wild-eyed the congregation and yelled: 'The minions of Satan are waiting to lift you in their arms and carry you off to hell! They're all around, ready to bore into your soul and turn it into maggots!' He'd lift up his hands, like he was holding up a baby. 'Yes! It will seem like lifting, it will seem like you're happier in the sins and lusts of the flesh, but one day you will look in the mirror and a zombie will stare back at you! You will be one of the living dead!' Those arms would come down, both fists banging the podium and then he would scream: 'Jesus is the Way, He is the only Way! "I am the Way, the Truth, the Light. He that believeth on Me shall live for ever!" If you stop following Jesus even for one tiny minute, you will become a murderous whore of Jezebel! A Judas!'

When they were still living in Seattle, before they came to England, his father's sermons had been gentler, no talk of Satan in them, Devil this and demons that. Then if his mother threw cedar in their baths, little branches like fans that made the whole bathroom smell strongly of steam and cedar, and the scent went right through Patrick's head so that even his ears felt clean, his father would smile and say: 'Alice is going native again.'

Things changed after they got here. Whatever string wrapped circles around his father, holding everything in like an Easter ham, was cut. Patrick remembered one conversation very clearly. It stood out because his parents were fighting, and this fight was so bad that his mother told him to take Charlene and go in the back garden. Patrick took his baby sister's hand, but they went no further than the back step. As they huddled up against the door, Patrick's cheek pressed against the wood so that later it left a red imprint, like a slap.

Patrick and Charlene had been colouring on pieces of scrap paper in the kitchen. Their mother had been helping them draw simple symbols with thick crayons – the symbol for mountains – triangles, the symbol for the four directions – an equilateral cross, and the symbol for *Umane*, the leftover power, the power that was left after the creation of the universe and all the earth, the two-legged, and four-legged and winged people. They were drawing *Umane* in red when Patrick's father came into the room. Immediately Patrick could sense the tension, as if this were something he should be drawing behind the garage, or hiding in the attic with a flashlight. His mother looked stiff, worried too, although not afraid. There wasn't the full-blown fear in her yet. Not yet.

Their parents began talking, quietly at first, Patrick's father asking: 'Alice, why do you teach them this junk?'

She answered, 'It's not junk, it's their culture.'

'We agreed our children would be Christian children,' he said.

'They are,' she said.

'Then why are you teaching them these pagan things?'

'For Petesake, Frank!' she exclaimed. 'This stuff is so basic it's in the Boy Scout manuals! So what are you going to do now, ban our son from going to Boy Scouts? Ban Charlene from Campfire Girls? Make sure they never go to a museum?'

Patrick could see his father had stuffed his hands deep into his pockets, so they balled out a little, like he was carrying a whole bunch of loose change. He could see restraint and tension in those pockets.

'We baptised them, isn't that enough?' asked Alice, her hands free, roaming the air as she argued with her husband.

'What have you been doing on Sunday in church, Alice? Do you listen with your ears closed? Baptism is just the beginning. We must keep our children pure so they grow straight in the Grace of God, in Christ's way.'

That's when Alice hustled Patrick and Charlene outside and closed the door on her children. Finally, her voice again. Low, hissing, like water. 'I want equal time, Frank. I let you teach them about your God, now I want them to learn about mine.'

'Yours! There is only ONE God, Alice, and that is the Lord Jesus! Now if you can't agree with me on that fundamental point—'

'I am sick and tired of that Lord Jesus!' she screamed at him. 'What has your Lord Jesus ever done for me? I'll tell you what! Kill people so they lie bleeding in the snow, dead mothers in the snow with babies trying to suck at their breasts! I tell you, Frank, Jesus didn't die for *your* sins!'

'No? Who did then, Miss Smarty Pants?'

There was a long silence. As if Alice were circling the big round kitchen table, getting on the side opposite to Frank, putting four-and-a-half feet of solid pine between them.

'C'mon,' he taunted. 'Tell me. Who died for my sins?'

He had her cornered; he spoke calmly. He had her afraid to speak, afraid to finish, afraid to tell him what she really thought. 'So tell me, about this wonderful person. Who was he? C'mon Alice, surely you're ready to spread the good news.'

'Forget it.' Her voice was low. 'Just forget it.'

Patrick heard the sound of tearing paper.

Patrick and Charlene crept back inside when the fighting stopped. Their crayons had been put away and their drawings torn up and put in the rubbish along with coffee grounds and banana peels from breakfast. Alice stood at the sink with her back to them, washing dishes, stiff, sloshing the plates and coffee cups in the hot water.

The church door opening popped Patrick's memory. A

man came into the church wearing a brown and grey jumper and carrying a trowel stuck with dirt. He absorbed Patrick, then Patrick's biker's jacket and pack, all while he walked down the aisle.

'Excuse me,' said Patrick, knowing the man was wondering why he was here, sitting waiting. 'Can you tell me who the vicar is?'

'I am,' said the man, turning around.

'Can you help me? I'm looking for a man called John Abernathy. He used to be a vicar in this area. He was a friend of my father.'

'John Abernathy . . . the name is familiar. When was it?'

'About ten years ago. My father was an Episcopal minister. He came here on sabbatical, to study. They were friends.'

'If you come inside, we're just about to have breakfast. Maybe I can help you.'

The pew creaked as Patrick picked up his pack. He single-filed behind the vicar, footsteps echoing like in a high cave. Patrick, who was a full six inches taller than the vicar, felt tempted to reach over his back and open doors for him. Instead he said, 'My name is Patrick.'

The vicar answered, 'Mine is Evan. Evan Jones.'

The vicarage – a warm, spacious place with high ceilings – smelled of toast and coffee and frying. The vicar swung open a heavy wooden door with dingy brass handles. Patrick followed him into a dining room with a long picnic bench able to seat at least twelve people, and a floor-to-ceiling bookshelf packed higgledy-piggledy with books and loose papers, to the kitchen entrance where they stood shoulder-to-shoulder in a doorless doorframe.

The vicar's wife fried eggs and bacon and tomatoes on a cast-iron plate on a huge iron cooker painted bright green. She saw Patrick but didn't miss a beat. She said, 'Breakfast will be in five minutes. The coffee's steeping in the pot. Evan, get the milk out and pour, please.'

When Patrick was first in England, he had a school assignment to write down ten things he liked about his mother. He remembered only one, and that was because everyone else was shocked: *she makes great coffee*. The way that she made it was to throw a handful of coffee in a saucepan of water, add a few crushed eggshells, and boil. A pinch of salt, and then strain it off. Thick, bitter, rich. Patrick drank it dosed up with sugar before school. That coffee and a stack of buttered toast took him all the way to lunch and beyond. The thing that amazed Patrick was that he knew some of the English kids drank tea. His mother wouldn't let him near the stuff, no way. She would say: 'It stunts your growth. It'll turn you into a woman. No tea.' Charlene could have cambric tea – hot water, milk and a little sugar – but for her brother it was always coffee.

Mrs Jones' coffee was thick and bitter too. Patrick put his pack under the picnic table and wrapped his hands around the mug. He buried his nose in the steam while Evan dug around in the bookshelf.

'Our directory,' he said, holding up a little white book. 'I'll do some phoning after breakfast and see if I can't find your John Abernathy.'

'Dad, have you seen my—' said a girl as she burst into the room. She stopped. 'Oh my God,' she said, and went back out. Somewhere in the house Patrick could hear a scale of giggles.

'Don't mind her,' said Evan.

Patrick kept his mouth shut, drank his coffee.

At breakfast, Evan and Marjorie's two daughters sat on the opposite side of the picnic bench and gawked at him as he ate greasy eggs and salty bacon and pulped tomato. He felt like the guest star of an unpleasant chat show. He imagined the girls were about the same age as Charlene, only they seemed so much younger, without Charlene's gravity. Patrick couldn't see these two managing to feed their father and a brother, keep house and go to school. He couldn't imagine them doing anything except giggle.

'Patrick is looking for a John Abernathy. Do you know the name?'

Marjorie shook her head 'no', not speaking, pulling a fork out of her mouth.

'We moved up here from a parish near Bath only two years ago,' said Evan. 'But this is London. We still don't know all the clergy in all the parishes. Probably never will.'

After breakfast Evan went into the kitchen for the telephone. Patrick stayed at the picnic table, staring at the bookshelf, cocking his head sideways to read the spines: *English Architecture, On Sakharov, Poems of W.B. Yeats, The New Testament in Modern English.*

After a while Evan came back into the room and said, 'I found him – he lives in High Barnet. He says he can see you this morning. I can drive you over there after the girls leave for school.'

Abernathy's house was set on a steep hill, one of a terrace of houses that formed a single chain of front doors a mile long, like spines on a stegosaurus' back.

Evan let Patrick off at Abernathy's gate. As he clapped the thin car door shut he saw concern in the vicar's face, a concern that hadn't been there before, so that Patrick felt like telling him, 'Don't worry, I'll be all right.'

'My my, it really *is* you!' said Abernathy as he took Patrick's hand and shook it. 'Come in!'

Patrick stepped into a narrow hall, peppery with must and the smell of cooking chicken. Abernathy led him to the back of the house, down three steps as wide as a man's shoe is long, to a little door on the right which opened into a sitting room papered dark green.

'I'm making a cup of tea. Would you like one?' asked John.

'No,' said Patrick, and sat down in an armchair with his pack between his feet.

The old vicar came back with a book in his hand and offered it to Patrick. It was a small black book with an old hardback cover, its spine worn with threads sticking out of the top. It said in gold writing: *Black Elk Speaks*. Patrick opened it in the middle. The book felt stiff, its pages unbroken, unread. He turned to the front expecting an inscription, but the page was blank.

'That's the book your mother gave me,' said Abernathy, rolling his vowels around his mouth. 'Maybe something made me keep it all these years so that I could pass it on to you.'

'You knew her that well?' asked Patrick. 'This is a classic.'

'She wrote a note at the back,' said Abernathy.

Patrick opened the book's back cover. Alice's scribbly handwriting jumped out of the page at her son, as if the message was intended for him, as if it were a message in a bottle. *To John Abernathy: Let him speak first. Alice Smoke Hunter.*

'Your mother,' said John, lowering himself heavily into an armchair covered in green plush, the silver green of rosemary, lowering himself without rattling his cup. 'Terrible thing. Shocking tragedy. I couldn't get over it when I heard.'

Patrick was silent. He wasn't going to agree. No matter how shocked Abernathy was, it would never measure up to his own grief.

'Alice Smoke,' John said, waving one arm. 'What a wonderful name she had. Such a kind and soft-spoken woman, but with a powerful presence. She'd stop a room talking when she walked in.' Here he stalled, looking up at the plate rail above the sideboard, at a little collection of china saucers in red and white, staring at them as if they helped him remember. 'There was something very dignified about her. It wasn't a *London* sophistication – designer clothes and silk scarves and such – but an *inner* quiet. A very spiritual person, your mother. But she didn't like to talk about it. Very difficult to draw her into conversation.'

Patrick thought of Abernathy's Red Indian letter. He didn't have to wonder much further about why his mother had shut off. 'Do you remember going home and changing your sermon?'

'What?'

'She kept your letter.'

'Ah, now that you mention it, I do remember something about that. I think . . . yes . . . we were talking about sacrifice. Alice had the idea – now what was it? – that Jesus' sacrifice wasn't enough to save our souls.' Abernathy laughed wryly. 'Your father wasn't very happy. I think it quite upset him that she thought that way.' The elderly man shifted in his chair, touched his forefinger to his specs. 'Your father – he's well, I trust?'

Patrick frowned and nodded.

'Good, good. He was – is – a passionate man. Forthright about his beliefs and expecting everyone else to see his truth. Sometimes he pounded the table a bit – not that that's a bad thing. I expect that's why you Americans are rather more successful at religion than we British. Perhaps we're too gentle in our approach. Your father was a real . . .'

Patrick waited for it.

'Let's just say he had a way of getting people to sit up and take notice.'

'Do you know how she died?' Patrick didn't want to talk about the Reverend.

'You don't know?' said John.

'No. He always said she just died.'

Abernathy seemed confused. 'If your father hasn't told you by now . . . I . . . I don't expect *I* should, somehow.'

Something exploded inside Patrick. What right did this man have to know his mother, to have stories and memories of her that Patrick didn't share, her own son? And then to say that Patrick himself didn't have the right to know how she died?

'Why,' Patrick made himself hold back, took a deep breath, 'do you think I came all this way, huh? I'm here because I *don't* know. Because I *have* to know or I'll go crazy!'

'Now, Patrick . . .'

'Are you gonna tell me? 'Cos otherwise I'll leave. I'll find someone else!'

'I just don't think it's my place to tell you. She's happy now, your mother. She's happy in the arms of Jesus. It doesn't *matter* how she died.'

'Tell me! I have a right to know. I *have* to know! Not just for me, but for my little sister's sake as well.'

Abernathy stared at Patrick. 'She didn't die a natural death. She was . . . killed. A person entered the house at night. I'm so very sorry.'

Abernathy's words sunk in Patrick like a lead ball dropped in cream. The words sunk to his very depths where they stirred loathing and anger and pity all at once. He felt deep anger at his father that he had had to hear this from a stranger, that his father had sealed the truth from himself and Charlene, sealed it against them.

'How did she die? Was she shot?'

Abernathy shook his head, stared at the carpet. 'It was a knife.'

Patrick knew where he had been on the night of his

mother's death. If he didn't know anything else, that memory was engraved in his mind, of waking up and being told he had slept while she died downstairs. Sheer helpless rage at his sleep – that he *hadn't woken up!* – had shaken through him over the years leaving a tatter of rage behind, a little square of rage sewn into himself so that at any time, any place, he could work himself into an angry frenzy if he thought about that night and his helplessness.

Then, for the first time when he was awake, Patrick imagined his mother's death in the way it actually took place, not in a made-up way that she died peacefully in her sleep, drifting off to meet her grandparents in the next life, wrapped in the arms of God. He saw the knife rise and plunge, rise and plunge so clear that he wondered if it was a memory. The image was silent, an image without a soundtrack. The anger he'd felt, the anger that had throbbed him to suicide, bubbled in his blood. Only this time it didn't paralyse him. This time it pushed at him like hands on his back, shoving him forward, making him stumble, shoving him again when he gathered his thoughts.

At the same time, Patrick felt resignation about what he now knew, as if Abernathy's news was inevitable. *This is what pushed at me in Seattle*, he thought. *This is what sent me across a continent and an ocean to get to this place.*

He asked, helpless to stop the shake in his voice: 'Was the man caught?'

'I expect there was an investigation. Really, we didn't hear any more than that she'd been . . . Well, your father took you and your sister back to America and that was it.'

'So my father just ran away? He didn't stay to catch him?' That explained the Reverend's refusal to let Patrick and Charlene visit their mother's relations in South Dakota. Frank didn't want to show he'd been a coward. Frank's children in their innocence would tell the truth: that they didn't know how their mother died. That they had left England in a hurry, not even a month after her death. His father had erased their mother, erased her to hide his cowardice, his flight from what had happened in that house.

Maybe Frank had never told Alice's relatives the truth about their daughter, their sister, their aunt. Maybe he'd hidden it all.

'Can you tell me any more?' said Patrick, who had a thousand questions now, but each one a bullet for his father living on another continent, carapaced in his church.

'It was in the papers. I expect if you go to the *Advertiser* office in North Finchley, they'll still have the articles on record.'

The close, musty heat of the house, a dark-green room crowded with knick-knacks, a windowless room . . . Patrick wanted to be away from John Abernathy. He needed to be out in the sunshine of the street. There was nothing here, nothing that would tell him about his mother, that would shed reason on what had happened. Nothing but this papery old man and his wire-rimmed spectacles. And anger.

Twenty minutes later he was on the bus to North Finchley.

If the bus-driver hadn't called twice to Patrick he would have missed his stop even though he stared through the window at the red and white sign that said *Advertiser*. It was only the bus-driver's calling, and an old lady sitting behind him prodding him in the shoulder that woke Patrick out of his thoughts. He mumbled, 'Thanks,' got off with his pack and crossed the street, not paying attention. A red BMW nearly knocked him over. Patrick flipped off the man driving the car and shouted, 'Watch where the fuck you're going, you motherfucker!'

'Asshole,' he said to himself as he finished crossing, and swung open the glass door into the newspaper offices.

After he'd explained what he wanted to the receptionist, a reporter took him to a place she called 'the deadroom', where grey metal shelves held old papers sorted by month and year, and left him to it.

Patrick found the right newspaper in a space of five minutes. His mother's death had made the front page of the *Finchley and Barnet Advertiser*. Here, next to a photo of Alice that Patrick had never seen, was her story for the world to read – for ten years a story hidden from her children:

An American woman was stabbed to death at her Finchley home on Tuesday night while her young son and daughter slept in their beds upstairs.

Alice Hunter, the wife of an American Episcopal minister, was stabbed seven times while her two children slept at their Lichfield Grove home.

The dead woman's husband, Frank Hunter, says he returned to the house at 2 a.m. on Wednesday morning only to find his wife's mutilated body in the rear downstairs bedroom.

A neighbour of the Hunters said: 'I heard her put out the rubbish late in the evening, but didn't hear anything after that. The house was completely silent.'

Police have set up an incident room and are appealing for information to be given to DCI Peter Neal.

Patrick crouched on the cold cement floor and stared at the picture – his mother smiling, high cheekbones, a pretty face that shone love at him, that stopped a room talking. He stared at the photo, searching the grainy black and white for emotion, to bring back the love he felt when she pulled him up onto her knee and hugged him, when she kissed the top of his head and said: 'Good.' But the picture didn't make her materialise. It could only bring back thoughts.

Patrick read the article again, and the words '2 a.m.' jumped out at him. What was his father doing? Where had he been at that hour? Why wasn't he home to protect his wife, his family – to protect the helpless ones, helpless in a foreign country? That morning's feeling of being a little red leaf in a river, of being guided by the flow, disappeared. Now he felt as if he were trapped in a torrent of rapids, that something had pushed him under and he didn't know when he'd bob up for air. He had to talk to someone. He had to talk to his mother.

He saw his sister's face as she said prayers for him on the night before he left Seattle. Kneeling on the floor he felt the need to pray for guidance, and he hoped someone would hear him. He pulled *Black Elk Speaks* out of his pack, held the little book, once part of his mother, tight to his chest. Tears ran down his cheeks and onto his throat. He whispered: '*Grandfather hear me, Grandmother hear me, take my hands and show me where to go. Take my ears and tell me what to do.*'

After that he stopped crying and wiped his cheeks on his shoulders, and hoped that even in this Godforsaken home of Christianity where no wildness was allowed to grow, where even the winds could hardly breathe, where an amber smog smeared the sour sky, that someone would hear him and send help.

He stood up, slowly, knees aching from kneeling, and went back to ask the reporter for some photocopies.

Patrick jogged with his pack on back to Finchley Central. As he ran, dodging pushchairs, people walking hand-in-hand, ladies wobbling on their clickety-clack heels, gathering stares and nervy sidesteppings, he thought up tortures to inflict on the man who had killed his mother. Skin him, and then pull out his fingernails with a pair of pliers one by one, and then his toenails, and then cut out his liver.

Hang him up on a meathook and with a rusty knife cut his dick off, then his balls, then run the blade from his neck to his toes until he looked like a living barbershop pole.

Hang him upside down, skin his feet, and then skin the rest of his body with a pair of fingernail clippers.

Stick him with pushknives until he looked like a porcupine.

Patrick thought these things as he passed a police station. He stopped, unfolded the white photocopy in his hand. He climbed the cement stairs up to the station door and walked into a small waiting room. He buzzed the door to the front desk and a plainclothes policeman in a white shirt and tie let him in. Patrick laid a photocopy of the newspaper article on the counter.

'I wonder if you could help me. This is an article about my mother. It happened ten years ago, but I'm in London for a little while over from Seattle. Could I speak to this Peter Neal who handled her case?'

The Desk Sergeant turned the article rightside up.

'You got an address here?' he asked.

'Yeah,' said Patrick.

'Leave your name and details. We'll see what we can do for you.'

A knock on the door interrupted Kitsy's play with Lucy. At fourteen months, Lucy could now hold a chubby crayon in her fist and scrub at a colouring book. The knock made Kitsy jump inside, and she stopped crayoning to listen. It was eight months after Michael had walked out on them, and Kitsy's heart still banged around whenever anyone called at the door. Only now she didn't jump physically. Now it was more like a start.

She went to the window and pulled back the curtain. It was that tall young man again, the one with the dark hair and long eyebrows who had stood there in the rain the day before. He caught her eyes and smiled, folded his hands as if he was praying, and begged at her with them, mouthing, 'Please, please.'

'What do you want?' demanded Kitsy when she cracked open the door. Patrick saw a slice of her face bisected by the door chain. With a tan she could have been an older version of a California girl.

'I want to give you something,' said Patrick, reaching into his pocket, and Kitsy wondered, *Does he have a knife?* But he pulled out a few pieces of folded paper and a small blue booklet.

'Have these,' he said, and thrust them through.

Kitsy took the papers. 'What do you want me to do with this?'

'Read 'em. I'll be back tomorrow,' said Patrick, and turned down the path towards the gate.

Kitsy watched him go through four inches of chain. She wanted to go after him, to give back the pieces of paper and the passport, to say: 'Get stuffed. Stay out of my life!' But then she'd have to open the door.

While Lucy took her afternoon nap, Kitsy sat at the dining table and read for the first time about her house and the people who had lived here ten years before – the minister and his wife and their two children. She flipped through the passport until she came to the front, until she came to the photo of Patrick Lance Hunter as a child of eight. She checked his birthdate. *When he was eight I was eighteen.* She went through the passport, page by page, examining his stamps for clues.

In the section for personal information, who to contact in an emergency, someone had written in neat capital letters, in pencil: FRANK J. HUNTER, FATHER & ALICE SMOKE HUNTER, MOTHER, followed by Kitsy's address and telephone number, which she hadn't bothered to change when they'd moved in.

She stared at that number which hooked her into a set of events, a circle of people whom she'd never met, whom she had never wanted to meet.

Ten years ago I was still in love with Matheo and just about to dump him for Michael. And these things happened only a few miles from where I was living in Camden Town.

What does Patrick Lance Hunter want from me?

Kitsy stood up and went into the kitchen. She made herself a cup of tea and carried it back into the front room. She took two sips, set in on the dining table, picked up the papers and sat in the window. She pulled back the nets and stared out, wondering, staring at a tree in her front garden, its white trunk straight and peeling, its leaves dark green on one side, and silvery on the other, a tree in full life, its leaves still that fresh green of spring with a bright translucency. She looked at the branches, how they touched and tapped in the summer wind, and thought how she saw only half of the tree, that the other part, the most important part, spread itself underground.

It made her want a tattoo of a tree with dangling dark roots.

She saw the tattoo engraved on her left shoulder: green and silver, and then saw Patrick's hand take her arm, and his lips kiss her tattoo.

Cradle-snatcher.

She got up and went to the dining table. She straightened the papers and the passport into a square pile. She put them on the sideboard next to a pair of brass candlesticks, and began to think what she'd give him to eat tomorrow (a French stick, cold beef and mustard and butter, pears and watermelon, cheese) after she let him in.

★ ★ ★

'Char?'

'Trick?'

'Is the Reverend there?'

'No.'

'Good. Look Char, I've found something out. I don't want to tell you until I see you. Are you all right?'

'He keeps looking in the mailbox every day. I don't know what to say any more. I'm so afraid I'm gonna get hit. Patrick?'

'What?'

'Well, the last time he punished me, he wanted me to pull down my jeans and panties. I didn't do it though. I ran away.'

'What?! Are you sure! When was this?!'

'Just after you left.'

'Oh my Christ, Charlene! I'm seven fucking thousand miles away and I can't get home for two weeks at least! You stay away from him, ya hear me? Go have slumber parties at your friends' houses or something. Promise?' Patrick felt sick at the thought of what his father might have done to his sister.

'Yeah. I'll try, Trick.' She sounded on the verge of crying, like it was taking all her control to stomach her need to weep.

'That fucking bastard. Look, when I get back, Char, we'll take a trip. You got it? Just you an' me.'

'Where?' she whispered.

'To visit Mom's people, OK? Way far away. You don't ever have to see that asshole again. OK?'

'. . . OK.'

'Stop cryin', Charlene! What're you gonna say if he comes in and sees you crying?'

'OK . . . Trick?'

'Yeah?'

'What day are you comin' home?'

'I don't know yet. Soon as I finish some business. Sooner if I can swing it. I'll call you, yeah?'

'Yeah.'

'Bye, Char.'

'Bye, Trick. Love you.'

CHAPTER 8

In an Icicle of Light

Patrick sat on a sleeping bag next to his pack, scarfing down a chicken pie with drippy filling, his fingers sticky with white gravy and grease from his french fries. He didn't have to climb over the wall today – one of the men had spotted him in the park and guided him to their secret entrance. Patrick kept a straight face as the man whispered passwords at the brick wall. Finally a little door swung back – a piece of plywood screwed onto bricks. Patrick crawled in after the older man, behind his smell of onions and drying sweat. Today Ronnie had built a little fire in front of his shack; it looked almost invisible in the sunshine, partly unreal as fires do in the daytime. He shoved several potatoes into the coals. Suddenly Patrick wished he could order out for pizza. There was something about those spuds roasting in the fire that looked so rustic, so unloved.

Now he sat under his tree, alone and a little bit lonely, waiting for night to fall, and for sleep. After England he'd never been a good sleeper – suffering from nightmares, sleepwalking, and in Junior High the problem vampired into insomnia. At least cross-country runs had taken care of that for a couple of years, but tonight sleeplessness was back. It was as if that night when his mother had died would revenge

itself on him every night for his deafness, for the blindness
that sleep had brought.

So now he waited, and wished there was something to
do. He wanted to distract himself from this engulfing feeling
of separateness, but there was nothing to do except to feel
and think. He picked up a stick and fiddled with
it, peeling off the bark. Would the woman let him in
tomorrow? He thought so. He had put her in that position,
calculated the shot so that the balls fell into their pockets.
He hoped she would let him in. She looked nice, like the
kind of person he would want to get to know, even if he
didn't need her, even if he didn't have a ghost to face. And
what about Charlene? Would she be all right? After the
telephone call he worried. He felt depressed thinking about
her little repressed sobs like a cat mewing. He'd always been
there before when she got thrashed. Now that she was alone,
he felt frightened for her. His father had gone too far. What
if he didn't stop, didn't hear from her crying that she'd
passed the point where pain and fear turn into numbness,
where you wish for unconsciousness just to make it stop?
Patrick knew his father was capable of this. The small, deep
scar on his cheek from the belt buckle proved it.

And what if his father came home all high on the Bible –
as he did – and saw Charlene sitting on the sofa watching
TV in her pyjamas – as she did – and there was no Patrick
in the house? No Patrick to walk into the lounge and be
angry, saying, 'What is going on here?' Or to notice closed
doors?

Patrick didn't speak much to his sister. If anybody asked,
he said they weren't that close. But now with the safeness of
thousands of miles between them, he admitted to himself
that he had shoved her away, didn't talk to her, because
they shared a room. Deep down he was afraid of what might
happen if he got too close. Now he could see that being

close to her didn't need to be physical. He felt afraid for her. *Charlene doesn't have no one to step into the firing line. No one can take the bullet for her.*

He wished that he didn't have to be in this park, sorting out this kind of business, that he could be going back home to get Charlene in a car, a bus, a train, anything out of Seattle.

I have two weeks, he thought. *Two weeks of long days to fill, to try to think what to do. Maybe I'll end up going home early. Maybe nothing will work out. Maybe Mom was stabbed by some lunatic who sneaked into the house. Christ, this city is packed with people – what hope do I have? Better to get home, get back to Charlene. Let the dead bury the dead.*

But then he remembered how disconnected he had felt on the day when he cut his arm, and he was afraid that those feelings would freeze him again if he didn't see Alice Smoke put to rest. Then Charlene would be left alone. Then she'd be the one with the knife. A chain of knives, twisted into his family.

No. Not that.

He took out a letter from his pocket, and unfolded the worn, yellow paper.

Dear Dotty,

I'm so happy being a mother. Patrick has grown so fast that it seems impossible that he's two already. Last night Frank was away on a retreat at Crystal Mountain. Our little home felt so lonely so I took Patrick into the big bed. You know, he spent the whole night with his head snuggled against my neck and his hands touching my face. He loves the feeling of skin so much. He's delighted when I'm changing clothes. He comes over and presses his palms against my knees and says 'kim' – his way of saying skin. Sometimes I look at this little guy and think he will be my savior, that if only I could run away with him now, just me and my little man, that I'd have the best of Frank, all his love and passion and a clean slate to teach this new person, and I'd avoid all the things that Frank's parents did to him, all that Protestant hardness. Why do some people think misery is holiness? It's not easy being a preacher's wife. Sometimes I wonder how we ever got married in the first place, and I wish I was back on the rez with you guys. But I wouldn't give up Patrick for anything.

Today I sat on the floor, Patrick in my arms. We both had dirty feet, black soles. It's hot and we'd been outside barefoot, letting our feet touch down on that little patch of grass in our yard, that little tuft of green hair. Everything else is cement, and that makes most of the dirt on our feet. Oil and broken stone, dust from other people's shoes, everything binded together like egg in a cake.

Patrick's face was red, his eyes were wet. He sucked on a big green plastic binkie. We rocked in the heat. I held him in my arms, cradled close to my chest like he was a newborn. But he's a big toddler now, grown tall. The heat surrounds us like a second skin. Like heat does, it presses on us. Reminds us that we are held in this world like I hold the baby, pressed into a comforting spot by the sky above, the earth under the floorboards, and cement foundations of this house, pressed together like Christmas cake by the four directions and their infinite relations, all pointing and pressing us together, invisible arrows of space.

We rocked and I hummed that mother hum, that toneless growl in the deep of my throat that I heard from our mother; something comes up on a short, deep channel and sounds in my chest, into his body, but not into the room, a sort of tin-cans-with-string communication. What's wrong what's wrong what's wrong? Why are you upset? I rock and ask. But he doesn't answer, just tucks himself closer in, seals his head closer against my armpit, sucks stronger at his nook.

I think he was disconsolate because he was tired, because he can't communicate. Images, questions, pictures form and evaporate, reform and disappear. Inside his mind it clicks and clacks, railway carriages hooking up, banging together, setting off for destinations, forgetting where they're going, forgetting the map. And it frustrates him so that he bites and throws things, and that frustrates me so I put him in a corner, and he screams red in the face so I call him out and cradle him here, like so.

This, sitting on the floor in the hall on my stained gray carpet on a hot July day, us the only pair in the house, clung together with our thoughts and emotions, this here is motherhood. This is the part I like.

Alice.

Patrick folded the letter back into its worn four squares, the lines where it had been folded so many years ago, the lines in the paper now so worn they were like cloth. He wondered how the letter came to be in his father's things, how many times his father had read it and folded it up, how many invisible fingerprints of his father's were smeared into the letter, mixing with his own prints now, and the faint, faded, smudged prints of his mother.

He tried to remember himself at two, pressing his palms against his mother's knees, against her skin which glowed warm, the colours of sunset oranges and reds coming up through the brown, bathing him in her heat. Then he remembered how she died, felt himself back at the house, warm in his little bed under a heavy heap of quilts and blankets, remembered his contentment. He tried to imagine what was going on beneath him as he slept, content in his child's dreaming, so far away from his mother.

He felt something stir in his mind, something he couldn't allow himself to look at. He stood on the stairs, small, confused. Like a word on the tip of his tongue, he tried to feel deeper, to think back. The black, formless thought slipped away like a fish's shadow.

Some saviour.

There was another letter too, the last of those unsent messages from before the grave (the cremation, actually. Bodies were too expensive to fly home, said Frank). Patrick pulled it out of a ripped-open envelope, stamped and addressed but never sent.

Mom must've told Dad to mail it and he didn't, thought Patrick.

Dear Dotty,
Last night I dreamed the Owl and I'm scared. I'm not supposed to believe in anything any more, but I know that there are some things you can't ignore. Frank came home yesterday with the news that the church is sending us on a sabbatical so he can preach in London for nine months. I wanted to be excited but all I can feel is deadness. I've got Charlene and Patrick settled here and made my friends. I don't feel so stranded any more like some Martian that's lost his UFO, and now Frank wants to throw me off-balance again by going to that Godforsaken place. The older I get the more I hate those greedy pilgrims – why couldn't they have left us alone? Why? Do I really need a steam iron? Do I really need power-drills?

I am slowly coming to a frightening place, beginning to believe that Mom was right when she said that a part of me could never be a part of him, that he'd never understand so many basic things about me. I told her that our love would make us understand. Now I'm wondering if I heard that on the radio in some dumb song. So much of what she said has come true. *There are parts of me he doesn't want to know, and I think he wishes they weren't there! Thing is, those are my foundations he's wishing away. He wants to replace them with his Jesus and his Bible. I thought he could just love me like I love him. Does any of this make sense?*

Maybe I'm upset because of my silly dream. I'm probably taking it way too seriously. I've had dreams before where nothing has happened. But this one was so vivid. Anyway, it's probably an opportunity for Frank and me to have a change of scenery. Sometimes I feel like I don't know him any more. He's gotten hard. Maybe it's that I didn't know him before, and I do now. Try to be happy, Alice! Maybe the trip will do us some good. If it doesn't, I'm going to have to do some hard thinking about coming home to you when we get back. My hope that we can make it no matter what everyone said is almost dried up now. Maybe that's what the Owl meant – warning me that my marriage is dead and that it's time for change.

Keep me in your prayers.

I love you,

Alice.

She had dreamed the owl, he thought. *So she knew what was coming but went to London anyway. Why didn't you run, Mom? Why?*

But Patrick already held the answer in him. She didn't run because she had willpower. A strong will which repelled her from her parents' home and bound her up with the handsome, charismatic Frank. A will which kicked against anyone who told her 'no', which held her head through the loudest fights, the strongest silences. Her will said she was going to try to make it work, one more time. That she would see when it was time to give up, slip out. She ignored the

Owl's warning, and she paid for that act of will with her life.

The letter said another thing to Patrick: he had been right when he tried to run away from his father all those years ago. If their mom had lived, he and Charlene would have moved back to the Great Plains with her and his whole life would have been different. He'd have different friends, go to a different school, have new relatives. And she wouldn't be dead and he wouldn't be stuck here now with the bums and the weirdos, and he never would have taken a knife to his arm.

Patrick folded the letter and put it in the envelope. Then he opened *Black Elk Speaks* and laid her letters at the back on top of her inscription. He turned to the front and in the mellow light of an early summer's evening, a fuzzy light like peach skin, he tried to read the opening chapters, to fit the clear, calming stories and prayers into the jumble of his mind. But by the time he'd finished, the light had melted blue and it still felt like pop-goes-the-weasel inside his head.

No way am I gonna be able to sleep.

Patrick put the book in his purple pack, got up and walked over to the fire. Ronnie was crouched next to it, poking at it with a stick, hunched into himself in a pink satin bathrobe.

'Mind if I sit here?' said Patrick.

Ronnie pointed his stick at the place opposite, a flattened circle of grass. Patrick sat. Ronnie turned the potatoes with his stick, a stout, stripped rod carved into a point at one end, and fire-blackened.

Patrick tried out different opening lines in his head: Did you get the money? Is that your dinner? Is pink your favourite colour? Where's everyone else? but he didn't have the energy for them so he sat in silence, staring into little flames snapping and eating the twigs and logs. The staring and the heat fixed him, almost in a drugged way so that he could observe his anxiety floating by, his wondering whether that woman at the house would let him in, whether the policeman would get in touch . . . all these thoughts going round and round, little juggling beanbags, and behind all these things, like a reflection in a black pond, stood Alice Smoke.

Patrick woke to a black sky, a sky so much night that it threatened to cover up the points of silver stars that poked through. He woke with a terrible urge. He managed to crawl on all fours out of his sleeping bag and into the bushes before he vomited his guts up. He swiped sharp-smelling dribble with the back of his hand, then threw up a hot second wave which brought with it another urge. He crawled over the cool earth, fighting off the blank screen of unconsciousness so that he didn't know which he saw: night or the back of his eyelids.

He crawled into a bush and managed to wiggle down his jeans and pull himself up into a crouch before splattering the ground in great violent squits. He felt as if a dying porcupine were dragging its body through his cramping guts, guts pulling in on themselves, trying to squeeze the prickly mammal out.

Damn that chicken pie. Damn those greasy fries.

Crouching in that bush with his pants around his ankles, Patrick wanted his mama like he hadn't wanted his mama for years. He ached at her absence. In his pain he felt a kind of surprise that she wasn't there. The feeling was like that day when he let himself in through the front door after school and called to the empty house so that his voice rang out: 'Mom! I'm home!' The words left his mouth as he realised she was no longer there to hear them. He let the words go and stood in silence, glad that he'd shouted for her because he'd never shout those words again.

Now when Patrick got sick at home he looked after himself; he'd gotten pretty good at dragging himself to the

113

bathroom for cold towels, aspirin, the toilet. Got pretty good at fixing his own food or waiting for Charlene to come and fix it for him. Sickness foods: peanut butter and banana and milk in the blender, noodles coated with Campbell's condensed mushroom soup, scrambled eggs.

He felt desperate for the warmth of home and Charlene's comforting voice, so desperate that it was a kind of mild panic.

With every effort of his aching and exhausted body he wiped himself with handfuls of leaves from a bush and pulled his pants up so that he stood, swaying in the night. A breeze blew up and breathed coolness on his face. That steadied Patrick enough to take one step, four steps through the underbrush, the drying grasses, back to his bag and pack, waiting lumps.

Feeling like his own planet independently spinning, he stuffed his sleeping bag into the pack and heaved it onto his shoulders. The swing and weight made him stagger, spread his feet for support. He walked wide-legged as a sailor, step after slow step, heading for the little exit, bumping into trees nose-first, walking through bushes, his eyes straining to distinguish the darker lumps that were obstacles from plain darkness.

At last he could tell he was at the wall by the little bit of earth built up at its base, the grass higher and harder.

'Oi!' said a voice in the night, and a torch shone over his body, feeling him with its fist of light, its invisible touch.

'Let me out.' Patrick fought down the urge to vomit.

'Phwah! You don't half pong,' said little Ronnie, now in front of him like a pink pixie, tossing light onto a path.

'I'm sick,' replied Patrick, drained of any other explanation.

After that, he remembered only the step he was taking at that moment, didn't recall how he managed to walk more steps than the one he took now. But somehow he crawled through the break in the wall, and then through a hole in the park fence, and staggered – puking up once against a telephone pole – down Sylvan Avenue and into Lichfield Grove where he let himself into Kitsy's gate. He collapsed on her doorstep, his pack a hard pillow against his back. He fought for control. When he was sure he wasn't going to barf, he rang the doorbell.

Only trouble rings at 4 a.m.

Kitsy walked through her house feeling her way along the walls, wearing darkness. She went into the front room, all footfalls and heartbeats, to the curtain's edge.

In the porch's spotlight, an icicle of light making a little patch for itself in the night, in that little bit of light was Patrick, his jeans stuck with grass, his skin as white as a page.

'What the fuck are you doing here?' she said to the windowglass and drew strength from the word 'fuck'. From the way he was flopped there, sprawled where he fell without bothering to arrange his limbs, she knew that she was in the position of power.

She went and opened the front door, got hit with the smells of sick and sweat.

'You're drunk,' Kitsy said.

'Not drunk,' he said. 'Food poisoning.'

He lurched up and ran inside, past Kitsy, making for the cloakroom that used to be at the back of the house. She shut the front door and went after him.

While he threw up in the toilet, Kitsy crossed her arms over her chest and sat in a chair outside the door, disgusted and curious, her toe switching like a cat's tail, her head full of 'just becauses' – *just because he gave me his passport, doesn't mean . . . just because he used to live here . . . just because I was going to let him in tomorrow, doesn't mean . . .*

'You can't stay, you know,' she called to him. The toilet flushed. He came out, still pale. He'd taken off his black T-shirt, held it balled up in his hands. He had four long scabs on the inside of one forearm, the skin pink and puckered like a grub's back. The sight of those scabs made Kitsy shrink inside, want to put distance between her body and Patrick's. *I shouldn't have let him in*, she thought. *I want him out*.

'Can't I even sleep in the back yard? I've got a sleeping bag.' He thought, *She's got to let me sleep there. She's the* one.

'What, and spew up into my roses every ten seconds? Charming.'

'Oh,' he said, drained, empty. He leaned against the wall and slid to the floor. 'I guess I feel better, maybe . . .' and rested his forehead on his knees.

Although he closed his eyes then, the memory of the brightness of them stood out to Kitsy. Maybe his eyes were brighter in illness against the deep shadows under his cheekbones, hollows that somehow echoed the hoods of his eyelids. His fingers were long and thick, the white crescents of his nails torn down to slivers with his teeth.

'Not your roses,' he said, looking up at Kitsy.

'What?'

'You read the article. You know how my mom died.'

'Yes.'

'How can you say this house is yours when that took place here? It's something that belongs to me. You can't erase it.' Patrick couldn't see why she refused to understand.

'So? Do you now own every place that has a memory for you?'

He stared at Kitsy then, his face completely blank, and she felt by that stare that everything she was, everything she'd said, everything she would say to him in future would be alien to him. They were speaking English to each other but from across a profound barrier. *Our language may as well be going through an interpreter,* she thought.

Later, when Kitsy looked back at the turning points in her life, she thought that this one had happened from a need to understand Patrick, to somehow connect with this person whose thinking was as different to hers as someone from Outer Mongolia, or Mars. This was what made Kitsy say 'yes' to Patrick. Or maybe it was instinct, that somehow this bloke was OK and wouldn't hurt her and Lucy. He certainly looked helpless enough to her. Kitsy knew she felt lonely and fed-up. She wanted some adventure in her life for once. She wanted to feel like she did on that day when she climbed the ladder up to her parents' roof, excited, a little scared, although deep down she knew she was safe.

Kitsy finally said to him from the height of her chair, staring down on him sitting on the floor, 'Take a shower first, then you can sleep in the spare room. It's the first door along the corridor on your left. By the way, I'm Kitsy.'

She stood up and went back to bed where Lucy slept, locking the bedroom door behind her. Then she lay awake, wondering about the wisdom of making him sleep in the dream room until she heard no more noises downstairs and fell into an uneasy sleep.

Only now did Patrick remember the day-dream he had had about this room.

It was the day after his mother's death. His father's friends gathered in the front room, sitting in a circle, filling up the settee and six dining chairs, his mother's china teacups, white china painted with purple pansies, balanced in their English laps. His father told Patrick to come to him and Patrick went. He stood before his father who put his hands over Patrick's head and the room started to hum with a hymn: 'Come bless us, Lord Jesus, Who vanquishes all darkness . . . ' The visitors sat still in their chairs with their cups not even rattling while they sang, calling for Jesus' spirit. Patrick felt comforted, as if he were in the middle of some good power, cradled in the love of these people.

Then his father clamped down on his shoulders with his hands, gripped them so hard that Patrick sucked in his breath and whimpered. He could smell his father's sour breath, his soapy smell, could smell the shampoo coming off his head as his father sweated, knew droplets of sweat were forming at the roots of his blond hair. His father gripped harder, calling: 'Deliver him, Jesus, from Satan's grasp! Deliver him from his mother's demons, the demons got from her womb! Deliver him from her pagan past, from the bloodshed of her savage family, oh Jesus, deliver him!'

Patrick cried and fell to his knees – 'Daddy, Daddy, stop! Stop!' He cried all the tears he'd bottled up in front of the mourners, all the tears he'd kept from them to show he was a man. They flooded over him, got into his lungs in great, gasping swallows, forced him to sit on the floor, to kneel and gasp for air, to wail when he found that air until his little boy's body collapsed completely into a shivering heap and Charlene, who was sitting on the floor near her father's feet, started to scream.

That was the beginning of a long fight. A long hatred started on that day. Charlene's scream pierced something in Patrick, like an icepick through a can of spray paint. In Patrick there was a small explosion of fire, of indignation, of bitter resolve so that he grabbed hold of his sister, wrapped his skinny arms around her chest and pulled her from the floor and from the room, away from his father and all his guests, with their evil eyes. He hauled her down the hall towards the kitchen.

As he passed the little room on his right he could see through the closed door, through the dividing wall, see fresh blood splattered on the lavender wallpaper, soaked into the bed's cheap nylon coverlet, rusting into the blue carpet.

As he stopped there, staring at the blank wall, a woman came up behind them and took Charlene from him, pulled them both to her body, her fatty warmth, and rocked them making the mother's comforting sound in her throat: 'Hmm hmm hmm hmm,' until they were soothed.

In the business and anguish of mourning, the upheaval of the sudden move back to the US, of starting school again without his mother's quiet love – in all that he buried his perception of the blood in the room.

Now he knew it was that perception that gnawed at his mind, that had brought him to the blade at his father's kitchen table. That perception, that day-dream – or vision even – was what told him that his mother didn't 'just die' as his father said, but that something wilful had happened. An event.

Lucy woke Kitsy at six the next morning by pulling the diamond sleeper from her nose. The slither as the gold shank slipped through its hole like a strand of spaghetti sucked up – that she could sleep through. But the pinch and pain of the back forced off – that hurt.

Pain and anger hung in Kitsy as she changed Lucy's nappy and put her into a little red dress. Kitsy dressed herself in old black jeans and a T-shirt.

'Wait,' Kitsy said, and shook her pointed finger at Lucy. 'Wait on the bed.'

As she closed the door, Kitsy could hear Lucy climb to the edge of the bed and drop down feet first. She whined to herself, 'Mammy, Mammy, Mammy,' but Kitsy knew Lucy wouldn't let herself out. The handle was too high.

Downstairs Kitsy checked on Patrick, opening his door a tiny bit. Through that slit she could see him snuggled down under the covers, his head sunk into the feather pillow, smiling.

At least one of us is happy, she thought. But then Kitsy realised that thought was more habit than truth, from Michael's disgruntled wife, angry at being imposed upon. It wasn't the real Kitsy, the woman who was starved for good company, the woman who wanted adventure, to bring spice home.

One of the most comforting smells Kitsy knew was that of toast and coffee and eggs frying in the morning. That was her dad's breakfast, the one he always made for Kitsy and her mum on Saturday mornings when she was little. Somehow that gesture stopped when Kitsy was about eleven. Now when she went there on a Saturday they didn't have cooked breakfast at all; cornflakes bowls were in the sink instead of the frying pans and saucepans that Dad used. Less washing up, she guessed. Washing up or not, on that day Kitsy wanted to cook her guest the full works – fried bread, grilled tomatoes, sausages, mushrooms, eggs.

Kitsy fetched Lucy downstairs, sat her in the high chair with a yoghurt and cereal and juice, and then set about slicing mushrooms, beating eggs in a bowl, boiling the kettle. She was happier than she had been at any time since Michael left.

So much for being an independent woman, she thought. *So much for not needing a man – even a kid off the street, chucking up on my doorstep in the middle of the night.*

Kitsy had just put the plunger down on the coffee when Patrick appeared in the kitchen door wearing a long-sleeved black T-shirt pushed up to the elbows, and jeans. His arms were completely smooth, and thick with muscle. He took up most of the doorway, his head missing the lintel by a couple of inches; slumped against the doorframe; rubbing his eyes, he looked thoroughly sleepy and relaxed, his body bent casually into a hard curve.

If Kitsy had been raised without manners, she would have whistled. He looked to her like someone from a jeans advert, with his tousled thick hair, so dark she couldn't tell if it was brown or black, and those classically-chiselled features that shouted 'Man alert! Man alert!' *This bloke should be out of my kitchen and advertising Calvin Klein underwear or Diet Coke*, she thought. Somehow watching this kind of beauty lounging all of its six-feet-plus frame in her doorway made up for any of last night's inconvenience.

'Coffee or tea?' Kitsy asked.

'Coffee. She doesn't like me drinking tea.' Patrick sat down at the table, feeling happy and cared-for in this place he had once called 'home'.

'Who doesn't?' Kitsy said, raising her eyebrows.

'My mom. Being back here . . . in this kitchen, it's like America doesn't exist. I know it does, but it's like it doesn't.' He yawned. 'Like all that time never passed.'

'But it *does* exist, Patrick. And *I* live here now. This is *my* house.'

'I know,' he said, and accepted the cup of coffee Kitsy poured for him. But his eyes weren't focused. Like water on wood.

'Sleep well?' she enquired as they pulled out chairs and sat down at the round oak table in the kitchen. She'd put on yellow placemats and yellow cloth napkins in blue napkin rings, blue-rimmed juice glasses, blue-rimmed plates. There was a plate of scrambled eggs spiced with thyme from the garden, mushrooms fried in butter, grilled sausages and bacon, a rack of toast, butter and marmalade. A pot of coffee and a pot of tea, a blue-rimmed glass pitcher of orange juice.

'Yeah. Slept really well,' said Patrick through a mouthful

of toast. 'The best since . . . well, cross-country season I guess.'

'You're an athlete?' *I should have guessed*, she thought. Kitsy gave a slice of toast to Lucy who was trying to smear spilled milk into the tray of her highchair. Lucy stuffed all of the toast triangle into her mouth. Kitsy fished out the blob of damp bread, took Lucy out of her highchair and put her on the floor.

'Sort of. I got long legs so Coach appointed me. Came up to me in the hall and told me to try out. Never ran before that.'

'Did you do well?'

'Got eighth at State.'

'What does that mean?'

'You know, State. All the high schools compete and you've got Regionals, then State, then Nationals. So it means I was eighth place out of all the runners in Washington State.'

'That's where you're from?'

'Yeah. Seattle.'

'Your mother – was she American?'

'About as American as you can get. She was a Lakota – most people say Sioux, though. Mom and Dad met on the reservation when he was a minister there for the Episcopalians.'

'She was a Red Indian?'

'No,' replied Patrick, restraining himself, trying to be polite. 'She was not a *Red Indian*. She was a *Lakota* of the Minneconjou band.'

The tone of his voice made Kitsy wonder how many bloody noses he'd received and given trying to get that point across.

The doorbell rang. Lucy began to cry, tugging at Kitsy's T-shirt and saying, 'Up, up, up.'

'Shh, shh, shh, sweetie, it's all right,' Kitsy said as they walked down the hall. She was afraid and excited it might be Michael. How would she explain her breakfast guest?

Kitsy opened the door to a uniformed bobby, his Panda car parked across the street.

'Is Patrick Hunter here, please?'

'He hasn't done anything, has he?' Kitsy said anxiously, thoughts of an axe-murderer in her kitchen chomping down her eggy bacon.

'Is there something we should know about?' the policeman said, raising his eyebrows.

'No.' She paused, then asserted. 'No, there isn't. I'll go and get him.'

Kitsy went back indoors. She looked at the eggs and sausages she'd laid on the table, and Patrick wolfing it all down. Now there was a cop banging on her door.

'There's a man at the door for you.'

Patrick looked up, surprised. 'For me?'

'I don't know what you've done but you can leave. I don't want any trouble,' she said, and pulled Lucy closer. Kitsy rested her cheek against Lucy's head, held her warm body close and took some comfort from it.

Kitsy followed Patrick back down the passageway and stood behind him.

'Patrick Hunter?' said the police officer.

'Yeah.'

'We tried to get you by phone but no one answered. Anyway, the officer you wanted to see is working the afternoon shift at Hornsey today. He'll be expecting you if you want to pop around to the station there at two.'

'Thanks. I'll be there.'

As the door closed, Patrick turned to Kitsy, wanting to reassure her. 'See? I'm not in any trouble so you can relax. The guy wants to see me about what happened to my mom. He dealt with the case.'

'You can understand how it would make me a bit nervous, a policeman turning up at breakfast and you haven't even been here a full night yet!'

'Do you want me to go?' He meant it sincerely. If she wanted him to leave, he would pick up his pack and walk out the door. If she really was his helper, she'd let him stay.

Kitsy could tell he asked the question honestly, that he understood her worry. That bit of understanding made her soften towards him.

'No, I'll let you stay a bit longer,' she conceded. 'But no funny business!'

He grinned at her. 'OK, no funny business,' he said, relieved he'd been right.

Kitsy had a little car, a midnight-blue Cinquecento that she'd bought when the new model came out, before she and Michael got married. She could imagine Patrick accordioning his body to get into its little seats, his knees ending up somewhere around his ears. It made her smile. But she was determined not to give him a lift to the police station at Hornsey. She wasn't going to be the fool again.

Back in the kitchen, Lucy wiggled down from Kitsy's arms and toddled over to Patrick. She grabbed his index finger and tugged.

'See, see, see,' Lucy said. He looked at Kitsy.

'She wants you to look at something,' she said.

Patrick slid off his chair onto the floor and shuffled on his knees across the linoleum to the sash window where Lucy wanted him to see out. He lifted her up by the waist and crouched there as she pointed: 'Twee! Bud! Cat!' Kitsy watched him, wary, her daughter clasped in this stranger's huge palms, his hands a wide belt around her little waist. The way his head bent to Lucy as they talked, it pulled at

Kitsy, made her conscious of Michael's absence. She got up and took Lucy off Patrick.

'You go and finish your breakfast,' she said.

He rose from his crouch and sat back at the table. With Lucy on her hip Kitsy began clearing away plates, stacking them in the sink. She wanted to be on her feet, thinking, not sitting staring at him, bewitched. Kitsy felt she'd been doing very well. She'd stood up to her mum and her entourage of fluffy white rats. She'd stood up to Michael too, in a way, surviving his walkout, getting rid of the telephones. She would stand up, too, to Patrick and his brown eyes and thick lashes, his long, expressive eyebrows. No problem. If there's one thing Kitsy had found growing up as an only child, and now being a single mum, it was that she liked her independence. She was an independent person who could stand her own ground.

So why am I doing this? she thought that afternoon when she found herself at the wheel of her little Cinquecento straining its engine up the steep north side of Muswell Hill with Patrick crammed into the front seat and Lucy strapped into her chair at the back. Kitsy parked near the police station and they all walked in and took seats on old wooden dining chairs that were so twisted that each had one leg higher than the other three. On Kitsy's chair, some bored person had tried to make up for the short leg by sticking chewing gum to the foot.

'Come in with me,' pleaded Patrick after he'd told the Desk Sergeant that he was expected.

'No. I'll stay out here with Lucy. She'll only make a fuss.'

A man came into the waiting room. 'Patrick Hunter?'

Patrick stood up, feeling anxious. 'Kitsy, aren't you coming?' he asked again.

'No. It's *your* family's business,' she said.

'I need *your* help!'

Kitsy felt complete reluctance – she really didn't want to get involved. But she couldn't help thinking that if something awful happened to her one day, and she needed help, then maybe someone would stand up for her. So Kitsy picked up Lucy and followed them in.

Kitsy had never been inside a police station before, never gone further than that front desk to hand over her licence for the endorsement she had collected for parking illegally on a zebra crossing. It wasn't a bit like on *The Bill*. For one thing, it was so grey and dingy – more like the inside of a tatty old school.

DCI Peter Neal took Patrick, Kitsy and Lucy into a little room where they sat on orange chairs with thin, vinyl-covered foam seats and metal legs, at a metal table with a fake woodgrain top.

'Tea, coffee?' DCI Neal asked.

'Tea,' Kitsy said. 'One sugar.'

'Nothing, thanks,' said Patrick.

The policeman disappeared and came back with two cups and a plate of biscuits. He sat down. He sipped. Kitsy sipped. They dunked biscuits.

'You've obviously grown since I saw you last,' said DCI Neal. 'But I can see it's you.'

Patrick didn't feel like making small talk. This was too important. 'I want to know why no one ever went to jail.'

'As I'm sure you can appreciate, a lot of that is confidential. There's very little I can tell you.'

'You know, I only found out she was knifed when I came over here. All my life I've felt . . . *taunted* by this place, like it's laughing at me or something. I get here and I find out why. All I'm looking for is an explanation!'

'I don't have one. We never charged anyone with your mother's murder.'

'Why not?'

'The killer didn't leave any fingerprints. Didn't force any doors or windows. We never found the murder weapon. We ran appeals for information and interviewed all the neighbours. We never had enough evidence to bring a case against anyone.'

'But you *must* have had suspects!' Patrick felt incredulous.

'Of course.'

'Who *were* they?' Patrick wanted to push this man into the wall. He wanted to shake him until his teeth rattled and an answer fell out, like a little black pearl.

'In any case such as this, the spouse is always the first suspect,' the policeman went on, seeming not to notice. 'The spouse, or close family, or a lover. Strangers just don't commit murders like this one.'

'My father?' For the first time, Patrick articulated his deepest fear, lit a candle in this unholy, dark part of his heart.

'We considered him.'

'Did he do it?' Even though Patrick felt afraid of the answer, at least it would be something to wrestle instead of these black holes in his mind, sucking out his identity, slurping the snail from its shell.

'No one was ever charged in this case. You must remember that, son. This murder is still under investigation. The file isn't closed.'

'But he could've done it.' He said it flatly, matter-of-fact, and felt as if he addressed the statement to himself.

'Don't go playing detective, my lad! I've only agreed to see you because I think you are owed that courtesy. Leave policing to the police.'

'All right!' shouted Patrick. Suddenly he felt lava-angry at the policeman's incompetence. 'I'll just go back home and not bother anyone any more, is that OK with you?' He jumped up and strode to the wall, stretched out his arms and leaned on his hands, his head hanging to his chest, his shaggy hair flopping down over his eyes. In his pain and anger he looked every inch the athlete, the muscles standing out in his back, his tall body. Kitsy noticed how toned his legs were under his jeans.

'I'm afraid there isn't a lot more you can do except put it all behind you,' said DCI Neal, trying to be soothing. 'Is your father still a minister?'

Patrick made an effort to be calm. He turned around and leaned against the wall, crossing his arms. 'Only part-time when the regular guy is on vacation. Mostly he's the youth-worker now.'

'So he's not still involved in that house?' said DCI Neal.

'What house?' asked Patrick, alert, hoping for a scrap of information, for a teeny-weeny little fingerpost.

'Of born-again Christians. Charismatics. Happy-clappies.'

Kitsy said, 'What do these people have to do with it?'

'It could be that some of them remember Patrick's father and mother,' he replied.

'And know who did it?' Patrick asked, knowing the man wouldn't say 'yes' but hoping for it anyway.

The officer shifted in his chair. 'Now I didn't say that.'

'Where is this place? London?' Kitsy asked.

DCI Neal shook his head. 'Wales. *If* they're still there. Abergavenny.'

'Do you have an address?' Patrick felt his heart leap up, begin to pound harder against the dread of the word 'no'.

DCI Neal coughed and shifted, looked as if he'd said too much.

'Oh come on!' exclaimed Patrick. 'I'm not going to do anything, for Godsake! I only want to talk to people who knew my mom, that's all. Are you going to take that away from me?'

'I'll give you the name of one of the people down there but I don't want any trouble. It's a small town and I'll be checking up on you. If you so much as tip over a barstool while you're there I'll have you deported.'

Patrick felt suddenly happy, and couldn't stop a grin taking over his mouth. 'OK, OK! I understand. Now who is it?'

'Her name is Dooley. Elizabeth Dooley.'

The policeman stared Patrick in the face. For many years he'd wanted to explain to this boy and his sister why they'd never found his mother's killer. Slowly he chose his words. 'With some of these cases, it's a question of resources. At the time of your mother's murder, we had a big hunt on for the killer of a titled woman found strangled in her BMW. All the attention was focused on her. Sadly, the press weren't interested in an American woman stabbed in her home in Finchley. Leads went cold.'

'So you're telling me,' Patrick sucked breath between his teeth, 'that because the *newspapers* weren't interested, you dropped it? I thought you guys were the police! Who reads newspapers any more anyway?'

'I'm simply telling you. You wanted explanations, so I'm trying to give you some.'

Kitsy saw anger come back into Patrick's face as his grin closed over. His jaw and cheekbones suddenly solidified, went polished-wood smooth, and – she thought – a little bit magnificent.

'C'mon, Kitsy,' Patrick said, suddenly wanting to be outside, to be free. 'Let's get outta here.'

He held the door open and Kitsy walked out with Lucy in her arms, unwilling to ruin this fine bit of theatre by staying. She wanted to giggle as she walked behind Patrick, the kind of giggle she'd given after escaping from the Head's office when she and Sally Fisher got caught learning to smoke in the loos. But she didn't laugh this time.

When they got to the car Kitsy suggested, 'Let's go for a coffee. My treat.'

He looked at her, hazy, his face older, more serious.

'All right,' he said.

They walked down the street to a little workman's caff. The smell of grease and cigarettes hung outside like a sign: *Food Poisoning Available Here.* It was one of those places the size of someone's front room. A few white plastic garden tables, black plastic chairs with bendy backs. Two men sat at a back table smoking, the *Sun* spread between them, drinking tea from polystyrene cups. Lucy toddled over to the display fridge, pressed her nose against the glass and stuck out her tongue, trying to lick at the black-cherry cheesecake slices on the other side.

Patrick and Kitsy didn't talk for a while. They watched the little girl exploring the shop, pulling out chairs, going back to the display case. Kitsy ordered coffee and cheesecake. They ate and drank in silence, Kitsy feeding Lucy tiny bites of the solid white cake with a brown-stained coffee spoon.

'So . . .' she said finally.

'So,' replied Patrick.

'I don't want to pry.'

'But?' said Patrick.

She reached over and touched the back of his hand. 'No buts. It's your business. Family business.'

He looked up and smiled at her for that touch, for the brief flicker with her fingertips. 'You'll do. I gotta find out more about this group. I wonder if Elizabeth Dooley and my mother were close.'

'I think the policeman dropped that in deliberately. He's not stupid. He didn't have to say anything about it at all.'

'You think so?'

'He said something he wasn't meant to say. I also think we should go home and get some rest. It's time for Lucy's nap.'

The ride back in the car was quiet. Kitsy turned the radio on for some noise. Patrick didn't talk. She concentrated on the road, the music, Alanis Morissette singing: '. . . *the mess you left* . . .' and in Kitsy's mind's eye there was Michael, sneaking out on his family to pursue a fantasy, one of Lucy's soap bubbles bursting into nothing as soon as he touched it.

At home Patrick went to his room. Kitsy settled Lucy in her bed and went to her room. She logged onto the home computer and onto the Internet. Kitsy surfed around for a while and then sent a few e-mails, checked for mail from TattooChat and logged off.

Tomorrow they'd get started.

Then she realised she'd made a decision. *Tomorrow.* That meant she was keeping him around. Why? Because of that taut body, those muscled forearms with their question-mark scars? His little-boy-lost look when he stared at her in the café? The way he went for that policeman, pushing for his answer, and for all of his eighteen years handling himself better than Michael at thirty?

Kitsy wanted to get her mind off herself and think about something that was bigger than what Lucy would eat for her tea. Patrick offered something she'd yearned for since childhood, since she pulled the bedclothes up over her head and read *The Famous Five* by torchlight and couldn't get up for comprehensive the next day. Patrick offered a challenge that would help Kitsy live up to the stud stuck in her nose. He gave her a chance to prove her new self, asking her to join him on the rock-face that he scaled, reaching his hand down to help Kitsy up.

★   ★   ★

That night they had a simple meal, mostly cold things – potato salad, sliced beef. The three of them sat at the kitchen table, cosied in elbow-to-elbow, and it felt right to Kitsy to be a part of a trio again, even if Patrick was only a stranger standing in.

'I think he did it,' said Patrick out of the blue as he ripped a piece of bread from the baguette with his big hands. He buttered it, tearing into the bread with a knife and a sticky lump of butter.

'Who?'

'Dad.'

Kitsy was silent. What could she say? It wasn't exactly a situation covered in Debrett's *Etiquette & Modern Manners*.

'Why?' she said finally.

'Stands to reason. He was here – he wouldn't leave fingerprints. She'd trust him to come in. He could creep up behind her and slit her throat. Oh God . . .' he said, and put his head in his hands. He looked up, his fingers tangled in his black hair, and stared his dark-brown eyes into hers. 'My sister's still there.'

'Patrick, you don't know that he did anything! The officer said *no one* was ever charged. Besides, why would your father want to murder your mother? Weren't they happy?'

'Happy? I don't know. Happy, I guess. They seemed like it. But I've got these letters from her, and you know, she doesn't seem happy. Wondered why she ever married him in the first place. Said when she got home she'd decide to leave him. But he was never violent to us until *after* she died and we went back to America! She'd never let him hit us. He said she spoiled us. Boy, he sure made up for it when she died! Late home from school? He'd bop you. No dinner? He'd bop you. You get used to it after a while. I even got used to him hitting my sister.'

'It was probably the trauma of her death,' Kitsy said, and

immediately sounded twee to herself like Claire Rayner, dishing out instant advice. Patrick wasn't listening to her anyway.

'She wasn't a Christian. That became a big difference. He was always nagging at her, "Go get baptised, go get baptised," but she never would. She didn't want anything to do with it. Whenever he brought up religion, she'd listen, but she wouldn't contribute.'

'And he was a *minister*? So being Christian was part of his job.'

'Yeah.' Patrick helped himself to more cold beef. Kitsy went to the fridge and brought out a fruit salad coated with yoghurt and put it on the table, dishing out a small bit for Lucy who was already into it with her fingers.

'Why would he commit murder then? If he was a dedicated Christian, it wouldn't make sense.'

'He could always beg forgiveness. Forgive me, Lord, for I have sinned, and all that *junk*.'

'I gather you're not a Christian then,' she said.

'I was baptised. If there was a way I could undo it, I would. And that goes for my sister too. I can quote you whole chapters from the Bible but it don't mean jackshit to me. You know what he used to do to punish us?'

'Hit you?'

'Besides that. Make us memorise verses that he thought fitted the crime, and then if we got a word wrong – smack! Right upside the head.'

'Charming,' Kitsy said. She'd heard enough. She didn't want to know about this horrible man. Kitsy's father was gentle to the point of jelly, even more so now that he was frail, spending all his time with his cacti in a little greenhouse off her parents' kitchen. He seemed as if he'd never had the energy for anger, and shrunk into himself during her mum's rages. She knew that getting rid of the phones had hurt Dad the most. It was something Kitsy didn't like to think about.

'So what's the plan for tomorrow?' She changed the subject.

'Tomorrow?'

'Where are you sleeping?'

'In the park, I guess.' She hadn't asked him to stay, and he didn't want to push it.

'Is that where you've been – sleeping rough in the park round the corner?'

He nodded. 'In the old stables. There's a whole gang of us.'

'Well, I'm not having you sleep in the park and then come around Lucy, so you'll just have to stay here.'

'Sure.' He smiled, remembering his dream, remembering how well she would help him. In front of him sat a new friend. 'Thanks.'

That night they had a quiet evening in. After Lucy went to sleep, Kitsy sketched tattoos and interpreted *Coronation Street* for Patrick who understood only one word in three. He was better with the *Only Fools and Horses* rerun. After he went to bed Kitsy stayed up to do the dishes, feeling like her own mother in Marigold gloves and soapsuds in the middle of the night, the only one responsible for the house in all its quiet. In those moments Flo's curse seemed to have come true: '*You'll be just like me someday, young lady!*' How Kitsy hated to be called *young lady*. She sighed. But someone had to do the dishes. At least Kitsy had control over the other curse, the one that went: '*You'll say the same things to your children one day!*'

When Kitsy passed Patrick's door she stopped. There was a smell like chicken coming from that room. And he was *smoking*. Kitsy knocked on the door.

'Patrick?'

'Yeah?'

'This is a no-smoking household. I expect that rule to be obeyed. You're not smoking a spliff in there, are you?'

'A what?'

'A spliff. Blow. Hash.'

He opened the door a crack and put his head around it. His shoulders and the top of his chest were naked smooth and he held a cloth-bound book in one hand, forefinger tucked into the pages to save his place.

'I don't smoke pot,' he replied. 'It wrecks your head and makes you dopey.'

'Well, stop doing whatever you're doing,' Kitsy said. 'Smoking is a major cause of cot death.'

'Yeah, OK. G'night,' he whispered at her.

Kitsy walked away feeling like she was walking on stilts. Patrick was the one person she couldn't tell off. That feeling scared her. *I'm tough now*, she thought. *I'm take-no-shit gangsta Kitsy. Oh hell, who am I fooling? People like that don't have houseguests and feed them baguettes and fruit salad. No, I'm a slightly-reformed middle-class housewife, and I'd better get used to it.*

Patrick slept badly in the room. In his nightmares a gang of thieves came to kidnap Charlene. His father let them into the house, and stared out the window when she screamed for help. Depressed and shaken, Patrick wondered whether he should take the information he had gleaned about his mother and leave.

'I've been thinking, Kitsy,' he said the next day at breakfast. 'Maybe I should just go home. Get on the next plane back.'

'But I thought you were here for a few more weeks?'

'I'll change my ticket. I don't feel right about leaving my little sister with my dad any more.'

Kitsy got angry. 'Don't you think that if you go now, you might blame your father for the rest of your life for something he might *never* have done? Don't you want to *try* to find out more about what happened to your mother while she was here? That's the only way you're going to get any answers, you know.'

He looked at Kitsy, surprised. 'What's it to you?'

'Nothing.' She felt her face flush. 'Fine! Go home then!' She walked over to the sink and turned on the hot water full blast, squirted in washing-up liquid, started swishing a teacup in it, agitated.

He was staring at her. She could feel it. *How rude, to stare at a person in her own home*, she thought. *I don't care if his father was dreadful to him when he was a kid. At least he could have manners.*

Kitsy washed and rinsed, conscious of how she stood, how her hands were red from the hot water and covered in suds, how her blonde hair fell in front of her face and strands caught in the diamond stud, how she bent over the sink, as if she were trying to hide. *I'm not going to speak. I'm not*, she promised herself.

He pushed his chair back. Brought over his cup and his plate, clattered them on the counter to the left of the sink.

Patrick spoke to her in a hard, brittle voice. 'What you don't understand is how *raggedy-assed* I feel, like someone took a magnum and blew my fuckin' leg off!'

He turned around and went out the back door into the sunshine of the garden. Lucy toddled after him. The door clapped shut. Kitsy could hear them playing, bouncing a ball. Patrick said a rhyme to her as the ball bounced. Lucy laughed.

His swearing made Kitsy shrink back, feel subdued. She finished doing the dishes, brushed her teeth and washed her face to feel more herself again. Kitsy didn't like the fact that he could do this to her. She liked it even less that he might suspect the effect he had.

She didn't like it, but he felt delicious.

CHAPTER 9

Dirty Laundry

She stared out of the window, her round little chin resting in her palm like a skin-covered rock. *Queen of all I survey*, thought Brune. *Keeping it all held together. Without me, it would disintegrate and I'd become invisible.*

'NO!' she said out loud. She got up and shook herself. She mustn't let the head-talk get to her. *I am their leader. I have no doubts.*

Over the window hung a large, wooden cross. Brune had nailed it there, placed it over the window deliberately. Long ago, before all this, a Tarot-reader told her that a soul would come through a window and threaten her life.

Something held her from going downstairs. She couldn't face those depressing hangers-on living in her house, the house that was rooted to her. It was as if they rattled around in Brune's own body, moving from room to room, organ to organ. Some of the housemates thought the building was haunted. But the only person haunting it was Brune, this house a result of every sacrifice, the force of her will. Why didn't she kick them out? Tell them to take their sad little carrier-bag possessions and be on their bikes.

She needed a Him. A Him to come into her, to invade her, to take over and chase back the head-talk, to wipe her clean and make her fresh, to make the sun come again the next day.

A Him to be her Jesus, to be her Lord. Through Him she worshipped her master. Each Him was her master, changed by the act to her Jesu-man. Oh, the bodies would be different. He would come to her as John or Frank (that beautiful Frank. He was the first. Inside her she felt the Master move. In Frank she felt that true at-one. At his feet she learned how to be taken over by her Jesu, to see it was Jesu claiming her, washing her with part of Himself.) Keeping the house going was the way to keep a constant supply of Hims, to keep her consecrated.

Why had Frank stopped sending her the stipend? It had been a few months now. She looked at the letter she'd written to him, couched in neatly embroidered words, outlined with unspoken threat. It sat in its airmail envelope on her bedside table, ready to be posted. Frank needed to be reminded of the stick that held the carrot.

She heard music start up in the Great Hall. It was time to go downstairs and lead her little congregation. Time for prayers.

Brune opened a wooden box, the top painted red with the Sacred Heart, pulled out a package of disposable orange razors and a small can of shaving foam. She hitched up her blue silk dress, long like a cassock, and put one foot and a hand-mirror on the bed. She spread a thin layer of foam on her labia and shaved herself there, gently, slowly, with an old pleasure, in the cold slip of foam, in the work of her fingers. Now she would hold onto this pleasure as she left the room, feel herself rub against herself as she walked downstairs and into the hall of waiting worshippers, their ecstasy of prayers.

Downstairs Brune would face the something silent that was brewing.

She had to have women in her house, grudgingly, to keep the peace. She liked them the least. When Chloë came knocking on their door, it was John who had admitted her. Brune never would have let another woman into her nest. Chloë had become part of the something that was brewing. She had power.

Now when the circles formed, everyone wanted to be under Chloë's hands.

'She healed me! She healed my migraine!' Amos shouted one day. The words sent shivers down Brune's spine. Chloë had stumbled over Brune's grave.

'*Jesus* healed you,' Brune corrected, trying to make a pleasant smile, trying not to be too snake-lipped about it. 'Her power comes from *Jesus*, Amos! Remember that.'

'Oh my God, did it really? Did I really channel something from Our Lord?' Chloë stood stock still in the same spot, relaxation and joy showing in the way her arms hung, in her big smile, in the sparkle of her eyes. 'I can't believe it!'

But Brune knew she could believe it, and would believe it, and everyone else would follow the hysteria, the myth of Chloë-as-healer, and then Brune's power would be gone. She'd seen it happen before. She'd stamped it out before.

'Just remember Who's at the *source* of your power,' said Brune. She clapped her hands, made everyone stand to attention and roar out a hymn.

That night she'd gone to bed with Chloë twisting in her gut, a worm in her, a worm that could only get fatter and bigger and longer until she had to purge it out, throw Chloë out of her house. But she couldn't afford to do that. The other woman brought with her money, good middle-class-stock money, a steady supply of it. Chloë fed them. She would also pay for the heating in winter, if Brune could stand it that long.

* * *

'If you're ready to go, could you give me a hand, please?' Kitsy called down to Patrick.

He ran up the stairs, taking them two at a time, feeling excited. 'You want me to take those?' He pointed to the two small suitcases Kitsy had packed. One for her, one for Lucy, plus a Tesco bag full of food. Patrick carried the cases downstairs while Kitsy went through her bag to make sure they had everything: bed and breakfast reservations, map, Barclaycard, cash, keys. She shouldered the bag, cradling Lucy who was still asleep, locking the bedroom door behind her. If, by some miracle, Michael came back while Kitsy was out, she didn't want him to get the computer.

Patrick and Kitsy had planned the trip on the spur of the moment, drinking coffee slowly at dusk, sitting opposite each other at the kitchen table.

'What about Lucy? There's nothing for her to do down there. She'll fuss so much I'll go grey,' said Kitsy.

'I'll help you look after her,' said Patrick. 'Or else I could go by myself.'

Kitsy bit at her thumbnail and considered. 'No, the train's too expensive. Cost you fifty quid at least, and then there's the B&B. If we go with the car I can put the petrol on Michael's Barclaycard – he hasn't cancelled it yet. If he wants to fight for custody one day, now he can at least say he's put a few quid towards something.'

'I can camp out,' offered Patrick. 'I've got my sleeping bag.'

'It'll be just as easy if we share a room,' she said, and Patrick stared at Kitsy. 'Twin,' she answered his unasked question. 'Unless you mind, that is. I can't camp out with Lucy to look after.'

'Sure, I mean, thanks.'

They left at 6 a.m. the next day, Lucy sleeping in her car seat, cuddled up to a little blanket and her favourite teddy.

Kitsy wanted to make the Severn Bridge by breakfast-time to avoid the worst build-up of traffic.

'You know who my favourite saint was?' said Patrick as they rattled along in the early-morning aloneness like a wheeled milk crate pulled by a piece of string.

'Judas?' Kitsy said.

He laughed. 'No, Thomas.'

'The doubter?'

'I don't think he was a doubter. I think he was a realist. After the Lord appeared and Thomas asked Him to show him the nail-holes, I think he was hoping it wasn't Jesus. That He'd really died – you know, like the whole scene was over.'

'That's interesting,' she said. Kitsy liked Christianity as a concept, its rituals and holidays, and didn't want to pick at its specifics.

'It's like grunge,' Patrick carried on, feeling he was on a roll with this theory. 'By the time Kurt Cobain had died, grunge was dead. But that's when the media picked up on it in a big way. Even though grunge had been tits up for a while. And that's like Thomas.'

'Tits up?'

'You know, dead. Gone. 'Cos after Jesus was dead, the disciples were a total mess. Thomas, now he knew the good times were gone. He'd got in on it when it was still the thing to do.'

'So what's your point?' she said, puzzled.

'My point is that's when it all began to go wrong. See, up until then you didn't have all the saints and shit. Then Paul started hanging on Jesus all his hopes, and went around telling *his* version of what Jesus was about. That's fine, I guess. But the problem came when it all got written down. Then the stories about Jesus and what He did and what He meant to the world were no longer legends. They became *law*.'

'Really?' answered Kitsy. She said to herself: *He must have been thinking about this for a long time.*

'Is that all you can say – "Really"?' Patrick felt disappointed and upset. She didn't seem to be paying attention to what he was saying.

'It's not something I've thought about.' Kitsy kept her tone mild.

'Well, *think* about it!' he urged. 'Christianity got stuck in a time-warp. The whole thing is thousands of years away and people are still taking it literally. Don't you think that gives them a great excuse to do whatever the fuck they want? They pray to Someone who hasn't even bothered to show up for two thousand years! There's no account of the spiritual world as it is *now*, as it still *exists*.'

'What spiritual world?'

Patrick gave up on her. He felt she'd closed the door on the conversation, refused to understand. 'Just forget it.'

He grunted and folded his arms. He shifted so that he stared out of the window into the green fields and jigsaw hedgerows. Kitsy glanced over at him, his set face, his hard stare away from her. She wondered at how he'd become so suddenly animated, how his passion had shot out a flame.

You immature little git, Kitsy thought, not understanding what Patrick had said. She assumed his flame burned at her.

They stopped before the Bridge for breakfast. Eating seemed to pick up their spirits. When they got to the Welsh side Patrick said, 'Hey – what's that sign say? Gaawaasanaythou? What kind of word is that?'

'Welsh. *Gwasanaethau*,' Kitsy said, giving the pronunciation her best shot. She garbled it, but felt like an expert next to Patrick's wide-eyed wonder. 'The translation is on the sign – it means "services" in Welsh. We're in a different country now.'

'Cool! International traveller or what! How come we didn't bring our passports? Hey – what's that one say? Akkuub dee daal . . . free recovery. Wow! I can speak Welsh!'

'Not quite,' she said sourly.

After that, Patrick tried to sound out all the signs in Welsh. Kitsy's annoyance turned to amusement as he started trying to give her directions in a made-up language.

'Hey, there's a sign for you,' he pointed as they got close to the town, driving past fields and hedgerows, stone walls and grazing sheep. 'Skenfrith Yaaanees gunraid? What a tongue-twister!'

Skenfrith Ynysgynwraidd? Even Kitsy couldn't take a stab at that!

At Abergavenny they drove past signs for duck eggs, coal and homemade bread, past the cattle market and to a B&B near Neville Street which they found after a few false turns.

Their room was crowded with two twin beds and an old, white-painted chest of drawers. Violet and green-striped wallpaper crowded it even more, as did the pink bedcovers. Patrick slung his dirty purple pack on one of the pink beds, and dumped Kitsy's cases and shopping on the other.

'I'd like to go wander around if you don't mind,' he said, wanting to get away, to stretch his legs and his lungs.

'Aren't you going to unpack your things?' she asked.

He stared at the drawers, then at his pack. 'What's the point? I'll only have to put it back.'

'I suppose you're right,' she answered.

Patrick bounced out of the door and Kitsy smiled at his enthusiasm. *So much for 'I'll help with Lucy'!* she thought.

Patrick was glad to be out of that little car, letting his legs yomp up the streets. He didn't care where he went. He knew he'd eventually get to the right place if he stuck to the sidewalks.

Kitsy's all right, but she gets on my nerves sometimes, he thought. *Hey! Those are supposed to be mountains over there, those tiny little foothills. No bigger 'n warts they're so small. It said they were mountains on the map. Jesus, what a country.*

He walked through the little town with crammed-together shops, sloping streets, the stores shunted on top of each other like boxcars after a rail crash, all uneven and speaking of a distant past. Patrick's sense of history was so much in the present that he could barely imagine what it was like to live even a hundred and fifty years ago on the open plains, his mother's people hunting buffalo with short bows and fast ponies, so skilled at the kill that they could ride into a herd and shoot an arrow directly into the great woolly animal's hump.

America then, mostly unbuilt, was still an open space with elk and bear left to hunt. The salmon ran thick in the Columbia, their silver bodies rubbing against each other, the water so pure you could cup it icy in your hands and drink. Now the Columbia River was brown, dead like the Thames, and it was hard to imagine that it had ever been roiling with fish. He remembered going down to the Thames with his mother, making a special trip to see it, this great dirty sore running through the city. He expected to be able to swim in it, or fish, and pestered his mother on the bus-ride down: 'Pretty please with sugar on top, Mommy, can I *please* have a fishing pole?'

How disappointed he was when he saw the brown sludge moving at a stately pace through the dirty city. Kitsy said there were fish in it now, even a dolphin sometimes. But cities got the rivers they deserved.

Patrick walked out of town, and the shops with their roofs joined in a snaking line of black shale. In their crookedness, their home-madeness, the shops spoke of times when people didn't have power tools, when they slapped mud onto sticks.

This place went back to history he couldn't even imagine, past Bugs Bunny at King Arthur's court, past those castles he'd only seen in cartoons, back to a time when life wasn't written down.

Once off the main street, things got more modern. He passed the bus garage, the Renault dealership, and the Tourist Information offices to climb a small hill. A blue sign saying 'River Gavenny' stood guard over a little trickle of water trying to survive summer, not filling its banks, its stone walls mocking the river's diminished self. People had thrown trash on the ivy-covered banks – old blue Wispa packets, dirty-yellow styrofoam hamburger containers. It made Patrick sad to see the disrespect to the struggling river, so he continued up the hill, veering off from the out-of-town road. He stopped to stare out at the hills around the town, burned brown on top, bare-naked, and that disturbed him too. Mountains weren't impervious. They could be robbed and left naked.

These people were Europeans, the ones who left these crooked houses, faced death crossing an ocean and stole and plundered and tried to exterminate his mother's people.

No. Not quite. These were the ones that stayed behind. What did that say? He felt grateful to them in a way, that they stayed here, that he met them in their sensible black shoes, men with weak shoulders and fat hips, women skinny and flabby with bare faces and bras that let their boobs bounce. He was grateful that he was meeting them here, rather than in his neighbourhood.

A man walked by, a big black man with a fierce face and dreadlocks, with a roll in his walk. He watched the man amble down the bridge's slope, and noticed how other people didn't move out of the way. The white people didn't cross over. In a town this size near Seattle they would have scattered, discreetly, crossed the street or walked onto the grass parking strip to put distance between them. Always that edge there, in white Americans. But here they had no guns. Here that fear didn't seem to exist.

He was up in the residential streets now, in among the houses that overlooked the town. A few cars buzzed along, dipping into gaps between parked cars to let each other through. A man going past carried a wicker basket over one arm. Patrick looked into it as he walked by – the man had filled it with onions, dirty carrots with stringy green tops tied together with a blue rubber band, and a loaf of French bread in a white paper bag.

No man Patrick knew would carry a basket.

He walked on towards the end of town, looking right and left, over the technicolour cars parked bumper-to-bumper, coating both kerbs of the street. He was ready to turn around and go back, when he saw a huge white Victorian house with bay windows and an unkempt front garden. No cars were parked out front. People obviously avoided parking there – why? Did they have some reason not to be associated with that particular house?

Nah, he dismissed. *Must be they don't have cars.*

Patrick turned his back on the house and walked on. The summer's day sun had become so strong that shadows from tree trunks cast onto the pavement and street could have been black crêpe-paper cutouts, the leaf shadows twisting miracles in their invisible wind, animated pieces of black against bright, bright grey. He wandered for about an hour, sometimes jogging, enjoying being alive in his body in the sun, savouring the summer smells of cut grass and sweet tree sap.

Back at the B&B he knocked on the room door. Kitsy opened it.

'There you are!' she said. 'Guess what?' She walked to the bedside table as he came in. It held a tiny kettle, cups, teabags, little plastic cups of UHT milk, and two packets of chocolate digestive biscuits. Kitsy hefted the kettle and flicked on the switch.

'Whassup?' said Patrick, sitting on the bed where Lucy sucked at a bottle of Ribena. The little girl stared at him with blue eyes wide open, an assessing stare.

'I found it!' said Kitsy. 'The house where those Christians live.'

'You did? How?'

'By asking around,' she said, pouring boiling water over a teabag. 'At least, I'm fairly certain it's the right place, from what people said. Coffee?'

'Yes, please.'

'First of all, Lucy and I went to the Tourist Information office. Did you know they have a castle here and a children's museum? They hadn't heard of this Elizabeth Dooley of course. Abergavenny is more like a big town than a village where everyone knows everyone else. So I walked to the church up the road from them and we went in. The organist was practising. Lucy loved the music, didn't you, sweetie?' she said, smiled at her daughter, then handed Patrick a cup and saucer, with two biscuits.

'So what happened then?'

'When the music stopped I started chatting to the organist, a nice old chap. He said that Elizabeth Dooley used to be a parishioner there. I don't know, but . . .' Kitsy sighed. 'The way he said it – there wasn't anything he said *directly* but it was as if there had been some kind of kerfuffle . . . maybe that's too strong. As if she left under a black cloud. Nicked the collection box or something.'

'Did *what*?'

'Not literally! Just done something dodgy, that's all. Left some kind of bad smell behind her.'

'Where does she live?'

Kitsy dug in the back pocket of her black jeans and pulled out a crumpled scrap of paper. She handed it to Patrick. 'It's somewhere on the hill, past the bridge over the Gavenny.'

Patrick unfurled the address, glanced at it and stuffed it into his front pocket. She watched his reactions, studied his face. In her there was steadily growing a longing to know more about him, to answer the blanks of unconceived questions she had, questions threatening to break to the surface. Her British reserve held them under, pushed them down against her blood in case she probed too deep and something painful popped out. With Patrick her emotions felt translucent. She was acutely aware that she didn't know how he felt – that she didn't really know how *any* man felt. Certainly she hadn't with Michael, or else his walk-out wouldn't have been such a devastating surprise. Maybe that was part of Patrick's attraction for her – that his American openness meant that at least she could make a good guess at his thoughts and feelings. He hadn't Michael's studied English mask.

Patrick looked up to find Kitsy staring at him. He touched his face. 'What?' he said.

She shook her head. 'Nothing.'

'You look like my nose has fallen off!'

They laughed together.

Kitsy said: 'I feel grotty after that hot car journey and walking around. I'm going to take a shower and then we can get some food.'

She shut herself in the tiny en-suite bathroom which had once been a walk-in cupboard, and Patrick turned to Lucy. While he tried to remember the words to 'This little piggy went to market' he listened to Kitsy humming in the shower. He wondered how she looked, soaping herself.

Ten minutes later she walked out in her black jeans and a clean T-shirt, a white towel wrapped around her head, her feet bare and pink. They decided to go to the park for a picnic, and when she'd combed her hair and slipped on a pair of black mules they set out through the town with Lucy's pushchair, following signs to the river. After a while they selected a willow tree and sat beneath its dipping branches, Patrick resting on one elbow, draping his legs down the riverbank's small slope. Kitsy sat cross-legged with Lucy in her lap. Between the business of feeding Lucy and arranging sandwiches, getting out white plastic yoghurt spoons and pouring juice into paper cups, she'd look at Patrick, stretched out, noticing the grace in him, completely at ease in his body, and how he seemed to own a great deal of the space about himself.

'Do you want me to come with you when you go to the house?' she asked.

'I think I should go by myself,' Patrick answered, glancing up at her.

Kitsy wondered how this time was different; why had he needed her at Hornsey police station, but didn't need her now? But his glance made her shrug it off. It didn't really matter. He'd come to her when it was important.

As it was they found the house together – a big, ramshackle old building with white paint grimy from years of dust and dirty rain, peeling window-ledges and rotting frames. The front garden, once well-kept, had blown to seed. Edging the dandelion lawn and overhanging the cracked cement path were hardy bushes grown out of shape – a laurel, a pink camellia, and tall and spindly roses with a few orange blooms on each bush. A honeysuckle romped up a trestle near the portico. The screws holding the ancient, grey wood into the brickwork had worked themselves out of their holes with the weight. The trestle gave the impression of hanging onto thin air; a whisper of wind would bring the huge, scraggly bush crashing down.

In an attempt to restore order, someone had placed two potted red geraniums on either side of a green door. They'd since been forgotten and heat had dried the compost into threads of bark. Now the flowers were more brown than red.

Kitsy stared dubiously at the tatty house from the pavement, but made no comment. 'Right,' she said, 'I'll leave you to it. Do you think you'll be back for dinner?'

'Sure,' he replied, distracted, his eyes on that dark-green door. He hoped that this place would be the answer to his prayers and dreams, that inside, it would billow with clouds of answers, white promises to inhale.

For a reason she didn't understand, Kitsy wanted to give him a hug goodbye. Instead, she turned the pushchair around and headed to town for an afternoon of touring the castle and museums.

Patrick knocked at the door and rang the bell. Inside he heard a woman say, 'No, *I'll* get it.'

When the door opened, a woman in a long, blue silk dress and long brown hair which hung loose over her shoulders stood there, staring out at Patrick with a closed, aggressive face.

'Does Elizabeth Dooley live here?' he asked. He didn't like the look of her.

'Who are you?'

'Patrick Hunter. I guess she knew my mom and dad.'

The woman's face opened in surprise. Although she was old by Patrick's standards, she was pretty. 'You're Frank Hunter's son?'

Patrick smiled at her recognition, revising his opinion, feeling hope. 'Yes! You remember the Rev . . . my dad?'

'You're so grown-up! Last time I saw you, you were only a child, and now look – a man! Come in – *I'm* Elizabeth. What brings you to Wales?'

Patrick followed her into the house. Inside it was dim, cool, and deliberately quiet. He noticed that the woman kept herself immaculate, nice hair, her fingernails varnished – a contrast to the house. He felt that she didn't notice its dilapidation, the way it crumbled and warped around her.

'I'm looking for people who knew my mother,' he told her. 'A policeman gave me your name. He said you might be able to tell me something about her.'

'Shocking, shocking tragedy,' said Brune, shaking her head forward, obscuring her face with her long brown hair. 'We were all devastated when it happened.'

'I've only just found out how she died. Can you believe he kept it from me for all those years?'

Brune shook back her hair. Her eyebrows went up and her eyes opened in surprise. 'Did he really?'

'Yep. He did, the bast—'

'*Bruuune!*' a woman called from another room in the house.

'I'm coming!' she turned and shouted back, impatient. She faced Patrick again. 'They don't call me Elizabeth here,' she said kindly. 'Please call me Brune.'

The single name stood out to him like an old stone on a hill. Although she wore prettiness like a toga, in grace, he didn't feel in his gut a twinge, a response to beauty. He wanted to be friendly with this woman who had known his mother well, so he deliberately ignored something about her which made him go a little cold – the blue eyes, hard, like big beads. They were empty black in the middle, a place where his universe could fall in.

'Come with me,' she said, smiling at him as if he were a long-lost cousin. She swept him along with her toward the back of the house. 'Your mother and I were *great* friends in London. We'd have high tea together – she loved our quaint little English traditions – and phone each other up – go shopping . . . you know, all those things women love to do together.'

She gave a little giggle. 'Guess what we did once? Your father was *so* angry . . .'

A teenage girl stepped into the corridor from a side room. 'Brune? Oh, excuse me – I didn't know you were busy.'

'Chloë – meet Patrick, the son of my old friend Alice. Chloë is one of the people who live here. We're a house full of God's children you know, worshipping and praising the Lord.'

'Hi,' said Patrick to the pretty, dumpy Chloë. She was short, with shaggy light-brown hair, and a dark winestain covering her right temple, snaking down to the corner of one eye.

'Will you be staying with us?' she asked.

Patrick gave Brune a questioning look. She said: 'That's an *excellent* idea, Chloë, but of course it's up to our guest to make that decision.'

Patrick felt tempted. He wanted to hear the rest of Brune's story and all the other stories she had to share with him. But then he thought of Kitsy and her generosity, and knew he couldn't do that to her.

'Actually, I'm staying with a friend in town. But I don't have to be back until dinner.'

'Wonderful!' warbled Brune. 'We've just finished morning prayers and I have a few free hours to spend with you chatting about the old days.'

Brune led him into a hall which ran the length of the house. Patrick took in its scarred wooden floors and white walls with cracked plaster. Too-short yellow cotton curtains dressed the tall bay windows at the street end, while windows overlooking the back garden remained naked. A worn blue corduroy sofa sat under the naked window in a small patch of sunlight, a small spotlight on a tomatoey stain and bits of fluff.

'This is my Great Hall,' Brune said with a sweep of her arm. 'Can't you imagine how *wonderful* it used to be in the old days, when they had balls and all the women danced in those *gorgeous* silk gowns and their diamonds? Can't you just *hear* the music?' she said, and twirled a few times on the wooden floor. Patrick glanced at Chloë who stared at Brune with her mouth slightly open, showing a set of white, orthodontically-corrected teeth.

Brune stopped dancing and caught Chloë's expression. She laughed at her. 'What's wrong with a little bit of fun?' she asked, and the young woman turned pink with embarrassment, that her thoughts should be so plain on her face.

'Come on!' said Brune, taking Patrick's hand and dragging him over to the sofa. She patted a worn blue pillow and told him to sit down. 'Now you must tell me everything. Did your father send you over here for some reason? Did he have any message for me, his wife's old chum?'

'He doesn't even know I'm here,' Patrick spat out. 'You know, I think—'

'Yes, what *do* you think, dear? I'm *dying* to know,' she said.

Her aggressive, almost manic way of addressing Patrick made him back off. He had been going to say, 'I think he killed her,' but her attitude made him stop. He didn't want to watch his newborn suspicions sink under her gushing. He changed tack. 'I think he'd be upset if he knew I was visiting you. He cut off contact with all her relatives. I don't know many people who knew my mom.'

'Maybe he didn't want to upset you,' she suggested.

'No, that's not it.'

'I'm *sure* that's part of it. He's a *good* man,' she emphasised.

Normally this would have been a cue for Patrick to jump in, guns blazing, to whack black gaping holes into his father's character. But something in Brune made him not want to disabuse her of her sickly-sweet ideal. He wanted to let her live with her fantasy, here in her falling-down house. She seemed so nice.

'I thought you knew my father better than Mom,' he said.

'Goodness, no! Of course I *met* your father first through his Bible meetings in north London. But when he introduced me to *Alice* we immediately became firm friends.'

'So what was that story you were going to tell me?'

'Oh!' she exclaimed. 'Let me think. It was rather a long time ago, I'm afraid. Alice wanted to go into the West End to get her nails done for a party she was giving at the weekend. I needed a pair of shoes and so we went together – to Harrods, naturally! We wouldn't be caught *dead* anywhere else! Well, we shopped the entire morning and were absolutely *exhausted.* Your mother was an *angel* while I tried on every single pair of shoes in the place and finally settled on a simply *elegant* pair of strappy sandals.

'After a bite to eat, she had her nails French polished by this little Malaysian gentleman who was an absolute *scream* and we could barely stop giggling all the way home! Well, when your father saw she'd had her nails done, he made such a commotion! But Alice was *wonderful*. She tossed that black hair of hers, stared him straight in the face, and told him that a woman needs to feel like a woman! She was magnificent!'

Patrick listened, enchanted. This was a side of his mother he'd never seen, or if he'd seen, hadn't noticed. He'd never imagined her like that. Maybe because Frank and Alice had been at loggerheads for a long time, he mainly remembered her as thoughtful and quiet – ready to smile and joke, sure enough – but not the frivolous Alice that Brune portrayed.

Just then, a young boy of about ten with small, intense brown eyes and sandy-blond hair strolled into the room carrying a catapult and a handful of flint pebbles.

'Mum, have you seen my elastic bands anywhere?'

Brune's animated face closed down as she turned to answer him. 'No. You can see I'm talking. Ask Chloë, or John. He might know.'

'Who's this?' the boy said. 'Is he coming to live here?'

'No. He's a visitor from America. Now go out in the garden and play!'

The boy deliberately dropped his handful of pebbles on the floor, and they clattered against the wood like buckshot.

'Pick them up!' she ordered. The boy stood, staring at her. Patrick wondered at his insolence, that he didn't duck, anticipating a punch, that he defied his mother in front of company. Patrick felt conscious of the precise place on his cheekbone where his father would have hit him.

'HUNTER!' she shouted at him and then froze for a moment, as if something had stunned her.

The boy stooped to pick up the stones with the fluid slowness of honey poured from a spoon. Brune regained her presence and scowled at her son, face angry and set, until he'd got them all and ambled out.

'Hunter?' asked Patrick, surprised. 'Is that his name?'

She turned and smiled brightly at Patrick. 'Yes, that's his name. I . . . ah . . . named him after your mother.' Brune perked up. 'Something to remember her by.'

'That's nice,' said Patrick, 'but . . .'

'What?' said Brune, and stared at him, searching his face for what he was thinking.

Patrick had been going to say, 'Her name was Smoke, not Hunter,' but then thought it would be tactless. After all, she'd named the child years ago. It would be pointless to bring it up now. Instead, he said, 'Nothing. I'm sure she would have liked it.'

'Tell me a little about yourself. Are you up at University yet?' Brune asked.

'Nah, I wanted to work 'cos we never have any money, but my job didn't materialise, so I thought I'd come here for a while.' He didn't feel like explaining to an almost-stranger – even one he liked – about how depressed he'd been, how not knowing the facts about his mother's death had driven him nearly crazy.

Brune stood up. 'Would you like to see the house and what we do here?'

'Sure,' said Patrick, although really he wanted to sit on the couch and listen to more memories of his mother.

Brune seemed to take possession of Patrick, looping her arm in his. She was a tall woman, taller than Kitsy, and walked easily with him, matching his strides in her long gown and sandals. She took him across the hall and showed him into the kitchen. Although it was a huge room, it was even shabbier and less well-equipped than the one at Patrick's Seattle house – containing only a few beaten pots and pans, the Teflon mostly scraped away, and a rickety old gas cooker varnished with a sticky brown glaze of sugar and grease. A man with a tin-opener worked at the counter opening a stack of Safeway special-offer baked beans. He glooped the contents into a huge saucepan, and tossed the empty cans into a cardboard box. Next to the beans were plastic bags of special-offer white bread.

'John, this is Patrick, the son of an old friend in America,' said Brune. John grunted, 'Hello,' and tipped another can into the pot. He looked like a pub thug with a bashed-in nose, stubbly haircut and hairy forearms. All he needed was a blue tattoo of a dragon.

'John's our cook and does all the shopping,' she explained. 'He's also an absolute *wizard* with the Psalms, aren't you, love?'

'You staying for dinner?' said John.

'No.' Patrick felt grateful he wasn't.

'That's all right then,' he said without looking up.

'John!' said Brune. 'Don't be cheeky to my guest!'

They left the kitchen and walked into another room off the hallway; this one overlooked the back garden. It was a large, airy square with a ceiling rose and an original cast-iron fireplace. In the centre, covering a large part of the black and scuffed hardwood floor, was an oval carpet, its red wool washed and hoovered to pink. A plain, dark-wood bookshelf held Bibles and hymnals, a few tambourines and an Oxfam gourd rattle. In a patch of sunlight in a brown armchair, the last remaining of an overstuffed three-piece suite, Chloë sat curled up in shorts and plimsoles reading a *New Testament*. She looked up and smiled at them.

'Sarah says she needs to see you as soon as you can manage it,' said Chloë. 'Bob sent her another letter this morning and she's pretty upset. She says she wants to go home and sort things out.'

'Tonight?'

'I think so. When I came downstairs to pray for her she was getting her bits and pieces together.'

'Why didn't you tell me earlier, Chloë, so we could *do* something?' demanded Brune. She turned abruptly to Patrick. 'She's *so* hysterical, that Sarah. I'll be back in a tick.'

Patrick sat down on the floor.

'You can have the chair if you want,' said Chloë, half-getting up for him.

'Nah, that's all right. So why do you live here?'

She sat down again. 'Because everyone here loves Jesus and I can be myself. I don't have to make excuses why I want to serve the Lord because they do too. Have you come to Jesus?'

'Nope,' said Patrick cheerfully. He was a million miles

away from his father and wasn't going to pretend.

'I'll pray for you,' said Chloë.

'You do that.' Patrick felt good to be able to say it. 'So what's everyone like?'

'We're a normal house really. We all pay rent and help with the food and the bills. We give what we can, just like the first Christians did. Except Brune, of course, because she owns the house, and it's all her furniture and everything. We have prayers in the morning and before bed. She can be quite strict with us when we forget God's words.'

They heard Brune's feet running down the stairs. She blew into the room. 'I'm afraid we've got a crisis!' she said with a dramatic opening of her arms, making Patrick stand up. 'Chloë, you'll have to go and sit with her for a moment while I finish here with Patrick. Take up your Bible and read to her!'

Chloë uncurled herself from the chair and ran out of the room with her Bible in her fist. Upstairs Patrick could hear a door open, a woman crying, and Chloë voice, soothing, before it shut.

Brune settled in the chair and Patrick sat on the floor again.

'So tell me a bit about your father,' she said. 'Is he still working in the ministry?'

'Not really,' answered Patrick, distracted by wondering whether Brune shouldn't be with Chloë and the other woman. 'After Mom died he didn't want to be a preacher any more, so they gave him other jobs around the church. At the moment he's a youth-worker.'

'He paid for you to come to England on a youth-worker's wage? He must do well for himself.'

'I paid for this trip!' Patrick protested. 'Look – he doesn't even know I'm *here*. Besides, he gets nothing for his job. We'd be better off if he flipped burgers.'

'I see,' she said, considering. Upstairs, Sarah's crying intensified and the sound leaked through the ceiling. Brune raised her eyelids, her thin eyebrows.

'What's wrong?' asked Patrick.

'She doesn't know when she's well off, that's what's wrong. She wants to go back to her simply horrid husband instead of staying with people who *truly* love her!' She paused, her head to one side, listening to the ceiling. 'I'd better go and sort it out. Are you sure you won't stay for dinner?'

Patrick thought of John's beans. 'I've got to get back.'

'You will come again before you return home?'

'Sure,' he said, feeling as if she knew more stories to tell. 'Maybe tomorrow.'

'That would be *divine*,' she said. They got up and she showed him to the door. As she opened it, she leaned forward to kiss Patrick on the cheek. And then, in an odd gesture, she placed her hand against his chest, as if to feel the muscles there, or his heartbeat. After a moment, he pulled away and stepped across the threshold. She gave a little wave and closed the door.

Patrick walked past the rose-bushes, the camellia, the laurel, not seeing any of them. He automatically turned right out of the gate and went down the hill, crossing the bridge over the Gavenny. Like that he walked back to the B&B feeling drained, exhausted, and very confused.

Kitsy and Patrick ate dinner at a little café which served big burgers for small money.

'It was as if she was telling me about a whole side of my mom that I totally didn't know was there,' Patrick said, as he chomped his way through a double cheeseburger with onion and pickle and described his time with Brune. 'I never would've thought in a million years that Mom would set foot in Harrods!'

'Just imagine if I died now, Patrick,' replied Kitsy, tearing at a Cornish pasty with a dull knife and fork. 'Lucy would see me as a giant who did nothing but talk in nursery rhymes and tell her to eat up her dinner. You were never able to see a complete picture of your mother, the picture you would have seen as an adult.'

'I guess. I always saw her at home, looking after us, making dinner and stuff. But even when she went shopping . . . I mean, she got her jeans from Fred Meyers. That's like getting them at Tesco. Not Harrods, for Chrissakes!'

'She obviously had a secret life on the side,' said Kitsy, waving the fork with a bit of pasty at the end. 'That's not so uncommon. Look at my husband, Michael. One minute it was happy families, the next minute we have a little argument and he never comes home from work! Now I hear through the grapevine that he goes to discos all the time and wears platform shoes. What's that all about?'

'I dunno,' he said. 'It's just that I have different memories of my mother, I guess.'

'Such as?'

'She wasn't stingy or anything, but she made things last. Other kids' moms never sewed up holes in their socks or cut up old jeans to make patches. It's not like anyone could tell they were patched either. You know, I never knew she wore nail polish! She kept her nails short – not bitten down but clipped. I can see them now – they were very white at the tops, like chalk.' Patrick shook his head and smiled. 'Boy, he must have been mad when he found out she'd gone and spent money on beautifying herself. 'Course, then he couldn't of spent it on some mission to the poor in Saudi Arabia.'

Kitsy laughed.

Patrick watched Kitsy feed her daughter a bite of pasty. Somewhere, in a distant part of him, he felt the gentle finger of an old memory, saw himself for an instant sitting on his mother's lap, heard her laugh and slip a tiny plastic spoon into his mouth.

He shook himself. 'Brune asked me back tomorrow. What do you think?'

'Good idea – why not spend the day with her? But I don't really want to stay here another night. We've seen the castle and both museums.'

'If I want to stay longer, I can always take a train back. Brune's already said I can spend the night with them if I want to.'

Kitsy didn't like that idea, but she kept it to herself.

After dinner they walked around the town in the warm evening air. The pubs had thrown open their doors and laughter and conversation drifted out like musical phrases. Abergavenny had a comfortable, at-ease-with-itself atmosphere which almost made it romantic.

As they walked, their arms swung in unison, the backs of their hands sometimes touching. It would have been a small motion for either Kitsy or Patrick to grab the other's hand, and both knew it. But each person waited for the other – Patrick, in his relative inexperience and Kitsy, anxious to read his signals properly. She wasn't willing to take the chance and get rejected, become bruised. Instead she talked excitedly and laughed a lot. Her eyes sparkled. Patrick enjoyed her mood, bouncing back her jokes. By the time they got back to the B&B, Lucy had fallen asleep in a backpack and they were tired and happy.

Changing into their T-shirts and climbing into their separate beds were anxious moments for both of them. *Should I kiss him good night?* she asked herself. *Should I make a move?* Patrick thought. Kitsy wondered what he'd think of her body, now more toned from the gym than she'd ever been. While she pottered about in her long T-shirt and knickers, he pretended not to notice the curve of her back, the femininity of her blonde hair shaken out of its ponytail, her hard thighs. Kitsy waited until Patrick's back was turned to give him a long look, memorising his naked legs and the triangle his broad shoulders formed with his small waist.

'Good night,' she said, as she turned over and snapped out the light.

'G'night,' he replied.

As Kitsy tried to unwind for sleep, her throw-away comment about Michael came back to haunt her. She began thinking about the time Sarah and Peter had come over for dinner, and their conversation about the spare bedroom, the room in her house where Patrick had slept.

'I'm convinced that it's got some kind of strange powers,' Michael had said, as he poured more brandy for Sarah and Peter. 'Kitsy?' he'd asked, and held the bottle over his wife's glass. She'd shaken her head.

'I don't know about strange powers exactly, but I shouldn't like to sleep in there,' Kitsy had said, resting her hands on top of her pregnant belly, on the little shelf it provided.

'It's the guest room where we put all the guests that we don't want to come back,' said Michael, smiling, drawing a puff on his Hamlet and blowing the smoke up to the ceiling.

'Tell me, Kitsy,' said Sarah, bending her head toward her hostess. 'Exactly *what* makes the room so spooky?'

Kitsy and Michael looked at each other. Kitsy had felt annoyed. She didn't like to talk about the room, didn't like to give it power by making it any more real than it was. Telling Sarah and Peter felt a bit like taking them on a tour of the house and not bothering to make the beds. 'You tell them, Michael,' she said.

'Well, to put it all into perspective I must start at the

beginning,' he said, pushing back the chair, smiling at his captive audience.

'Just tell them about the dreams,' Kitsy said.

'No, dear. If you tell a story you must tell it *properly*, from the beginning.'

'Come on,' said Peter. 'You've got us on tenterhooks now.'

'We think a woman may have died in that room, that's all,' said Kitsy.

'That's all? That's a bit of an understatement, sweetheart! She was *murdered* in there,' said Michael.

'We don't know that for sure!' Kitsy protested. 'It could have been *anywhere* in the house.'

Sarah and Peter sucked in their breath. Peter felt the tiny feet of a cold shiver patter up his back. 'Stabbed,' relished Michael. 'And they never found her killer.'

'Nobody told us when we were looking to buy this place. We bought it when the bottom fell out of the market and it seemed a bargain. Nobody said anything about a murder then,' Kitsy explained.

'We had to find out ourselves the hard way,' he said.

'Actually Michael, that's not entirely fair. Our neighbour Barbara came out with it that summer when we were working in the garden. She was the last one to see the dead woman – alive, that is – when she put out the rubbish at night. Barbara was coming in and the woman was putting down the milk bottles. Next thing you know, Barbara gets woken up by a policeman at her door saying her neighbour's been murdered and has she heard any screams.'

'No, really?' said Sarah. She had the shivers now.

'My God!' said Peter.

'Anyway,' said Michael, 'it doesn't stop there. No way. We're here in the house, calmly minding our own business, and we decide to redecorate our bedroom. So we put two camp beds in the little room downstairs to sleep there for a couple of nights. Only we didn't get much sleep, did we, darling?'

'We tossed and turned all night,' agreed Kitsy.

'At one point she rolled over and hit me on the head! That woke me up, and I shook her awake.'

'He told me that he'd had the strangest dream,' Kitsy took up the tale. 'He dreamed that he was in the Army, playing for the band, and he saw an Irishman in a little leprechaun suit with a green feather in his hat, and under his arm was a big package.'

'On the package,' said Michael, leaning forward on the table, 'was a cartoon drawing of a bomb – like in Bugs Bunny, one of those ACME bombs – and a skull and cross-bones. Then *she* says to me, "Oh my God, I dreamed that the Army band got blown up." Anyway, what could we do? We made cups of tea and went back to bed. But the next evening it was all over the telly – the Army band had been hit by the IRA, and one of the bandsmen got killed.'

'I thought it was paint fumes,' said Kitsy.

'How could you?' said Michael. 'It was obvious!'

'Then why did we go and put poor Mary in there when she came to visit me?' asked Kitsy.

'Oh God, Mary,' Michael groaned.

'What happened to her?' said Sarah.

'Yeah,' said Peter. 'What happened to her?'

'You tell it, Kitsy,' Michael commanded. 'She was your friend.'

'*Was*. Isn't any more, thanks to that room. We'd known each other since Sixth-Form College, but we'd lost contact and I was hoping to patch things up – you know, have a few quiet days in my house to talk about old times.'

'She stayed in there three nights, didn't she?' said Michael.

'Yes. You have to admire her guts, really. Every time she tried to get to sleep she got the most terrible splitting headache. In the end I gave her the whole packet of paracetamol to keep by her bed.'

'She didn't overdose, did she?' breathed Sarah, wide-eyed.

'No, of course not!' said Kitsy. 'But she didn't get a lot of sleep either. And when she did, she had the most vivid dreams about her boyfriend splitting up with her, saying how he really hated her, that he thought she was ugly and a big fat blob.'

'She did have a bit of a weight problem,' Michael remembered.

'That was on the first two nights,' said Kitsy. 'Then she dreamed she got this brilliant job but the company folded. That wasn't very nice because she had an interview to go to the following week.'

'Did you ever hear from her again?' asked Peter.

'No,' said Kitsy. 'But I bet the dreams came true.'

'That's no reason to fall out, just because she had bad dreams,' said Peter.

'Maybe you should get the house blessed,' Sarah suggested.

'Yeah,' agreed Peter. 'Get it blessed.'

'I've *told* Kitsy that, but she doesn't listen to me,' Michael said.

Kitsy felt uncomfortable again. Now the onus was on her, the bad feeling was on her; it was all her fault for not allowing a priest in the house to do his hocus-pocus.

'I can't believe,' she said, tentative, 'that our murdered lady is going to react kindly to a priest coming in and trying to turf her out. It'll probably make the problem worse.'

Kitsy had known her protest was lame, but that was how she felt. And Michael and all his friends could lump it.

'Patrick?' Kitsy asked into the night.

'What?'

'You know the room I put you in at my house? Are you

sure you're all right to sleep in there?' She felt guilty. At the time he'd been an unwelcome stranger. Now she knew they were friends.

'Yeah, I'm fine. Why?'

'I think that might be where your mother died.'

'I already knew that,' he said.

'And you slept there anyway?'

'Where else was I gonna sleep? Besides, she'd never hurt me,' he said.

'But the memories?'

Kitsy fell asleep waiting for Patrick's answer.

CHAPTER 10

Dark Medicine

Patrick walked up the broken cement path, wondering what the day would hold. He'd eaten a late breakfast with Kitsy and Lucy, then wandered around town for a while, aiming to get to Brune's house after morning prayers had finished. Finally he'd felt he couldn't stand it any longer, and slowly hiked up the hill to knock on the dark-green door.

'Come in, come in!' Brune welcomed him. Today she wore the same kind of floor-sweeping silk dress, only this time in emerald. 'You've caught us at a rather bad moment, I'm afraid,' she said as she ducked inside. Then she added in the loud whisper a person uses when they are slightly tipsy: 'Sarah's still threatening to go, and the bathroom's flooded. You don't know anything about plumbing, do you?'

'Afraid not,' said Patrick, wishing he did. He wanted to help her out. Today she looked even prettier than yesterday, the green in the dress showing off the red highlights in her brown hair, making her complexion seem pink and porcelain. He wondered why her eyes had seemed hard yesterday, and guessed it was because he'd been a stranger.

'We'll need another strong pair of arms if it gets any worse. We're in the library at the moment.'

Patrick followed Brune into the room with the armchair

and bookshelf. Chloë had sat herself in the chair. Patrick noticed Brune's mouth tense up and frown.

A woman in her mid-twenties with a long pasty face, stringy blonde hair, black at the roots, and bad teeth sat cross-legged on the pink wool rug next to a short, fattish man with a red beard and a tonsured head.

'This is Sarah, and that's Amos. You've met Chloë,' introduced Brune. 'This is Patrick, the son of an old friend of mine. His father is in the ministry.'

Without being asked, Chloë got up from Brune's chair and sat on the floor. As Brune took Chloë's seat, her emerald dress and the way she moved as if she were on stage brought liveliness to that quiet place. She waved an arm at Patrick, indicating the carpet. 'Sit down anywhere,' she said, as if a row of red velvet chairs waited for him.

Patrick settled cross-legged between Chloë and Amos, a little bit separate from the group. Brune turned her attention to Sarah, staring at her, not blinking, very intense. 'Look at me, Sarah,' she commanded, and Sarah, who picked at a piece of blue Plasticine embedded in the rug so that she *wouldn't* have to look at Brune, lifted her head and tried to stare back.

'Now *why* would you want to leave us?' asked Brune. 'Here you can feel our unconditional love, our Christian love from Jesus. And what has Bob ever given you except pain and sorrow? He won't let you worship, he forces you to commit sinful acts, he entices you to miss the Sabbath – the *Lord's* Day. Here you have everything; all is provided for you in Christian fellowship.'

Sarah took a deep breath. She debated her words, and finally said, 'But if I go back to Bob, maybe I'll have a chance of getting Jamie out of care.'

Upstairs, Sarah's things were packed in the two-wheeled old lady's shopping trolley which she'd first brought with her when she'd answered Brune's advert for 'Christian life in a Christian household' in a newsagent's window. It wasn't that Sarah was particularly devout, or versed in the Bible when she applied, but 'Christian' reminded her of the summers she'd spent in York with her grandmother as a little girl, her grandmother's peaceful house, and prayers before mealtime. To Sarah, a Christian house must have some of the same tranquillity, and her life had been low on tranquillity for several years. She'd met Bob in a pub, and for the first year most of their lives had taken place there – from their wedding reception to the pub quizzes and darts matches, the one-armed bandits for the occasional flutter.

After Sarah had Jamie, all that changed. She couldn't join Bob in the pub any more, but her husband carried on as if nothing had happened, as if the event which was Jamie belonged to another man. Finally, Sarah had had enough of Jamie's crying and Bob's absence, so she'd put the baby to bed early and nip out for a quick social drink with her friends. That was all – a quick fifteen minutes. Then it drew into a half hour, two hours, and finally lasted until closing time.

Someone must have twigged that Bob and Sarah didn't have enough money for a babysitter, because one evening they came home to find the Social and the police on their doorstep. They'd been there for three hours watching the flat, observing the absence of activity, and listening to Jamie's crying when he woke up to settle himself back to sleep. Sarah rushed in to make sure Jamie was all right and a policewoman grabbed her. Another copper shoved Bob on the floor and cuffed him.

After Jamie was taken away, Bob and Sarah began to row. They rowed before he went out on his paper rounds and after his minicabbing shifts, they rowed in the pub, they rowed over their cups of tea and when they climbed into their double futon at night. Sarah said she'd be better off drawing income support by herself, and he said, 'Go ahead.' The next week she'd gone up from Cardiff to an away quiz in Abergavenny and seen Brune's advert in the window.

'Are you *strong* enough, Sarah?' asked Brune, still staring. Sarah ducked her head at the question, and her nose went red, as if she was about to cry. 'Would you be able to fight off Satan and all his temptations *by yourself* and bring Bob to Jesus? Because Jesus is the only one Who can give you your little boy back, not Bob. Jesus is our *saviour*. A sinner like Bob *can't* save you and little Jamie!'

'Bob says he has a job now, and he's been there for two months and he's doing very well. Maybe . . .' Sarah said. She thought about his sweet letters, written in his own Bob Sweeney way: short, the joined-up writing a bit wobbly, but with all the right words. *I'm sorry about the rowing. Things aren't right without you here. I've got a job now at the garage three days a week.* And the latest: *If you come back we'll get Jamie out together.* When she read those words, Sarah knew she had to leave.

'Let us join hands,' Brune commanded.

Patrick didn't like it, but he gave his right hand to Amos and the left one to Chloë. Brune bowed her head and closed her eyes, and so did the others. Patrick stayed alert, watching them.

'Lord Jesus, help Sarah to see that You are the Way, the Truth and the Life, and that there is no life apart from You. Help her to see that we are the ones who truly love and care for her. We love you, Sarah,' said Brune.

'We love you,' echoed Chloë and Amos.

Then for a moment, the little circle was silent. Patrick watched their faces, Brune's intense will, Chloë's smile as she said, 'We love you,' Amos' expression an imitation of bliss – as if twisting around his facial muscles could make it happen – and Sarah, beginning to cry behind her closed eyelids, tears leaking fat onto her lashes, squeezed out and down her cheeks.

He was struck by Brune's power to make Sarah cry. Brune reminded him in some way of his father. *Maybe*, he told himself, *it's because they use the same words.* But it went deeper than that. Once he'd seen his father work on his High School prayer group. Frank was like an imitation of Brune. Frank reached for her intensity, her power. It was as if in Brune, Patrick saw the teacher and in his father, the student.

The circle broke and everyone looked up, all their attention focused on Sarah, waiting for her decision. Brune leaned forward in her chair watching all of them, behaving as if this was the most important moment since Creation.

Sarah began to sob. Chloë put an arm around her. Sarah leaned into it. 'It's all right,' Chloë comforted. 'You know we all love you. Why don't you stay?'

Sarah sat up and snuffled, wiping at her tears with her T-shirt. 'All right then,' she agreed. 'I'll pray about it some more.'

'Excellent!' cried Brune. 'Sarah, stand up so that everyone can give you a hug.'

Sarah stood up, her head bowed, smiling sheepishly. Brune stood slowly, as if she was the Queen, and gave Sarah a long squeeze. Patrick too, got to his feet.

'I'll tell John we'll have something a bit special for lunch.' Brune and her emerald-green dress swept out of the room.

Chloë and Amos gave Sarah a hug in turn. Patrick felt uncomfortable and separate from the trio. He didn't know what to do, so he went to the window and looked into the back garden. Hunter stood outside in the long grass, his shorts' pockets bulging with stones, a loaded catapult cut from a forked branch in his left fist. He aimed it at a tree, pulled back on the elastic, and let the stone fly through the leaves. A blackbird flapped away.

Go speak to Hunter.

Patrick looked at the others, lost in their little drama, and left.

Hunter played outside because he didn't know what else to do. He liked the sunshine and the smell of the long grass in his back garden. He liked the purr of the lawnmowers and getting down on his tummy and watching the insects crawl over the long grass-stalks, the spiders, the inchworms, the ants. He liked parting the grasses to examine the matted webs of root beginnings, as if he could find some small mystery, an intrigue there. But Hunter did this because he had no other children to play with.

Summer wasn't his favourite season; autumn was. If he'd been allowed to visit his schoolfriends he'd have been kicking a ball or shouting games, not down in the grass making up insect soap operas to keep himself amused. Although he liked summer's heat, and not feeling winter's cold in that big house which never had enough money in it to heat it properly, autumn marked the beginning of school. She couldn't keep him from that.

Even so, Hunter loved his mother fiercely, protectively, with the love of a boy who has no other person to love or to love him back. He understood that this was his mother's house, and that everyone else in it was a lodger. They appeared on the doorstep with rucksacks and boxes, leaving without saying goodbye weeks or months later. That at least was consistent; eventually they would each leave. At the moment he didn't like John. In Hunter's opinion, John cooked rubbish, and he didn't understand why his mother made them all praise John so much. He also didn't like the way she smiled her fake smiles at John more often than at the others, as if she wanted something from him. He didn't like the way John smiled back.

'Hi, Hunter,' said Patrick, closing the back door and sitting on a cement step next to the slight, sandy-haired boy. 'Whatcha up to?'

Hunter stared at Patrick, but didn't say anything. Last night his mother had told Hunter to go to his room. He'd gone upstairs and waited, wondering what she wanted. She'd closed the door and stood while he sat on his bed, drumming his heels against the floor and bouncing a little to make the springs squeak.

'We're going to have a guest tomorrow,' she'd said. 'It's that Patrick who was here today.'

'Is he going to live here?' Hunter asked his mother. This was new. He'd never been consulted before.

'No. He's not like us. He doesn't believe, so I don't want you talking to him.'

'But Muuuum! I talk to other kids at school and most of them don't believe.'

'That's unavoidable. Honour thy mother, Hunter. You're going to obey me and that's the end of it. Do you understand?'

Hunter understood. He kicked his feet harder. *Squeak squeak*, complained the bed.

So when Patrick said to him on the step, 'What's wrong? Can't you talk?' Hunter turned his back to him, took a stone from his pocket, and aimed it at a baked bean tin he'd set on top of a tree stump. He let the stone fly. The tin thunked and tumbled into the grass.

Patrick felt nonplussed. He'd never been dissed by a little kid before. But he wasn't going to let Hunter get to him, and so he sat down on the steps to watch.

'Mum said I'm not meant to talk to you,' Hunter muttered after he'd knocked over the bean tin four times.

'Really? Why?'

'I can't tell you because I'm not meant to talk to you.'

'Oh.' Patrick wondered what was wrong. What had he done so that Brune ordered the boy to stay away from him? 'What if I give you . . .' Patrick rummaged in the pocket of his Levis, bringing up a fistful of change. He picked out a golden pound coin, and spun it with two fingers on the cement stairs.

Hunter stopped slinging stones at the tin, and stared at the gold coin flashing spinning circles in the sun.

'Where is she?' he asked in a low voice.

'Fixing the bathtub.'

'If you come to my camp, she won't be able to see us,' Hunter whispered.

'Sure,' Patrick whispered back. 'Where is it?'

Hunter crouched down and ran around the side of the house. Patrick crouched and followed. Hunter crawled behind a great lilac bush, and Patrick squeezed in behind him, sitting with his knees under his chin on the swept-clean dirt. In one corner of Hunter's hideout was a small row of tins, their labels peeled off, some holding rocks, another rusty nails, screws and old washers. Patrick clunked the pound coin into a can of dirty penny pieces.

'Great fort,' whispered Patrick.

'No one knows about it,' the boy said proudly. 'They don't come over on this side. And if I aim my catapult through those leaves –' he pointed at a gap in the lilac's canopy '– the birds can't see me either. I actually killed one once!'

'Wow,' said Patrick. He remembered his slingshot stage, when being able to hit anything he aimed at was the ultimate test of skill, a testament to his own self-sufficiency, that he could find food and feed himself, that he didn't need his father any more. But unlike Hunter, Patrick knew about death first-hand, about the permanence of life lost, and didn't kill.

Patrick understood why Hunter had taken him to this spot. The dimness under the leaves, the cramped quarters, the brushed dirt, all lent itself to little-boy adventures. Hunter would sit in his camp for hours at a time, making up stories of a friend to play with, or a brother, bursting with secrets to share.

'I don't know why she doesn't want me to talk to you,' he confessed now.

'Neither do I,' Patrick whispered back. 'Did you know my last name is Hunter? Your mom and my mom were really close friends, and so when my mom died, she gave you her last name.'

'Then we're a bit like brothers,' said Hunter.

'I guess so,' admitted Patrick.

'She's stupid.'

'Why?'

'Because she thinks that John really likes her because sometimes he goes in her bedroom, but I've seen him go in Sarah's bedroom too.'

'Oh,' said Patrick, and understood why Brune didn't want Hunter talking to anybody. 'I guess that is pretty stupid.'

'Mum's pretty clever most of the time. Whenever anything goes wrong, they all ask her what to do and she tells them.'

'I see,' Patrick said.

'You want to see my penny collection?' Hunter tipped the can of coins into the dirt and spread them around with his palm. 'Some of them are really old.'

Patrick picked up a selection of pennies and stared at them, one by one. 'This one says 1923.'

'That's not the oldest. I have one that says 1894. I found that one near the stump when I was digging for treasure last year.'

'That *is* old,' said Patrick.

'I had more money a few days ago but Mum sent me to post a letter for her. Do you know who Frank Hunter is?'

'Why?' said Patrick, suddenly sharp, alert.

' 'Cos that's who the letter is addressed to, and I was wondering,' Hunter stared hard at a coin, 'you know, because I don't have a dad . . .'

Patrick gave a short laugh. 'That's my dad and you wouldn't want him, trust me.' Then an awful thought occurred to Patrick. He asked the boy casually: 'How old are you, Hunter?'

'I'll be eleven in October.'

'*Huntaaaah!*' Brune's voice called. '*Time for luuuunch!*'

At this, Patrick's heart beat hard, as if he'd suddenly changed places with the boy, was ten years old again and his father searching to give him a beating. He clawed back into himself, took command, became the leader of them both. He whispered: 'You go out first, then I'll sneak around the front and come in a few minutes later. Remember, don't tell anyone or we'll get in trouble.'

Hunter nodded and crept out on his hands and knees, crawling through the grass until he got to the corner of the house where he stood up, walked over to the bean tin and put it back on the stump. *Good boy*, thought Patrick, as he watched him from behind the lilac leaves. He heard the back door shut and sat in silence, his mind turning over the boy's age. Patrick knew he had to find out what was in that letter.

As he waited, crouched, Patrick heard the flutter of wings. He looked up to see a hawk land on the fence. Patrick stared at the bird, which eyed him back. *What are you here for?* Patrick asked the hawk in his mind. The bird swivelled his head and blinked, opened his wings and flew up into the thermals. There he circled, the feathers on the tips of his wings pointing like spread fingers. Patrick's mother had told him that the animals, insects, trees and birds were all his relations, and not one was greater than another. Patrick was no more important or less necessary than the hawk riding the thermals, or the rabbit the hawk would be bound to catch. This teaching was directly opposite to his father's conviction that God had made Patrick with the purpose of being lord over all the earth, to tame it and subdue it.

Seeing the hawk made Patrick remember that all life carried meaning; all he had to do was allow himself to be taught. It didn't occur to him to think of the hawk as an omen; instead he watched its circling, its patient waiting. It looked as if the hawk was simply enjoying itself, riding lazy circles of warm air with all the attention of a Sunday driver. But the hawk was in action. It wasn't sitting perched in a tree waiting for a rabbit to hop by. Instead it searched, watching for another creature's inattention. And then came the hawk's moment in the plunge and rush of the kill.

Patrick stared at the bird, black against summer's pale blue ceiling, and tried to think about how he could be more like the hawk. Already Patrick was in action. Now he needed patience in his search, and silence. *Maybe I should have hidden myself more with Brune. Maybe I shouldn't have shown her who I was. The rabbit won't even see the hawk's shadow.*

But it was more complicated than that. He needed to know Brune's relationship to his mother and father and that meant revealing his identity. No, what he needed to learn from the hawk was patience. He had to watch and to listen and to understand these people.

The sound of the back door closing as Hunter went inside for lunch reminded Patrick that he was still stuck in a lilac bush. He ran doubled up along the side of the house, jumped over the garden gate and walked into the front garden as calmly as he could manage. He knocked on the front door and when Chloë answered, excused himself by saying he'd gone out for a cigarette.

At the moment Hunter told Patrick about the letter, Chloë was fending off an advance from Amos. After the hugs, Amos had turned to Chloë and opened his arms. Not wanting to offend him, but suspicious that his motives weren't entirely based on Christian fellowship, Chloë opened her arms as well, but only a measly little mean bit, to send him a signal. Amos didn't receive it, his signal-receiving system fogged over by what he wanted to do with Chloë. Even though she didn't pull him close, even though she tried to escape as soon as the hug-action circuit completed itself, Amos was too intent on getting close to the young woman to allow himself to understand.

'Amos!' Chloë protested. 'Don't be like that.'

'Like what? God didn't say you can't hug, did He?'

'Let me *go*, Amos! I'm not like that!' Every moment that he held onto her became more unbearable. She felt as if she was trapped in a tunnel, or a small hot cave. She didn't like the bestial way Amos' red beard scraped against her face. She didn't trust the man behind that beard, not really. OK, she loved him in a Christian way as she knew Jesus wanted her to love other human beings, but this invasion . . . how was she supposed to put him off and still be loving? Chloë froze between instinct and intellect, her instinct telling her to pull away, her intellect asking her to be delicate about it.

But when she smelled Amos' breath, its coffee odour left over from breakfast, sour coffee and empty stomach juices, when Amos took her hesitation as affirmation that they wanted the same thing and squeezed his fat arms around her back, pulling her into him so that her pelvic bone was forced against his big belly and into his groin, Chloë's instinct won. She broke out of his arms and backed off, a scowl frozen on her lips and in the vertical creases between her eyebrows.

Finally Amos understood, and it made him angry. 'What are you so high and mighty for?' he hissed at her. He jerked his head toward the kitchen. 'It's not as if *they're* not at it!'

'What?' said Chloë, surprise taking over from anger.

'Didn't you know, you dozy cow? John's been shagging Brune for ages!' Amos said.

'You're *revolting*!' she shouted at him, the last curling wisps of Christian spirit blown from her mind. 'Stay away from me, understand?' She turned and walked quickly out of the library, then ran up the steps to her room and slammed the door.

She boiled inside. Chloë hadn't been a pretty girl at school, but once she was out in the wider world, she'd begun to receive advances from men. Except they weren't from the handsome ones. *They* wouldn't look twice at a girl with a huge mulberry stain on the side of her face. Only the ugly ones, the old ones and the disfigured ones made passes at Chloë. She wasn't so stupid or naive that she didn't understand. Perhaps that's why she made an extra effort to see into a person's soul, to understand what their spirit was like. Chloë felt this was why she was able to have some small effect in channelling God's love for healing.

But that didn't mean she was going to let herself become easy prey. Chloë tried to be as dignified as Joanna Lumley. She loved how the actress held herself, so contained, as if she'd eaten the world. Maybe she'd never be Joanna, but she could pretend what it would be like, and learn not to settle for less.

When Chloë decided to live 'a Christian life in a Christian household' she felt reassured that the men – and women – who lived there would share her motives and morals. But if Amos was right, then she lived in a house of hypocrites.

That she hadn't seen this in her housemates after four months made Chloë question herself. There again, it could be Amos who was lying.

Chloë sat cross-legged in the middle of her little bed picking at a Laura Ashley duvet cover her mother had given her, wondering what to do.

Although Patrick itched to get to the telephone, to call Charlene and tell her to look out for Brune's letter in the mail, after seeing the hawk he knew he had to see through his day with Brune; he couldn't simply walk out without an explanation.

So Patrick sat through lunch at a long rectangular table which had once been a door. True to Brune's dictum, John had cooked something besides beans on toast. They ate a mouth-searing chicken curry over sticky white rice, the chicken diced smaller than chunks in a can of catfood. Across from Patrick, Hunter ate steadily and stared at his new friend between bites. Patrick didn't like spicy-hot food, and pushed most of the meat around his plate. Brune didn't notice. High from her success with Sarah, drunk on her own manipulative power, she carried on an animated monologue.

'That's what we're all *here* for, isn't that right, John, because we're all theosophers at heart. The love of God – that's what binds us, one to another, and makes us special. Paul commands us to set ourselves *apart* from the world, to come out and be *separate* . . .'

Chloë shifted in her seat, staring at her plate. Patrick wondered if she was feeling unwell, or if she hated hot curry as much as he did. He caught her eye and Chloë gave him a thin smile, as if she didn't have the energy for it. Brune carried on her chatter.

'It's good to have Patrick sitting at the table sharing the

Lord's food with us, don't you think? Patrick's mother and I were great friends. Almost sisters, we were that close. We shared *absolutely* everything when she was living over here. When Patrick was at school we used to take his little sister ... *Charmaine* –' here she paused, and smiled, congratulating herself on remembering Charlene's name '– to see all the sights. Patrick's father was a *very* handsome man, and they made such a lovely family in church every Sunday, both of his parents *devoted* Christians.'

Patrick's mind froze for a moment, stunned. His ears carried on hearing Brune's chatter. 'Patrick, your family was the kind that anyone would envy! What woman wouldn't want what your mother had, may she rest in peace. A handsome Christian husband and two *adorable* children . . .'

Patrick began to feel uncomfortable. Still, he kept smiling, letting Brune carry on as he shovelled in a mouthful of chicken curry, chasing it down with half a glass of water, hoping it wouldn't give him food-poisoning. Then he stood up. 'Excuse me, but where's the bathroom?' he asked and listened to Chloë's directions, conscious of Brune staring at him, wondering at his sudden reaction. Patrick used all his concentration to keep his face pleasantly impassive, turned his back on the little group and walked out to lock himself in the tiny old water closet. He sat on the toilet seat with his chin in his palms, trying to analyse what disturbed him so much.

Like mosquitoes biting on a hot summer night, it seemed to be a list of tiny mistakes, whining by. He tried to strain them in his mental net, wondering if one would draw blood.

For instance, at the dinner table. Whatever his mother had been, she would *never* have made any pretence of being a devoted Christian, especially to a friend as close as Brune claimed to be.

Was Brune really Mom's friend? he asked himself. *If they'd been that close, she would have known Mom's last name was Smoke, yet she named her kid Hunter. Then there's the whole business of his age.*

The nail polish, the shopping – none of that tallied with his memory. Brune's stories began to take on the false ring of a metal lid beaten with an old stick.

Now he thought he understood what he could learn from the hawk. Like that bird, he needed to fly above the situation and use his vision to see the total landscape, to spy out the little truths and grab them. Patrick knew now that he shouldn't swallow everything whole, but pick and choose among the facts, then find a quiet place to digest.

When Patrick came out of the loo and went back to the kitchen, everyone had left the table. Chloë stood at the sink doing the washing-up.

'Need a hand?' offered Patrick. He wanted to talk, to find out what someone *else* felt.

'There's a tea towel over there if you'd like to dry,' she said gratefully.

Patrick was the kind of person Chloë wanted to be with; she liked his tall body, solidly built, his black hair and a face that spoke to her of some deep secret and maybe a soul that was a bit wild as well. That Patrick had asked to help made Chloë feel glad; so she wasn't entirely revolting.

'This is some house,' said Patrick, wiping a dinner plate and stacking it on a rickety shelf. Its plastic veneer of fake wood called attention to its cheapness, the compressed sawdust inside.

'Hmm,' said Chloe noncommittally, thinking of her mother's airy country house, handing him a glass. She tried out his accent, hardening her 'r'. 'And that sure was some dinner.'

He smiled. 'As we'd say in the US, totally gross.'

Chloë laughed. 'Disgusting!'

'You looked like you were going to puke in your plate!'

'I wasn't feeling too well.' Chloë weighed up whether she should reveal part of herself to this stranger. Who'd mind? She'd probably never see him again. She whispered, 'Amos made a pass at me.'

'Yuk,' said Patrick, fully sympathetic. If Amos had made a pass at his sister, he would have kicked the fat ugly son of a bitch down the stairs.

Chloë walked to the kitchen door and closed it quietly before coming back to the sink. She said in a low voice: 'And then he said that Brune is having an affair with John. Do you think he's lying, just to get me to do things with him? I know she was a friend of your mother's and everything, but . . .'

'What difference does that make? Nah, I think Amos was telling the truth, even if he was using it as a line on you.' Patrick thought about what Hunter had said. 'You could see it at the dinner table. He's jumping her bones all right.'

'You could tell? I couldn't and I've been eating with them for months! I suppose I never watched for it. Brune's always on about fornicators and adulterers, Sodom and Gomorrah. She knows the Bible so well, I'd never take her for a hypocrite.'

'So where's Hunter come from?' he said, disdainful. 'Planet Zog?'

'I never asked,' said Chloë, beginning to tackle the curry saucepan. 'I always assumed she was divorced.'

'Maybe, maybe not. You'd think if she was divorced, his dad would come around now and then. Have you ever seen him?'

'No.'

'Does she get letters from America?'

'Sometimes. Why, do you think his dad is American? That would be a reason why he's never here.'

'Could be,' said Patrick. He felt sorry for Hunter, stuck

in this house, playing games by himself. 'He's a lonely kid, don't you think?'

'She's a bit strict with him,' the girl said, rinsing the pan under the hot tap. An old gas boiler rumbled in a cupboard behind them. 'He should have some friends around but she doesn't allow him to play with anyone. I try to talk to him but he doesn't say much. He doesn't help himself, always sneaking up on birds and little animals, trying to kill them with his catapult. It puts me off.'

'So what does John do around here, besides Brune?' asked Patrick, wiping down the curry pan. Chloë laughed and picked up the rice pan.

'You're wicked, you are. He's like a handyman. Every day something different goes wrong in this house. It's falling to pieces. John's constantly pottering about fixing some leak or broken toilet and mending fuses. Sometimes he works in town doing odd jobs.' Chloë sighed.

'What's wrong?'

'I don't know how to talk to Brune about this. When I came here it was because I wanted to get away from all the games people play. I thought that in a Christian household everything would be above board, not that they'd be sneaking around behind everyone's backs.'

'Maybe you expect too much. Most people are jerks. There's only a few nice ones out there.'

'But we're meant to be Christians! Not sinners!'

'*Especially* Christians,' said Patrick. 'People, like, well – they shoot too high. And then they can't see what's with them on the ground.'

'I think sometimes I don't always fit in with other people.' There, she'd said it, something which had been hovering in Chloë's mind for the past year but which she'd been too afraid to speak, in case the speaking of it made the shadowy doubt a reality.

Patrick stared at Chloë, surprised by her glimpse inside herself. He thought at that moment that Chloë was pretty, an attractive person. Some inner warmth shone, in the red and gold highlights of her hair, in the pink of her cheeks. Her vulnerability, her trust in revealing such an intimate part of herself made whatever preconceptions he'd formed about this strawberry-marked girl fall away. In Chloë he felt a recognition about something in himself. Like him she was a truth-seeker.

'I dunno,' said Patrick, searching for something to say which would match the depth of her statement about herself.

'Well, I do. It's not because of this . . .' she touched her right temple with her fingertips, as if she stroked a baby. 'Mum actually was going to pay for surgery. Perhaps I should have it done . . . But I want people to like me for *me*. And the only way they're going to do that is if they can see *past* the stain.'

'Is that what you call it, a stain?'

'I suppose I think of it as a mark. But to people who can't see *me* . . . it's a stain, something which should be washed away. Actually, I'm a little bit grateful to it. I've learned from their stares when people have seen only the other side of my face and then this.'

'So what does my expression say?' teased Patrick. She stared at his face, which he'd deliberately relaxed, mouth straight, eyebrows in their black, fine arching lines, eyes wanting to laugh. Chloë knew what *she* wanted his face to say. If it had been Patrick in the library instead of Amos she would have stayed in those arms for as long as he was happy to hold her. It made her wonder about her own Christian resolve and what she would be willing to overlook for true companionship. *Maybe I shouldn't judge the others*, she thought.

'C'mon,' prompted Patrick.

'Er . . . you wish there were leftovers so you could have more of John's vindaloo?'

'No way!' hooted Patrick. 'Forget that shit!'

'What was it then?'

'Well, that was me, doing nothing.'

'I should have guessed.' She smiled.

'Anyways, I don't think you should be so hard on yourself,' he said, serious now. 'Go get the operation if your mom's paying for it.'

'You think so?'

'Sure. You won't forget that other stuff. Why not be the same as everyone else for a while?'

'Maybe,' said Chloë. For the first time she could imagine herself in the hospital room, sitting on a trolley bed in a paper gown waiting to go down to an operating theatre. The idea frightened her. She didn't like anyone touching the mark on her face; it was too personal. She still couldn't imagine herself without it. But what Patrick had said made sense to her, more than all her mother's gentle suggesting, the magazine articles clipped out and sent in large white envelopes.

Chloë handed Patrick the clean saucepan. 'I'll wipe down the surfaces and then we'll be done. Thanks for giving me a hand. Oh – I nearly forgot. Brune says she'll be upstairs reading if you want to go up and have a word.'

Patrick didn't, but he had to go and see Brune. He didn't want to stay here much longer – he needed to find the hawk's quiet place to digest – but he knew he must leave the door open to come back. Under his shoes Brune's house felt as if it shifted, as if Patrick trod on a giant undulating plastic mat as he walked up the stairs.

When he knocked, Brune called out, 'Come in.' She was lying on the bed in her long green silk dress, propped up on one elbow, expectant.

He stood in the doorframe, unwilling to step inside. 'I've got to be going now. My ride back to London will be waiting for me.'

'Ohhhh, that *is* sad,' she said. 'You're going so soon? You won't be staying the night with us?'

'I . . . I've got things to do there. You know, stuff,' he stammered, suddenly afraid she could see his thoughts, his raw suspicions laid out like parcels of dead meat.

'I see,' she said, sitting up and walking across the floor-boards in her bare feet. She shut the door, forcing Patrick to step inside. 'You're very handsome, you know – just like your father.'

'Thanks,' he muttered, wanting to bolt. Since lunch, she'd put on blusher and lined her blue eyes with a hint of grey pencil. Her brown hair hung thick, loose and shiny to her shoulders. She stepped closer to Patrick, her hips swaying, skin rustling against the silk gown. He edged away.

'I'm not going to bite you,' she assured him with a coquettish flick of her eyelashes, long and curling upwards under mascara.

'I know,' he responded, wary.

Brune stretched out one hand. Her nails were neatly rounded and painted pink. He stood tense as she put her fingertips to his bicep and traced the outline of the muscle there, from elbow to shoulder. At his shoulder she didn't stop, but drew a line with her forefinger across Patrick's collarbone.

Patrick stepped back from her. Brune tried to stare into his eyes but he looked out of the window, out over the houses and into the sky, hoping for a sight of the hawk.

'What's so fascinating out there?' she asked and stepped toward the window, her green dress swishing against her legs.

'Nothing,' said Patrick, wanting to escape. He looked at

the door painted plain white, chipped and showing under-layers of orange and green, like a glimpse of a woman's slip. She turned her back to the window and placed her palms on the low sill, dusty, the white paint bubbled in hot summers, frozen in winter. She half-sat there, the slippery dress falling over her legs to show them in outline, a tiny patch of darkness at the top of her legs. Patrick realised she wasn't wearing any underwear, was naked under the silk.

'Will we be seeing more of you?' she asked. 'It seems a shame. You've come all this way for *such* a quick visit. I'd like to get to know the son of my dear friends.'

Get to know me? In what way exactly? 'You'll probably see me again before I go, if I can get a ride back here.'

Brune's eyes flicked to the bed, to its rumpled pink duvet, half-folded back. 'Good, good. That would be nice. If I can be of *service* to you in any way at all . . .'

'I'm OK, really. You've helped me already. Sorry, but I've *really* got to go. Maybe I'll catch you again some time. Tell John thanks for the lunch, right?' he said as he opened the door and strode out onto the landing. He ran down the steps, brushing past Chloë who was on her way up. She flattened herself against the stairwell wall to let him pass.

'Are you going?' she asked.

'Yep,' he replied, without pausing, pounding down to the bottom and jumping from the third stair on to the hall carpet. 'I'll look you guys up the next time I come to Wales, all right? 'Bye, everybody!' he called and slammed the front door as he left.

Brune stood at the bannister drumming her fingernails against the newel post, staring down the empty row of hardwood steps. Chloë, who had been watching Patrick run out, now looked up at Brune who stared past her. Chloë noticed the make-up and wondered what Patrick and Brune had been doing in that room. She couldn't imagine them together, or that Patrick would allow it.

Outside, Hunter heard the door slam and ran to the garden gate. When he saw Patrick stride down the path and onto the street, his small fingers tugged and yanked at the rusty bolt. But by the time Hunter had freed the catch and stumbled out onto the pavement, Patrick was halfway down the hill. Hunter stood on the street, afraid of calling after his new friend in case his mother heard. He willed Patrick to turn around, watching his tall back and black hair disappear.

Hunter felt as if a part of God had walked out of his life. Barely keeping down the tears he crawled into the lilac bush where he and Patrick had shared secrets a few hours before and curled up into himself, tucking his head between his knees, rocking on his tailbone until all his feelings went away.

CHAPTER 11

Yelling After the Wind

On his way back to the B&B, Patrick met Kitsy at the bridge holding Lucy around her waist and throwing sticks into the Gavenny.

'Oi, Patrick!' she called when she spotted him. 'We're playing Pooh Sticks. Want to join us?'

Patrick walked over to Lucy, picked up a twig from the pavement, and put it in the little girl's hand. She threw it awkwardly, letting go too late.

'We're just about to go for a tea break,' Kitsy said. Together they walked up to the High Street and through the market to a café. Patrick began to feel subdued, as if the weight of all he'd learned in Britain pressed against him. They barely talked as they went.

'So what happened? Tell me everything.' In the café Kitsy eagerly scooted her chair in close to the table and leaned on her forearms, touching her tea cup. Then she took in Patrick's arm around the back of the chair, pulling it to his chest as if it were his comfort – a stiff, wooden chair. The tired, black-eyed young man stared at her, completely passive.

'Oh Patrick,' she said, and reached gently across the table, past his unopened can of Coke, touching his forearm with

191

the tips of three fingers. He pulled his arm closer into himself. 'What's wrong, love?'

'Is there a place,' he asked, hesitating, 'away from here? A forest? Some water?'

'We could drive to the sea – it isn't far. But I don't think you'll find any forest there.'

'What about the mountains? Do any of them have forest left?'

'Of course. The Brecon Beacons are close by.'

Kitsy paid. Patrick picked up his Coke. When they walked out of the café the air was thick with flying ants. They settled in Lucy's hair, on Kitsy's T-shirt, in Patrick's hair. Kitsy waved her hands in front of her face, tried to steer the pushchair through a pile of cabbage boxes. Everyone around them waved their hands in the air too; the stallholders with sheets of newspapers in their fists.

Patrick hated the stench of the street-market. He felt queasy with it and the heat of the pavements on this overcast day, breathing in air the same temperature as his nose and lungs. Overripe cantaloupe, broken watermelon, the smell of hot, rotting meat. When he moved away from one smell, he got hit with another – the black smell of a butcher's van revving its engine as it crept along the packed street, and when that had gone, the glue smell of printer's ink and hot photocopiers from one of the shops. As Kitsy and Patrick shuffled away from the flying ants, waving and walking, picking the bugs off their clothes and hair, from Lucy's clothes and hair, rubbing their fingertips against the little ant bodies to get them away, it seemed to Patrick he'd be trapped in this market for ever with its stink. In all those years of getting hit by his father, of school-fights and punches in the stomach, he'd never felt so faint as he did now. He snapped open the Coke and gave a long suck at the cold fizz, then held the can to his forehead. The drink didn't make him feel any better, but the red and white can, an American institution, made him come to himself a bit, remind himself who he was. He didn't have to take his father's bullshit, or Brune's bullshit. Not now. Not ever. Still, Brune's advance had made him tired, sapped his energy as if she'd attached a vacuum cleaner to his psyche.

The stallholders gave up on their paper whisks and decided to pack it in. Patrick and Kitsy reached the end of the market to the clap of wood on wood as people shut up shop.

'Let's go and get the car,' said Kitsy, and turned to Patrick. She read his face for an answer, but it was unfocused, distant. She wondered if he'd even heard her speak. He walked slowly. She didn't like the way his hands hung. They were too still; they didn't follow the rhythm of his stride properly. She felt solicitous towards Patrick, protective.

While Kitsy and Lucy went into the B&B to pay the bill to a landlady who wore her head in a pyramid of profiterole curls, Patrick sat outside on the step and waited. Twenty minutes later, Kitsy came back with Lucy on her hip to find Patrick quite still next to the pushchair, his hands slack between his knees.

'Right,' she said, all business. 'That's that.'

Patrick looked up at her as if he was too tired to explain again something he'd explained forty times before. Kitsy saw that look and knew she'd have to take the lead. She thought of Michael; Patrick's expression reminded her of him, how he used to be exasperated with her when something small would happen, like the key sticking in the front-door lock, as if it was his wife's fault that she hadn't brought the spare set, hadn't planned ahead for the key-sticking event.

Kitsy couldn't take that look from Michael. It always made her physically frustrated. She'd escape from him and busy herself doing the dishes, or changing Lucy's nappy, some such thing. But from Patrick the look didn't bother her, and knowing that made her feel free and realise her reaction had all to do with power, with somehow being *under* Michael, but being *next to* Patrick. She could walk away from Patrick now and it wouldn't matter, nothing would happen. In the state he was in, he probably couldn't even muster a swearword. She *wanted* to stay. No cement held her. The feeling of power and decision went to her stomach, so that she knew if she ever saw that look again from Michael she'd remember this moment with Patrick and tell Michael just how she felt and what he could do with his sour faces.

They drove for a full half-hour without speaking. Kitsy enjoyed the silence so she felt her way to the motorway, sometimes doubling back on herself, doing U-turns, going around roundabouts twice, following signs to the Brecon Beacons and then Sugar Loaf Mountain. It felt fun to have a man in the back of the car who didn't comment about her driving. She looked in the rear-view mirror to check for raised eyebrows but Patrick just stared out of the window, slumped in a corner, letting every tree, house and car slide by.

'What's got you down?' said Kitsy at last.

'She's got this kid, Hunter. She says she named him after my mom but then I find out she writes letters to the Reverend.'

'What! Are you sure?' Kitsy took her eyes off the road for a moment to turn to glance at his face.

He nodded. 'Hunter told me. It's like, she told me all those stories about my mom, you know, but I think she's lying. Why would she lie? I guess I need a quiet place to think. Where are we going?'

'You said you wanted to see the mountains.'

Kitsy drove in silence, respectful of Patrick's desire to be alone with his thoughts, and turning over in her mind what he'd found out. Lucy had fallen asleep with her dummy in the carseat, her head soaked with sweat, the hair gone dark, the colour of burnt caramel. Today was hot; it wasn't the right weather to be travelling at high speed in this tiny metal box.

Patrick watched the foothills in the distance draw closer. They weren't what he'd expected – big, shaggy things covered in fir. These looked more like the hillocks that come before the real things, the bumps the earth threw up in practice. These weren't even hilly enough to be called bunny slopes. In skiing terms you'd get a little momentum up before the whole thing flattened out and life came to a standstill.

Every inch of the hills had been worked, stripped down to pasture between groves, the pastures cordoned off into squares by grey walls, which, as they got closer, he could see were built by hand from the fields, chunks of stone shaped and laid on top of each other in snaking pillars held in place by gravity.

Kitsy turned left and began to climb. The car stitched back and forth along the narrow roads. Sometimes, when they met another car she would slow and pull over, almost on top of the roadside ditches swarming with blackberry vines and rose bushes, most of the roses gone now, and orange and red rosehips bulbing out to show where the flower had been, the blackberries heavy and thick, full of purple juice in the little black sacs.

Seeing the blackberries reminded Patrick of his mother's autumn ritual. They'd get every saucepan, every bucket in the house and walk through the alleys of West Seattle, going from vine to vine, Mom, Patrick and Charlene. When their pans and plastic ice-cream tubs and cottage-cheese containers were full they'd walk back with their armloads of treasure and spend the rest of the day picking over the berries, throwing out the half-red ones, encouraging little green spiders to go away, and little brown spiders too, and the great green June bugs which tasted bitter if you accidentally popped one in your mouth – something that had happened to Patrick only once.

The berries would go into a great cauldron for *wojapi* – berry pudding. But the highlight of the day would be blackberry pie. On blackberry-picking day his mom would make two pies; they'd eat one pie plain for dinner, and another pie – spiced with cinnamon this time – with vanilla ice cream for dessert.

Thinking about it made him feel sad, that she never had time to pass down her recipes to Charlene, that what she loved and he loved had died for all autumns when she died.

As the car got higher up the mountain, Kitsy passed fewer of the low, sloping stone farmhouses until they were about halfway. Then, on the right, there was a car park with a few cars in it.

'We're here,' she said, pulling up the handbrake. 'I don't know what you want to do now, but I've got to stay near the car to be with Lucy when she wakes.'

'I guess I'll go for a walk,' said Patrick, stretching, pulling himself out of day-dreams. 'Is this public land or what?'

'It's all privately owned.'

That worried him. 'So how do I know some farmer's not going to come out with his hunting rifle and tell me to git?'

'Because Welsh farmers don't carry hunting rifles. They have walking sticks and dog whistles. And they don't say "git". Look, see that sign down there?' Kitsy pointed to a stile and a small wooden fingerpost tacked onto a tree. 'That's a footpath.' She smiled. 'Stay with those signs and you won't be shot.'

'*Get* shot,' said Patrick. 'And it's not so funny if you went to a High School where they do handgun checks on your locker practically every other day.' *And your best friend from grade school gets gunned down in a driveby*, he added to himself.

'Who's joking?' said Kitsy, catching his serious mood. She watched him go, his long back, his beautiful, muscled back, and long legs, athlete's legs. 'Try to be back in an hour, OK?' she yelled after him, and felt as if she were calling after the wind.

Patrick stepped over the stile and onto a narrow dirt path. Immediately he was in woods, in a grove of hazel, birch, oak – the little forest floor a carpet of dry mulch waiting for fall's orange, red, and yellow leaves. He knew the place must be beautiful in autumn, just as he knew that many people had passed through here, that he wasn't the first, only one in a long line of solace-seekers. The grove was too tidy. There was none of the virile wildness of mountains at home, of hiking into a spot and hoisting your pack into the trees so the bears wouldn't get it once the campfire burned out. Someone had cut patches of the hazel close to its roots with a saw, their bootprints frozen in dried mud the color of ash. The path under his feet was swept clean of leaves; the lower branches of some of the trees had been cut away leaving smooth, knobbly scars.

He didn't expect to see anything much bigger than a songbird. Certainly, no eagle hunted here, no mountain cat carried off rabbits and stray dogs, and the streams – well, as far as Patrick was concerned, they were probably allowed to exist as decorations. No salmon. No trout. But at least it was a place where he could breathe. Although its history was palpable, thick with the ghosts of working hands and the small thud of walking feet, at least here there was room to think, to be, to feel the power flowing in his body, his blood circulating, to be still and away until he wanted to return.

Patrick began to run, to let his feet lead his body. At first, he was out of breath. But then he hit his stride, and his body went loose, his feet kept flipping the ground away and his lungs held the air in easy breaths. He ran, looking at the ground, lifting himself over rocks and roots, letting his body think and his mind rest.

As he ran, it seemed the forest was thick with his own ghosts. The running and the smell of damp grass, a light, mushroomy smell – that smell was like a meal to Patrick. It charged him as he ran and made him remember.

There was a hike his mother took him on out at the Olympic peninsula, his father carrying Charlene some of the way until he told Alice to take the boy on without him, that he'd meet them back at the car. Patrick skittered along the ocean path, running ahead, stopping, climbing halfway up a tree, swinging and dropping himself down from one of the branches, his mother walking steadily behind him in her jeans and white tennis shoes, wearing a red wool coat that she'd always had. He remembered the tree roots that bumped up through the earth like fingers making 'here's the church, here's the steeple', or like the rungs of some organic ladder that grew itself. And then the smells began to change, the crushed seashells mixed with sand, the ocean's raw saltiness invading the forest's dark calm before they burst into light, the ocean throwing its blue light at them, its dappled mirrors of sun overlapping. He stepped over logs castaway from the shipping lanes, raw timber that broke free of a cordon towed off to Japan, now on the beach and silver with weathering in a bed of grey sand, crushed blue mussel shells, bleached-white silver dollars and clam shells, and down to the beach.

His mother sat on a log and watched him play, turning

over heavy, water-smoothed stones looking for crabs and clams. Then she called to him to come over, picked up a Madrona stick, and dug a few shells out of the sandy bank. Patrick had never seen mussel shells so big and thick – at least four inches long and a quarter-inch thick, worn inside to mother-of-pearl, outside a blue as bright as the water itself. She told him this had been a place where the tribes held *potlatches* – feast days to celebrate salmon running, a marriage, a giveaway – and these were all the shells from the mussels they'd eaten.

Patrick wanted to take some shells home as a memory for the day.

'Respect our people,' she said. He knew she meant 'no'.

As Patrick ran through the Welsh forest, he knew Charlene was also here, although more faintly, as if she hid behind a tree counting to fifty for hide-and-seek, and then she'd come out, disappointed to see her brother, that he hadn't hid for her to run and find and tag. 'Paaatrick!' she'd yell at him. 'You're s'posed to hide!' But hiding was a pain in the ass, and once he realised that there was no one to force him to play with Charlene, he simply gave it up. Now Charlene was the only person in Seattle he missed.

The day which had been hot and bothersome in town began to cool. Patrick looked up through a break in the trees and saw a high head of grey clouds gathered. In the distance, the sound of thunder drumming cut through the heat, then a white flash, and another, deep call from the clouds. He heard the drops before he felt them, filtered through the trees; they dripped through his thick hair and landed cold on his sweaty scalp. He heard the rain splat in fat drops where it found its way past the leaves to bounce on the forest floor, and leaned back into the tree, felt himself snuggled and comforted by the heavy air, by the noise of the rain around him. He closed his eyes and breathed in the wood's smells,

now intensified by the damp, made stronger, more mouldy
– the smell of wet hay, the smell of running water and hot
rocks, of bruised leaves. He leaned back into himself and
had the urge to pray, and he felt lost.

If he'd been raised traditional, he'd have made his cry for
a vision by now. Maybe he'd have a helper, or have dreamed
a dream, instead of sitting here under this tree, thousands
of miles away from the land that was his blood and bones.

And then it came to him strong, so that it was a certainty
in him, that this was the testing time. OK, it wasn't in a pit
in *Paha Sapa*, the sacred Black Hills, with his uncles around
him, but it was a testing time all the same.

He felt his mother's presence here. The rain hit the hot
forest and raised itself into steam, into a thin mist that
covered his face and neck, his shoulders and legs like a thin
gauze.

Then he felt clearly, so it was as if he saw it as a photo-
graph or a piece of sculpture, that the earth under his bones
was still the same Mother and his Always-Mother, feeding
him for the rest of his life; whether he hunted that food
himself or bought it at Safeway, it still came from the same
sacred source. His Grandfather *Tunkashila* was here too,
surrounding this earth He made, so that Patrick was
included wherever he went, was related to it all.

Patrick stayed in that spot, went down into himself there,
down so far that he didn't notice a couple of hikers cross
through the trees fifty yards away. He stayed there, inside
himself, until a dump of green acorns dislodged by the
storm, fell, and bonked him on the head.

Then he stood up and ran through the rain until it
stopped.

Patrick began to feel a kind of oppression invade him as the
little car put the West and Wales behind it and began to

enter the outskirts of London. Tall buildings began to grow up around him, white surprises standing in a carpet of red-roofed houses, buildings that loomed up, grew to their full height and disappeared behind the car for him to forget.

While he was in Wales, on that little lump of mountain for that brief solace, he could hold his experience with Brune at arm's length, could refuse it. But now, as Kitsy raced back to the house, the house of his nightmares, he had to think about what had happened in Abergavenny, and what he could do next.

He wanted revenge for his mother's death, wanted it full, and fitting. Like to like. Before meeting Brune he'd imagined his mom's killer to be a masked stranger, a robber in the wrong house. But the more he thought, the more he digested, the more he *knew* – the clammy cold of suspicion told him it could all be much closer to home.

When Kitsy parked on the kerb in front of the house in Lichfield Grove, she felt the relief that comes with being finally at home, back among her things, with the freedom to walk into all the rooms, to wander into her garden and pick raspberries, to take ice cream from her own deepfreeze and eat it straight from the container with her own spoon.

Kitsy slung her bag over one shoulder and picked up Lucy. Patrick pulled the pushchair out of the boot for her and they stood at the door as she put her key in the lock, listening to it slide in, click against the little pins. Kitsy shoved the door open with one foot, took a step inside and froze. She pulled Lucy close to her shoulder and looked at Patrick, wide-eyed.

She could tell he smelled it too – the smell of someone smoking, someone who has been smoking a long time: stale smoke, fresh smoke.

Patrick dropped his pack near the door, its stained-glass

windows making the little hall a pattern of azure, cerise, vermilion – the bright colours illuminating the fear on Kitsy's face. Patrick pushed past her, brushing against Lucy who began to struggle in her mother's arms, wriggling harder to get down.

He walked into the house, listening. Waiting in the hall, Kitsy threw herself open to all sound: the clock ticking, the hum of the refrigerator, cars passing, the voices of a group of children going by.

Patrick came out of the living room and looked at her, holding his palms up, and shrugging his shoulders. He turned again and walked toward the back of the house. Then Kitsy heard the voice: 'Who the bloody hell are you!' and instantly she knew the smoker.

'Michael!' Kitsy yelled, slamming the front door and walking down the hall. 'Get out of my house!'

Her husband sat at the kitchen table dressed in a black tracksuit. In front of him was Kitsy's only bottle of claret, half-gone, and a dinner plate from her best china service, thick with cigarette butts, burns on its silver and blue enamelled rim next to cheese scrapings and cracker crumbs. Kitsy felt choked with anger. He'd ruined that plate!

Lucy stared at her father, but Kitsy could see she didn't recognise him, that five months had nearly wiped him off her memory. The cloud of smoke cottoned against the kitchen's low ceiling began to float into the hall. Patrick watched it crawl across, a thin mist.

'What the fuck is that?' Michael said, pointing to Patrick. 'Your toyboy, is he? You letting his filthy hands near my daughter?'

'That's it. I'm calling the police,' Kitsy stated.

'Police won't chuck me out of my own home. After all, I'm still paying all the bills for your little extravagances. Think I don't check my credit-card statements?'

'You think you pay for Lucy because you still cover the mortgage and get a Mothercare bill through every now and then? Well, you don't! My savings from when I was working puts food on this table, and when that runs out it will be the dole!'

'Want me to go next door and call for the cops?' asked Patrick.

'Oh!' said Michael, all sarcasm. 'It speaks, does it? A bit young for you, don't you think? Fucking jailbait now, are we?'

'*Get out!*' Kitsy hissed. 'You lost the right to know what I do when you walked out. Now I do as I please and like.'

Michael stood up, pushing the chair away with the backs of his knees. It made a rough, coughing sound against the linoleum, an announcement.

Kitsy turned to Patrick and dumped Lucy on him. The child began wailing, stretching out her arms to her mother, trying to grab at her but torn away, the little fists opening and closing in spasms.

'Take her to play with her toys,' Kitsy ordered.

Michael watched Patrick take Lucy down the hall, watched his daughter screaming 'Mummy! Mummy! Mummy!' and didn't do anything. Kitsy despised him for not running after her, for not trying to push past his estranged wife to comfort his child. She felt that inside Michael there must be metal shavings, or chips of ice like when an ice cube shatters, because she wanted to run after Lucy, to hold and soothe her, to take the child in her arms and whisper into her hair, 'Shshshsh,' until everything came right.

Instead, Kitsy faced off Michael at the kitchen entrance, half-listening to Lucy's screams and sobs retreat to the living room, half-listening to Patrick's words, words that meant nothing, were only the tone of his voice, even, trying to be light, and smiley, and in control.

Kitsy closed the kitchen door and mentally measured the number of steps from Michael to the knife block, and how long it would take him to get there. She looked at the bottle of claret, wondered if it really worked, cracking it against the countertop to come up with shards of a green weapon dripping with red wine, in readiness to drip with blood. Kitsy stood and faced him like a boxer, fists on her hips, feet as wide apart as her shoulders.

'That *obscenity* on your nose – that's the diamond off your engagement ring, innit?'

'Innit,' Kitsy replied. 'So what.'

He drew a breath. Kitsy could see he was trying to hold himself in, all the pieces that were flying about inside of him, all these little black metal bits of emotion.

'I'm moving back in,' he announced.

'NO!' Kitsy shouted. 'You *cannot* disappear for five months and then turn up, abusing my best china—'

'– *our* best china!'

'– *my* best china and expect me to take you back with open arms!'

'Well, I didn't think you'd move loverboy in so quickly, did I?'

And you've been faithful? reverberated in Kitsy's head, but she wouldn't concede. For the first time in a long while, Michael wanted something from her. He wanted his cooked meals and his cosy sex, his dinner parties and Christmas. And he was *wrong*.

'I want to see Lucy again. I want to play with her again,' Michael said.

So that's what he wants, she thought, and relaxed her stance, knowing the tension was over. If he was there to hurt her, he'd have done it already.

Kitsy walked past Michael and went behind him to the refrigerator. She opened the door, knelt, and began digging in the vegetable drawer, knowing he wondered what she was doing, knowing that he stared at the back of her neck. She pulled out carrots first, and that made her smile. Kitsy remember how she and Sally Fisher when they were sharing their first bedsit used to giggle at some of the huge carrots on display in Tesco. Kitsy had said she wanted a man who wouldn't feel threatened by one. *I should have stuck to it*, she thought.

She pulled out two onions, twisted off a stalk of celery, set six Italian plum tomatoes on the counter, closed the door, stood up, grabbed the bottle of claret from the table and the plate of cigarette butts. All the time Michael stared at her, not saying a word.

'Go on then,' she said finally. 'But only ten minutes, and you're *not* staying.'

Michael went. *Like a dog off its lead*, she thought.

Patrick came into the kitchen. 'He's in there with Lucy – is that OK?' She read concern on his face, and something else. Affection. He walked over to Kitsy and put his hand on her shoulder. She turned to him and looked up into his face, gathered him to herself in a hug, tucked the top of her head under his chin. He responded stiffly; a little bit of strangeness still hung between them like a shred of a wet sheet. Then he relaxed and pulled her in too, and Kitsy felt all the physical strength of him recharging her, as if she absorbed his strength into her stomach.

When Patrick and Kitsy separated it was reluctantly, her mindful that Michael was still in the house, that she didn't want him to intrude on whatever was growing between herself and Patrick. When she pulled away, she felt as if she'd been asleep in those arms. She felt refreshed, replenished, as if she'd had a massage or taken a long bath.

She picked up two onions and handed one to Patrick. 'Could you help me peel this before I go and kick him out?'

Patrick stood next to her, picked the blonde onion up in his hand, cupped it in his palm, waiting for the knife. Kitsy handed him a paring knife from the knife block and he stabbed it into the onion, and then scraped at the skin. They stood shoulder to shoulder for a moment, each working at their small tasks, smiling at each other instead of talking. It felt very intimate, so that Kitsy wanted to stay with him in the kitchen, the sharp smell of onion biting at her eyes, and savour the way they stood now, thinking of some way to put it into the bolognaise sauce.

'Chop that as small as you can. I won't be a moment,' Kitsy said, and headed to the living room to deal with Michael.

For Kitsy and Michael, it had all begun to unravel with a row over sex.

Michael wanted. Michael wanted. But Michael didn't get.

After that horrible, painful birth which everyone said she'd forget but was still etched with laser-light in Kitsy's imagination, after breastfeeding Lucy, giving all her energy to Lucy, filling her mind with Lucy's cries, her burps, slow smiles, nappy rash, tummy ache, with cuddling Lucy and getting up in the middle of the night for Lucy, Kitsy didn't have any time for herself. Everywhere she went she came across a dead cup of tea, cold, gone green-brown with a scum of milk fat floating on the top. She never got to finish one. They were always a quarter drunk before the next cry, the next demand came around.

Kitsy was grateful she didn't have twins.

Michael wasn't grateful at all. Not for the least tiny thing. Michael went to work all day at the office, shaved his spots and played the game, and came home to a house that was a bombsite. Every time he went to put something down, he had to watch out that he didn't knock over a cup of cold tea or put his papers on a half-eaten piece of Marmite and toast. This wasn't order! Kitsy left him to sort out his own supper. *She had time enough to make something for herself,* he'd think, resenting her.

Every other day she was down at the Brent Cross Mothercare flashing his Barclaycard around, only now she didn't have an income to help pay for all the rubbish she dragged home. Who needs a babybath, for Christ's sake? All you do is put the baby in the big bath and bend over. Simple.

And the one thing that *was* a pleasure for Michael, Kitsy didn't want to give any more.

On the night of the big row, Lucy was asleep in her cot. Michael and Kitsy sat on the couch watching *Eastenders*. Kitsy still wore huge maternity leggings then, and long jumpers to cover a spongey stomach.

When Michael leaned over to kiss her, Kitsy snuggled up to him in the chilly room, hugging him, enjoying his closeness. Michael kissed more deeply, more insistently. One hand moved to her breasts, heavy with milk. He began to squish the left one. To Kitsy it felt as if she were being mashed, without even the delicacy a farmer would give to his cow. She pictured herself as a big black-and-white cow, the farmer's weatherbeaten forehead on her flank. Yes, that farmer would be more gentle than Michael. Even a milking machine would be more gentle than Michael.

Kitsy shifted position, thinking that would make her more comfortable. Michael shifted position too and his tongue and hand became more arduous, more insistent. Kitsy knew what would come next, and it had something to do with her raw, newly-healed stitches down below.

She felt overwhelmed almost to the point of being under attack. She made her tongue keep moving. She had to go through with this; she had to find out if what gave her pleasure once could give her pleasure again.

But it didn't. It hurt. A tiny splash of panic started in her arms and built itself into a wave that spread to her stomach, her groin, back and legs.

Suddenly, Michael stood up in disgust. 'Jesus Christ, Kitsy! It's like trying to make love to a corpse!'

Kitsy drew her knees up into herself, and wrapped her arms around them. She watched him and felt like a spanked child. She'd dropped a milkbottle on the step and now it would have to be swept and scrubbed. How could she explain that he needed to be tender? She didn't have the words.

Michael went over to the sideboard and pulled out a drawer. He took out a cigarette and a lighter and lit up.

Kitsy watched him smoke. Inhale, exhale. Inhale, exhale. The end of the cigarette curled smoke into the room.

'If you have to smoke, go in the garden,' she said.

'If I want to smoke I jolly well will, and I'm not going into that fucking freezing garden to do it.'

'Smoking is a major cause of cot death.'

'So fucking what. One cigarette is not going to kill her.'

'I won't have it in the house!'

'You won't cook, you won't clean, you won't screw – what *will* you have in the house, Kitsy, eh? Go on – tell me. Only I don't feel as if I'm welcome in *your* house, darling. And that's funny, because I'm paying for it!'

'That's not fair. I do all the cooking and cleaning when I get a chance. And I do all the looking after Lucy.'

'Well, you wanted a baby.'

'*I* wanted a baby? So you didn't want a child, is that it? What *you* mean is you want to come home and kiss her when she's all scrubbed and happy and put into bed, then you want me to bring your slippers and your tea on a tray so you can watch television and ignore me and never say a single word!'

'That doesn't sound so bad,' said Michael, taking another puff.

'Oh, piss off!'

Kitsy rose from the couch and ran upstairs to the bathroom. She locked herself in and drew a hot, steamy bath, poured in lots of peach body oil, and soaked in it trying to avoid looking at her stomach and the crooked fingers of brown stretch-marks which fanned their way up to her bellybutton.

Kitsy felt rock-grey, leaden, brimful of sadness which seeped up through her mind like rising damp until all she could feel was sorrow that her marriage was over, that her love for Michael had vanished.

How did I ever feel love in the first place? she wondered. What was it like? Was I happy? Did we laugh together? It's all been so earnest. Why don't we ever laugh? I'm angry. *He* didn't sacrifice a magazine-beautiful body. *His* flat stomach hasn't ballooned and deflated leaving scars. *His* breasts didn't stretch out of all recognition and feel like two cement lumps for a week when his milk came in. There wasn't a single mark on *him*! Oh no. *He* could walk away now and no one would ever know he'd once been part of Lucy. Or me.

She was so angry she couldn't look down at her body, at the price she'd paid for having a child. But it wasn't the scars or the bloating or the enormous breasts that she packed every morning into industrial-strength bras which made her angry. Of the two of them, she was the only one to pay the price. *That* pissed her off.

Kitsy added scalding water from the tap when the bath went cold, soaking until she got prune feet. Then she dried herself and went to bed. It felt too big and too cold without Michael in it, smelling too much of soap powder without his sweat and hair.

At one in the morning the house was stillbound. Kitsy

woke, anticipating Lucy's cry. She stayed in the dark listening to her heartbeat, to herself breathe. She'd created a warm pocket under the duvet, a place in the quiet morning to think.

The short sleep, the bath had washed out her anger. She looked down at her relationship with Michael from a great height and saw it all, as if it were trapped in a paperweight. In the cosy room, the room decorated by her, the purple curtains in the bay tied back and graceful with their swags and tails, the coving, the ceiling rose, so homey and welcoming, she felt self-sufficient.

If I were free to raise Lucy here on my own, I could make it, she thought. *We belong here, it's our home, and Michael is more of a long-term visitor. Nice to have around, nice of him to contribute, but not absolutely necessary to our survival. And if he's going to turn nasty, to smoke and go against me, if he's going to try to wear down my self-esteem by thinking how superior he is because he has a job and brings in the money, then we're better off without him. I'll go on income support. It's not being poor that matters.*

Feeling snuggled and content under the covers, Kitsy turned out the light and went back to sleep until she had to get up and breastfeed Lucy.

When Kitsy awoke that morning, she felt more refreshed than she had done since she was only a couple of months pregnant and could still sleep on her stomach. It was as if some great decision had been taken.

She changed Lucy and blew bubbles on the baby's stomach, making her laugh a belly-laugh, taped her into a plastic-and-paper nappy, buttoned up a clean babygro, tied on a bib and carried Lucy across her shoulder singing, 'She'll be coming round the mountain when she comes,' as she walked downstairs to give the little one her breakfast.

It wasn't until Lucy had eaten her mashed banana and

Kitsy had drunk her morning cup of coffee – strong, lots of milk, two sugars – then had changed Lucy's bib and wiped the baby's pink chin, that she took her daughter into the lounge and discovered a smashed mug. It had hit the cast-iron mantelpiece and fallen onto the hearth, scattering shards of crockery across the carpet.

The bastard, she thought. *He didn't even bother to clean it up.*

Kitsy carried Lucy back to the kitchen and grabbed a pan and brush from under the sink. 'Whatever are we going to do with him?' she asked, and Lucy burped, bringing up some of her banana as they walked to the lounge. That made Kitsy smile. 'Precisely!' she said. She wiped Lucy's mouth, putting her down on the carpet to sit and stare.

So we have a row, Kitsy thought, tidying the shards into the pan with a stiff-bristled brush. *Does that mean he has to go around breaking things? Good job Lucy isn't crawling or I'd have his guts for garters, leaving all these sharp bits around.*

By lunchtime Kitsy felt lonely without Michael. Every day she had the urge to phone him. Some days she gave in, some days she didn't. Today there was only so much of one-way conversations with Lucy that she could take.

'Is Michael Baines about, please?' she asked the receptionist after putting Lucy to bed for her nap.

'I'm sorry. He's off ill today.'

Kitsy slowly put the receiver down. *What did Michael do while I was in the bath? I thought he spent the night downstairs on the couch!*

As she punched in Peter's number, something tugged at her gut, so that her stomach felt like a black hole, yawning into nothing. At long last he answered.

'Hello, Peter. Have you seen Michael?'

'Er, hold on a moment, Kitsy.' She heard him put his hand over the receiver, shutting her out. His muffled voice sounded urgent. Kitsy strained to hear, but could make out nothing. Then he came back on the line. 'Kitsy, look,' he began, and Michael shouted in the background; 'You can tell the bitch I'm not coming home!' It was Michael's angry voice – a voice she'd only heard him use twice during their four-year marriage, in spectacular firework shows of blazing purple popping temper.

'Peter, what's wrong? Let me speak to him!'

'She wants to speak to you,' said Peter before he covered the mouthpiece again. Kitsy wondered what could be so wrong that her husband had involved Peter. Why would he go over to Peter's house and tell him about their little tiff? Why were the pair of them behaving like two schoolboys making a prank phone call?

'What do you want?' demanded Michael.

'What do you mean, what do I want? Why aren't you at work? Where did you sleep last night?'

'Here.'

'Why? Why didn't you sleep here?' All the while her mind ran around the possible answers: a woman with curly, long chestnut hair and a fifteen-year-old's body; a revulsion of Kitsy; a hatred of Lucy and her dribbly face, her yellow pooey nappies; a hatred of his new fatherly role; the fact he didn't have a son.

'Do you really have to ask?'

'Yes! For God's sake, grow up, Michael. We only had a little tiff.'

'Is that what you call it, a little tiff? You call throwing a brick at me a little tiff? I call that attempted murder!'

'I didn't throw a brick at you!'

'It certainly felt like one.'

'Michael, *what* are you talking about?'

'First you tell me to fuck off, then when my back's turned you throw that huge mug at my head and nearly crack my skull open! I'm surprised you didn't fill it with boiling hot tea first!'

'Me? *You* smashed that mug against the mantelpiece because you had a temper tantrum and then you left it for me to tidy up! What if Lucy were crawling and picked up a piece and choked on it?'

'You actually believe that?'

'Yes!' said Kitsy.

'I've had enough of this conversation,' he said. The line went dead.

When Kitsy got off the phone she went straight to the kitchen bin. She took off the swingback lid and fished out shards of the shattered mug with her fingertips. She dug past banana skins, soup tins, the remains of Lucy's goopy brown breakfast, coffee grounds, until she had every shard lined up and sticky on the worktop. Kitsy picked them up again, looking closer. On a piece that had once been the mug's bottom she found it: blood, a little scraping of it so that it could have been discoloured nail polish gone matt.

Kitsy put the shard on the windowsill next to an African violet in a red plastic pot. Half its green leaves had rotted black, the other half had yellow spots on them, the flowers dried up and crumpled. She made herself a cup of tea and stared at the shard, and then at the plant, wondering: *Why would Michael hit himself over the head? And if he didn't do it, who did?*

Patrick and Lucy and Kitsy sat at the kitchen table, not saying much, the two adults busy with their own thoughts while Lucy learned how to suck a long strand of spaghetti into her mouth, suck chew, suck chew, her mouth ringed red with tomato, her yellow bib orange with tomato. The doorbell rang.

Kitsy and Patrick looked at each other.

'Want me to get it?' he offered, afraid it would be another policeman or Michael again.

Kitsy liked it that he offered, that he took on the Man of the Family role, the protector.

'No,' she said. She went to the front-room window and pulled back the curtain to see a woman's bottom in Crimplene trousers.

'Your mother's been trying to get through to you,' said Barbara when Kitsy opened the door. 'She's been driving me crazy, stacking up messages on my answerphone. Where have you been, anyway?'

'Wales.'

'With him?' Barbara cocked her head towards the door and smiled. 'He's a bit of all right. Where'd you find him?'

'Chucking his guts up on my doorstep.' Kitsy smiled too.

'Well, when he's done on your doorstep, send him over to mine.'

'What's the message?'

'First she wouldn't say. Then she went all around the houses, and at the end of the day, I gathered you're not to mess things up – whatever that means.'

'So Mum's at the bottom of it, is she? Guess what, Barbara? Michael's been round. They're in it together.'

'Do me a favour, love. Get your phone reconnected, eh? All this is doing my head in.'

'Yes, I will. Sorry she bothered you.'

When she got back indoors, Kitsy found £100 in twenties and tens in a stack on the kitchen table, weighted down with a butterknife.

'What's this for?' she asked.

'Dues,' replied Patrick.

'Dues?'

'You know, like in cross country. You put money in a box

to help with the cookies and pop after the meet. And I need to make a phone call.'

'Not to the States? There won't be much left to buy biscuits if you phone home.'

'No. It's a local call to Barnet.'

Kitsy could see the disappointment in his face that she'd said he couldn't phone home.

'I hope you haven't left yourself too short.'

'No, I'm tall enough,' he said. They both laughed cramped, nervous laughs at his weak joke, and at finding themselves alone after the stress of the day.

'Where's Lucy?' she said.

Patrick stared at Kitsy, as if he'd just discovered something, as if something had occurred to him and he wanted to work it out.

'Hmmm?' he said.

Kitsy looked at him, wondering what he could possibly be thinking. 'I'd better go and find Lucy and give her a bath, then put her to bed. We can make our calls then.'

'Kitsy?' He'd picked up the salt cellar and held it between his palms, rubbing it back and forth as if it were a stick.

'What?'

'I like being here with you.'

She laughed, and he smiled back. 'Thanks,' she said. 'I like having you here.'

Kitsy put Lucy in her own little bed after her bath. That itself told a story, putting the child farther away, letting her sleep by herself, not warm together, face to face, all softness and gathered heat, the smell of each other and the house soap, spaghetti on their breath, and the comfort of the rhythmic breathing together, of waking up in a little 4 a.m. panic – *where's Lucy?* – Kitsy adjusting her eyes into the night until they picked up the bright blonde hair, capped on the pillow, still.

That evening, Kitsy got out the telephones, unwrapped the cords, and took them downstairs to the living room to be plugged in. Patrick made his calls. Then she telephoned her mother and said, 'Hello, I'm back,' before setting the receiver on the hearth until it stopped squawking. 'Goodbye, Mum,' Kitsy said and hung up, hoping that Karmic Retribution didn't really exist, that she wouldn't ever be talking to Lucy's hearthstones.

'I'm going up to play around on the Net. Want to come?' Kitsy said to Patrick.

'Sure.'

As they walked up the stairs to her bedroom, Kitsy in front, Patrick at her back, she was conscious of what she was doing, where she was leading him, what that could mean, and a little bit nervous because of it. But still she took each step, pushing down on the wooden stairs with the balls of her feet, enjoying the effort of going up, of being in front.

Kitsy booted up the computer and sat in the swivel chair. Patrick stood at her shoulder, leaning over her back, one hand on the desk. They played around on a couple of websites, Patrick standing over her, so close she felt as if she was touching him.

'You call up the next page,' Kitsy said. Patrick clicked the mouse and then turned to her, as if he was going to ask a question. They leaned in at the same time. Their mouths met at an awkward angle, but then Patrick put his hand on the back of her head and pulled her in square on.

Kitsy felt surprised by the strength in that hand, by its expression of need. Something in her tightened, and welled up, responded to him with a hunger that she thought had gone with the shadows of her early twenties. But there it was, blowing fierce and hot, making her stand up to meet him, strength for strength, to hug him strong and kiss him rough.

Patrick pulled off his T-shirt. There it was, that chest she'd fallen in love with on the first day when she'd watched him standing in the rain: smooth, ropey with muscle, with a scant scattering of black hair under his navel, a fingerpost. When he unbuttoned those jeans and she pulled them down to his ankles, she felt privileged to share the heat of sex with a guy who could have been the Levis man. And she wasn't school-girl frightened. She wasn't worried. Kitsy was entirely pre-sent in the moment, able to kiss and lick her way up his legs, pausing at what had grown too big for his Jockeys. When her jeans were off, when he'd stripped her down, she wrap-ped her arms around his neck and her legs around his middle. They fell on the bed to meet each other stroke for stroke.

That night Kitsy found the self she'd sent away when she was breastfeeding Lucy and Michael had made his rough approach. She stood in awe of the feelings which had walked back into her body as if they'd never gone. She enjoyed every bit of her pleasure, and that enjoyment fed the pleasure in darkening and widening circles of healing.

At about 4 a.m. Kitsy woke up, warm under the covers. She stared at Patrick in the dimness, the never-quite-dark of London filtering through her curtains. At that moment she loved his nose, its high bridge, like one of the Roman centurions at the British Museum, and his wide lips. She must have stared at him too hard because he woke up, and then . . . well, everyone knows about men in the morning.

An hour later they sat on the back step with mugs of coffee in their hands, Kitsy perched between Patrick's legs and leaning back against his chest.

Like that they watched dawn come up and toss her pink blanket across summer's eastern sky.

CHAPTER 12

A Place of Reckoning

In a way it felt odd, and this thought interrupted him, pushed at a little trapdoor in his mind when he was in bed with Kitsy, that he'd made love in the same spot where his parents had slept ten years before. Although the room didn't have the same tinge of malevolence (like a drop of yellow food colouring in a glass of tapwater) as the little room downstairs, still, it brought to him new thoughts, memories, of what his parents were like together.

Alice didn't yell at Frank. When she got angry, her voice dropped until it was a hard whisper, the sibilant hiss of a television with the sound turned almost off. But mostly she stayed silent, the muscles tense around her mouth. There was something sour there on her tongue. Something making her pucker up around Patrick's father. With the children she would relax. She'd laugh a lot, sit cross-legged on the kitchen floor, Patrick and Charlene in one arm each, and watch the laundry slosh around in one of those tiny, glass-doored English washing machines.

That's how he remembered things going tense – the noises in the house had changed; some stopped altogether, and new noises happened instead.

She always seemed to be stuck at the sink, doing dishes.

219

Patrick saw a lot of her back, her hands – red from the hot water – flicking between sink and draining board, the plates clicking against each other in the wire rack, the smell of suds and water.

He wished he could remember more. He could picture her back, almost make it stand in front of him, the black sweater, her wide shoulders, her straight waist and her bottom full in jeans busted through under the back pockets, white tufts of thread making an 'O' frame around her white cotton underwear. She wore those jeans even though Frank always wanted her in long, flowing skirts. Wore them with the hole undarned, rebellious in not sewing it up. A place in his mother said 'no', and this hole represented that place. She would not budge.

Then, last night as he slept next to Kitsy he dreamed he was a little boy on a plain, standing on hard earth in short grasses with a toy bow in his hand shooting little arrows up into the sky. He shot his arrows, five of them at least, and not one came down. They were all stuck in the clouds somewhere, his little toy arrows.

When he woke up with this image in his mind, he wondered about it and then understood that the arrows were stuck in the sky because each one had hit something. The clouds obscured the arrows but still, he'd done a thing; something had happened.

That morning, Kitsy left Lucy with Barbara and took off with Patrick to Camden Town. They browsed through the shops and drank cappuccinos by the canal. Patrick watched the canalboats come through the locks and wished he could jump onto one and float away, forget what he came here for and enjoy the scenery. It kind of reminded him of Pike Place market, the closest thing London got to all the hawking and selling and busking, the arts and crafts on display on the stalls. It also smelled. Not the salty fishy smell of Pike Place, but an urban smell of burgers and petrol fumes and canal skunge.

'Here,' said Patrick when Kitsy came back from checking out a book stall. He handed her a tiny nose ring with a red stone that he'd bought when her back was turned.

'Oh, thank you, Patrick! It's lovely!' She took out the diamond she wore and tucked it in her pocket and skewered in the curly back of her new piece of jewellery. She stood on tiptoe and gave him a kiss.

'It's nothing,' he said, feeling a bit embarrassed.

'It *is* something. It's from *you*,' she said firmly, and pulled down his head for another kiss, one that lingered.

They went home reluctantly, and held hands on the tube. Kitsy felt good with Patrick's big paw in hers. Patrick was amazed that she *wanted* to hold his hand. The girls he'd slept with at parties could barely remember it at school the next day, and if they did, they were usually the kind of girl he wanted to avoid. He couldn't get over that he and Kitsy had slept together the night before. If she *hadn't* taken his hand in hers, he'd have had a difficult time convincing himself that it ever happened.

They hadn't been home long and collected Lucy when the doorbell rang.

'That must be her,' said Patrick. He got up from the floor.

'I'll go and put the kettle on,' said Kitsy. She scooped up Lucy and headed for the kitchen.

When Patrick opened the door, he remembered the woman's face as it was ten years ago, and then the image was gone, replaced with the lines, the heaviness that had crept in, a soft pouch that hung under her chin. She wore her hair in a bob now, not short and butch like it used to be. She had make-up on, and that oiled her skin, made it shine more than he remembered it shining, and her short-sleeved sweater stretched tighter over her upper arm and across her large bosom than it rightly should. But when she smiled at him and said, 'Patrick? Is that you?' he knew that it was her again, the woman who had comforted him on the day following his mother's death, who had taken him and his sister into her arms and hugged them in the hall, and walked with her arms around them into the kitchen to sit and drink Coca Cola and eat chicken drumsticks, and not allowed anyone to drag them back into the living room again.

'Did you find the place OK?' said Patrick, realising that now he looked *down* at Christine Miles; the angle made a difference, made her less authoritative.

'John Abernathy gave me directions,' said Christine Miles as she walked over the threshold. 'He didn't really need to. I still remember that day. Oh!' she said, and threw her arms around Patrick and gave him a big hug, as if he was a long-lost nephew.

Patrick hugged her back, and hugged her hard. When they separated Christine had tears in her eyes. She wiped them with the back of her hand.

'If I had known I'd be so emotional, I would have brought tissues!' she joked as she smiled at him, her eyes red, the back of her hand smudged with little black smuts from mascara. 'You were such a strong little boy, and now look at you, such a tall young man!'

They settled in the living room. Kitsy brought tea in a teapot and chocolate digestive biscuits on a plate, and then left them to talk while she took Lucy in the back garden.

'You know, it's as if all these years I've been waiting for your call. When John telephoned me last night saying you wanted to see me, it was like a confirmation of something I already knew.' Christine reached over and put her hand on Patrick's forearm. She leaned in. 'You and your sister were ever in my prayers,' she said. She looked at Patrick's face for a moment, then settled back into her chair and lifted her cup, and sipped, the steam from the cup curling along the sides of her flabby button nose, making her blink.

'I only just found out how she died,' said Patrick.

'So John said. Apparently he had to tell you. Never had the stomach for that sort of thing. I think when John was studying for the priesthood he somehow managed to convince himself it was all going to be theology. He was in love with the idea of God, and maybe not so much with the messiness of His creation.'

'I'm trying to piece things together,' said Patrick. 'Until I came here I never really thought she'd been . . . murdered. OK, they had fights but most of my friends' parents fought worse than *they* ever did!'

'Wait a minute,' said Christine, sitting up straight on Kitsy's settee, setting the cup and saucer on a side table with spindly legs. 'You think your *father* killed her?'

'Don't you?' said Patrick, taken aback by her surprise.

Christine leaned forward and put her elbows on her knees and her hands over her mouth, and she stared at Patrick, her eyes wide. He stared back at the murky blue, as if her eyes themselves, those squashy pingpong balls set in blood, as if the organs to her soul would tell him the truth.

'I don't know what to believe,' she said, her mouth moving behind her hands.

'You said you kept us in your prayers,' he pressed. 'So you must have suspected something.'

Christine uncovered her mouth and sank back into the cushions. 'That was because of their cruelty, of that ceremony and your mother's blood still in the house! And Frank led them doing it, too. That was the last straw for me, seeing you children treated like that. I broke off the association. I often wonder what John Abernathy would have done if he had been there. He was fond of your mother, you know. No, that was awful. And Lizzy Dooley sitting there like a dog at his feet, lapping it all up.'

Shocked, Patrick said: 'Elizabeth Dooley? She was there – on that day?' He felt angry at Brune, that she'd never mentioned it.

'I don't expect you'd remember. She wore a Burgundy skirt and a knitted jumper with a moth-hole the size of a tuppeny bit in the back. She stared at your father all day long. Sat right there!' She pointed to a chair to the left of the fireplace. 'Bang opposite him. She didn't say a word. Stared like a lovesick calf.'

Patrick felt the itch of memory fill his mind,the straining to connect. He thought of her face and how he'd known what she'd looked like when she was young . . . and the connection fused with an image of Brune here, in this room.

'HER! Yes – and she had really big black circles around her eyes, didn't she, like Uncle Fester from the Addams family!'

'That's right. She'd been like that for a few months, really run down.'

'You know they have a kid?' he asked, wondering how Christine would react.

'No! Are you *sure*?'

Patrick nodded. 'She even called him Hunter.'

'Oh, my goodness.'

'He's half her, half him. Doesn't know who his dad is. Guess he's not missing much.' Patrick shivered inside, thinking of what it would be like for his father and Brune to join forces – Brune with her lust, his father with his temper. It was bad enough living with one of them – Hunter and himself and Charlene were proof of that. Brune and Frank together would be living hell.

Christine tried to put in a positive word. 'Your father's prayer meetings were the start of the first truly Evangelical group in Barnet. He brought radical ideas with him from

America. He was a rousing preacher. He touched us all, including me, with his healing circles.'

'But he couldn't *do* it himself!' said Patrick, raising his voice, upset at the old lie. 'That's the con! He imitated people he saw on TV, but he didn't have any real healing power of his own! If you wanted healing in *my* family, you went to my mother. She had a touch. It was more than just a mother thing. She could touch you and make you actually *feel* better.'

'But she wasn't Christian . . .'

'So?' Patrick was impatient that Christine should think that mattered. 'So what? You know, every time I got stung by a bee, I went to her. She pulled out the little stinger and then sucked on the skin for a moment, then closed her eyes and put her hand over the spot and in a minute, all the pain would be gone. One time I didn't go to her, y'know, and it swolled up like a great big softball! My mom had magic. She had the touch, all right. Even Dad used to go to her for headaches and stuff, when he was too lazy to get up and take a Tylenol.'

'Maybe your father had a different magic,' said Christine. 'Maybe it was in the power of his words, in his ability to bring people to Jesus.'

'He was *jealous* of her. She was a *pagan*! She wasn't no Christian and yet she had it, she could heal, and he couldn't! I think he was so jealous it ate him up, and that fed and twisted his mind so that he turned against my mother. Heck, she was a long-ass way away from her relatives, with two little kids. If she fought with him, she kept it quiet. She didn't want us to get hurt. I bet that's why no one heard anything. She kept quiet when he stabbed her so we wouldn't come downstairs.'

There came a long silence. The words 'he stabbed her' lingered in the still air.

'Has he ever hurt you?' asked Christine finally.

'Heck, yeah.' Patrick nodded and thought about Charlene, how vulnerable she was, and wondered if his father had discovered the missing letters yet, the missing passports. 'Hell yes,' he said again.

Christine sighed and shifted on the couch. 'I want to say something about how the years change us. But I don't know how. Maybe that ability to hurt was always in him.' She cleared her throat, held her fist to her mouth and coughed. 'Well,' she said. 'How can I help you now?'

'I was kinda hoping you'd be able to say something that would connect them . . .'

'I think that a child connects them rather well, don't you?'

'. . . to the night before. That night she was murdered, down here, while we slept upstairs not knowing anything.'

'I'm sure Lizzy came late to the gathering. I'm fairly certain that she wasn't here when I arrived.'

'If she was in on it, she wouldn't hang around for Mom's body to be discovered.'

'Your father found your mother's body that night after he came home.'

'What was he doing out?' Patrick demanded, hoping for a fleeting moment that she could give him a real answer.

'Church meeting? I don't know. He must have a legitimate alibi or he'd be in prison by now. Look, I'll go home and have a think about it, shall I? Sometimes, just before I fall asleep, God gives me answers. Are you still a Christian, Patrick?'

'Not when I can help it.'

'It's not such a bad way, my dear. All we're required to do is love God and each other. That's not so terrible, is it?'

'It's the people I don't like – no offence, Ms Miles.'

'None taken.'

Christine Miles rose from her chair as stately as a hippo

surfaces, with the same slow buoyant grace. 'I've got to go now. Down on the Strand there's a homeless person in every doorway. Someone has to feed them, and if the churches don't do it, they'll starve. One lad died last week. I bent over to give him his cup of tea, touched his cheek and discovered he was dead. Mind you, last winter we went down every other night through that nasty cold snap, and I wondered *then* how he would make it through.'

She opened her arms and hugged Patrick. 'I'll be in touch,' she promised.

Patrick showed her the door and then went back into the living room, flopped himself down on the settee and stared at the chair to the left of the fireplace, a straight-backed, wooden dining chair with a red plush-velvet seat. He imagined Brune sitting in it, looking like she did in her Elizabeth Dooley days, and he imagined her in that red skirt, with black, Uncle Fester circles ringing her eyes. He set fire to the image and watched her burn, watched her melt like a wad of SaranWrap, like a doll made out of plastic bags, watched the black, acrid smoke curl above her head and stain the ceiling, smelled her poison in his nose, but mostly watched her melt, her head going first, utterly disappear into her torso until that curled back too, evaporated into smoke until there was nothing left except a little brown ball of sticky sludge, the size of a melted Rolo staining the bright red plush.

'Patrick?' called Kitsy from the hall.

He got up and went to the living-room door and stopped, turned around and looked at the chair again. But there was no Brune, no brown stain, only a red chair in an empty room full of afternoon sunlight.

Later that night, Kitsy lay in bed next to Patrick playing with his hair. She'd never seen hair like it before on a man, hair so thick it was difficult to burrow through with her fingertips and press his scalp. If she squinted, it wasn't like hair at all, but like ruffled feathers on a bird's breast – something large, a raven maybe.

While Kitsy admired his hair, Patrick worried about Charlene. He couldn't put away his growing anxiety, that he should be finished with this place, that he should be on the next plane out of London, Seattle-bound. He tried to separate the feeling from what he knew about his father, tried to look at his anxiety objectively. Would he experience this fear if he didn't think his father had killed their mother? Was it purely a discomfort at separation from his sister? Or was it a true intuition?

Patrick decided to call Charlene the next day. He'd catch her before school, before his father woke up.

'Tell me about your mother,' said Kitsy, snuggling up to him.

'Like what?' he said, putting an arm under her neck and around her shoulder, pulling her head onto his chest, distracting himself with the feeling of skin.

'Like how they met.'

'He was a missionary on the rez in the seventies. She came from a good family – tribal bigwigs, I think. I don't know for sure – he would never let us contact them. We're not allowed to speak to our aunts.'

'So you wouldn't find out the truth.'

'Or so *they* wouldn't. Mom's parents didn't want her to marry him, I know that. But she did anyway and they moved to Seattle after he finished. I think he thought he was marrying some kind of Indian Princess – his shot at royalty. She was only eighteen when she fell in love with him. He was twenty-five.'

'All he got was a scared little girl.'

'I guess. She wanted to go back home to visit during the festivals but Dad wouldn't let her. Said they were pagan witchcraft. She tried going to local salmon feasts, but Dad said to her, "What do you want to be with all them Muckleshoot drunks for? They're not your people." We only went once.'

'He actually let you *go* to something like that?'

'Well, it was part of Seafair, so I guess he thought it was only dimestore Indians. But they all came out in their regalia. And the drums – I still remember the drums. She got up to dance . . .'

'She did?'

'Yep. In her jeans and Keds, she got out there and joined the line. All the time Dad was squirming. He kept bugging us to go with him to get Cokes and hot dogs. But me and Charlene – he could've asked us to go to Disneyland with him and we wouldn't have budged. We just wanted to look at Mom. There was something magic in the way she looked. I can't describe it even though I can see it as clear as if it was happening. She's out there bending and stepping and swaying, you know, her hair swishing back and forth to the drums. I guess because it looks like she *belongs*. Even though she doesn't have a bead or feather on her you can tell she's finally found water. You can tell that she's at home. Not at our home though. I mean *home*.'

'You mean her parents on the reservation?'

He thought for a moment. 'No. I think it's more than that. It's the mountains around the place where you were born. It's the kind of thunderstorms you have – you know, they're different here than the ones in Seattle.'

'Are they?'

'Yep. It's the kind of light you get after the rain. It's the food you eat. The way people smell. The language. Like all these English accents – it gets kinda lonely after a while. And having to explain yourself when everyone at home understands.'

'I'm sorry, Patrick.'

'Why? It's not your fault.'

'No, I suppose not,' admitted Kitsy.

'Anyway, I don't want to talk any more,' he said, and touched her cheek with a forefinger, letting it ask for a kiss.

When Patrick called Charlene at three o'clock the next day, he knew he was taking a risk. He was beginning to become disconnected and those English accents, however well-meaning only made him feel more alienated, more floating. He needed to talk to his sister, to find out that she was all right, that the only person who truly shared his blood was safe.

The long pause between the first and second rings were comforting in a disembodied way, that he was connecting with a tone he'd heard all his life, that he was connecting with home.

'Hello?' Charlene asked softly. Her voice was low, with an early-morning fuzziness.

'Char – it's me. Are you safe to talk?'

'Oh my God! Patrick!' She coughed and cleared her throat. 'When are you coming home?'

'As soon as I finish up a few things. Listen, I want you to keep an eye on the mail for me. There's a letter coming for the Reverend from England. You've got to make sure you get to the mailbox first every day until it arrives, and when you do you need to open it and tell me what it says.'

'I can't call England! If he finds out, he'll kill me,' she panicked down the line.

'OK . . . Lemme see. Hold on a sec.' Patrick covered the receiver with his palm and called to Kitsy: 'What's your e-mail address?' When he'd given it to Charlene and she'd written it down, she promised to go to the school library or the one downtown and send him a message once the letter arrived.

'Another thing, Charlene. Remember the box under his bed? I want you to read all those letters and see if there are any other ones from England with signatures from a Brune or Elizabeth Dooley. Do you understand?'

'Yes, all right.' She sounded distant.

'Charlene? This is important!'

'He's coming!' she whispered and hung up. Patrick listened to black silence, waiting for the dial-tone, imagining the scene in Seattle, Charlene trying to cover for herself that nothing had happened, his father's suspicions and shouts. Suddenly the line came alive again and Frank Hunter's gruff voice swarmed into Patrick's ear, demanding: 'Who's there? Who is this calling? Patrick, is that you?'

Patrick's heartbeat accelerated, as if a starting pistol had gone off beside him, slamming its harsh report into his eardrum. With a forefinger he pressed the button on Kitsy's telephone and cut the Reverend off. He replaced the handset as quietly as he could, hoping he'd succeeded in showing that no one was there, that it had all been his father's imagination. But Patrick knew that no matter how groundless Frank's suspicion, Charlene would pay for his whim – a slap across the face, being chased around the house with a belt . . . and then there was this new idea of Frank's that Charlene should take down her panties to be punished.

It wasn't right. It was so wrong that it made Patrick feel trapped, and a lump of frustrated anger balled in his throat, that he might have caused his sister pain. What right did he have? Wasn't it enough to live in the present? Did he really need to dig up the dead and buried? But he knew the answer was 'yes'. He had been destroying himself in Seattle with the not-knowing. At least here he felt a little peace. But at the price of Charlene's safety? He hated his father for putting her in jeopardy over a telephone call.

However, there was one thing that Patrick didn't question.

He knew that if Hunter had sent the letter as he'd said, and hadn't kept the money his mother had given him to spend on stamps, then Charlene would get to the letter first. His sister was resourceful, with depths of cunning, determination, and intuition which come with years of dodging abuse. She'd cut school to find out what time the mail arrived, and then make up some excuse why she had to leave class each day at that time. She would turn her charm on the mailman, maybe meeting him on the sidewalk so that he didn't have to walk up to the house. And once his father had gone up to the church, she'd swallow her terror at going into his bedroom, and push back the door to kneel at his box. There she'd delicately go through each letter, unfolding, gently refolding, staring at the postmarks and signatures, gathering to one side what she needed, and maybe even replacing the contents with blank sheets to give the envelopes some padding so that they felt and looked the same. Then, when she was done, she would replace everything in exactly the same order, slide the box back under the bed, put every carpet crumb in its place, and run back to school to hide the letters in her locker, so they'd be safe in the awful event that her father found out.

Patrick went into the living room to give Kitsy a five-pound note for the telephone call. Thanks to her generosity, he still had most of the money he'd carried with him on the plane. Kitsy sat on the floor with Lucy who got up, toddled over to a side table and picked up a china figurine of a man and woman dancing.

'Put that back on the table, sweetie,' Kitsy told her. 'That is Mummy's precious statue.'

Lucy ignored her mother. She held the figurine over her head and gazed at Kitsy, defiant.

'Lucy! Put it DOWN!'

Lucy didn't budge. Instead she stared first at her mother,

then at Patrick and cocked back her arm, ready to throw it. Kitsy jumped up and wrenched the statuette from the toddler's fist and carefully placed it on the mantelpiece. Then she took her little girl's hand in her own and smacked the back.

'No! I said you mustn't touch!'

Lucy stared up at her mama, her source of every comfort, and began to wail. She wrapped her arms around one of Kitsy's legs and hugged it tight, tears streaming down her chubby face, her cheeks gone bright red, as if she'd been sunburned.

'Muummmy!' she bellowed. 'Uuuupp!'

Lips set in a grim line, Kitsy bent and prised her daughter off the leg and lifted her in her arms, Lucy laying her head on Kitsy's shoulder, snuffling now. Patrick stared at the little drama and it triggered something in him, a loathing at what Kitsy had done.

'Why did you do that?' he asked her, trying to hide his anger.

Kitsy felt surprised at his question. 'It was Royal Doulton. I received that as a wedding present!'

'Why did you hit her like that? Was it so important to make you hit your own flesh and blood, your own *daughter*?'

Kitsy felt taken aback. Under the unexpectedness and intensity of his question she spun out an answer. 'She's got to learn that some things you don't touch. What happens when she goes into other people's houses and doesn't leave their things alone?'

'But this isn't other people's houses. This is *her* house,' he said, icy in his anger.

'If you think you can stand there, a guest in MY house, and question the way I bring up my daughter then you can get your things together and leave.'

'Fine,' he spat at her, and found himself marching to his

room, the fiver balled in his sweating fist, to pull out drawers and unzip his purple knapsack and begin to stuff things in.

In the living room Kitsy see-sawed between two emotions: 'This is completely ridiculous,' and, 'Get this interfering little shite out of my home!'

She listened to him stomp around, slamming drawers – *her* drawers – amplifying every movement in his anger. Patrick didn't know what had hit him a few moments before, and why he'd reacted so harshly to what Kitsy had done. But he knew that her small action, which was also her right, had peeled off a scab on him and poked a dirty finger into the pus that lingered there.

Kitsy appeared at the bedroom door, Lucy on her hip.

'Stop packing, Patrick,' she said.

'No,' he muttered, his face set and square, his thick black hair flopping forward, his long black eyebrows scrunched down over his eyes. Kitsy felt keenly that she was talking to a man-child, that she would have to be calm, get to the root of what was going on.

She tried, gently: 'You've got to understand – I have to be able to bring up my daughter in the best way I know how. And that includes discipline. I have to be both her mother and father. Don't you see?'

'No.'

'Stop packing. Let's talk about this.'

'You're the one who kicked me out.' He pouted, stuffing the jeans she'd washed and folded into the gaping main pocket.

'We have to talk,' she said again, and had to stop herself from adding, 'Don't behave like a child.' She tried a different tack. 'You mean too much to me to go like this.'

'Do I? Then how could you do that in front of me when you know what went on in this house? When you know how my father treated me? Do you know my sister is probably crying right now from a beating he's given her because I called and he happened to walk in as she hung up the phone. Do you know what he *does*?'

'I didn't *beat* her, Patrick. I slapped the back of her hand. Don't you see the difference?'

'Hitting a kid's all I see. An innocent little kid who picked up a dumb piece of glass which *you* left on that table! When she's curious, you hit her!'

'But there's a difference between what I just did and beating a little kid, or your dad abusing your sister.'

'It *feels* the same!' he shouted at her, and the tears came into his eyes. He could feel the water but he fought back the drops.

Patrick stood in that room, stiff, burning, and aching with rage, his hands in fists and his stomach in knots wondering, Why? Why does Charlene have to go through hell?

He felt the rage break into tears and shouted at Kitsy: 'Go away! Leave me alone!' but she wouldn't. Instead she sat on the bed and picked up Lucy's My Little Pony from the floor and handed it to her daughter. Lucy had forgotten her crying and was fascinated by Patrick's mood. Kitsy pulled Patrick by his back beltloop, tugging at him until he yielded and sat, his face turned toward the wall at the head of the bed.

Kitsy waited. After a while she said, 'Did you know smacking is banned in Denmark? If they catch you, you can go to jail, I think.'

'Good for the fucking Denmark people,' he sulked.

Kitsy took a deep breath and held it. He was a man in so many ways, but at the moment she felt as if she was trying to bribe a nine-year-old boy out of a tree with an ice lolly.

'I know you're worried about your sister,' she offered, 'so I'll try not to smack Lucy while you're around, all right?'

'Yeah, right. So you'll take her out in the back yard or

upstairs or something and do it there instead.'

'Nooo,' she said, as patiently as she could. 'I *won't* smack her – I promise. I think you're wrong and I'm crazy to let you have your own way over *my* child, but while you're here I'll abide by that, OK?'

He turned his face to her, and she saw that his tears had broken and made single silver lines down his brown cheeks.

'Oh Patrick, I'm sorry,' Kitsy said, and her apology was not for her smack on Lucy's hand, or for their quarrel, but for what he'd left behind, and for what he still carried.

That evening, as if in respect for his mother's death, for Patrick's old suffering, for the pain he said Charlene still had to endure, they treated each other kindly. They spoke in soft voices, moving slowly, saying, 'Please,' and, 'Thank you,' for little incidences – passing the salt, rinsing a plate. Kitsy put Lucy to bed and they kept the house quiet. Patrick read an old Stephen King novel that Michael had left behind while Kitsy practised drawing a tattoo of two hands holding.

When they went upstairs to bed they lay together naked and still, skin on skin in the silent closeness in the warm summer night. As Kitsy washed into unconsciousness she wondered where her skin ended and his began until, for a moment, the difference in touch melted and it felt as if no barrier existed between their blood, muscle and bone, and sleep drowned all her wonderings.

In the two days that followed, Kitsy and Patrick took with them some of that night's quietude. The affection between them ripened and sweetened like the apples in Kitsy's tree, turning from hard little sour green golfballs into fruit. They began to be able to be in each other's company without saying anything, comfortable with the spaces between words. Patrick had never experienced that before; his High School dates had wanted to giggle, or chatter, anything not to be in that place of awkward silences. So he was able to rest and digest like the hawk, and muster the patience he needed in order to wait.

Every morning and afternoon, Kitsy would turn on the computer and get into her e-mail account. She would keep the connection open sometimes for two minutes at a stretch, but whatever arrived was junk mail, or silence, not the 'ding' of news from his sister. Patrick sat next to her, anxious, each time counting back the days and saying: 'How long does it take for a letter to get to the States?'

Each time Kitsy answered back, 'I don't know, Patrick. I've never sent one.'

'It can't be that long,' he'd say. 'How much do you think, a week? Two?'

'They don't call it snail mail for nothing.'

On the morning of the third day, something arrived with a strange mailbox address, dinging once, almost insignificantly.

'There she is,' said Kitsy, handing him the mouse and turning away to make the bed.

Patrick double-clicked on the box with the same excitement and unease he'd felt opening his report cards, hoping for a nice surprise, looking forward to reading his sister's words but dreading it too. Charlene wrote:

Dear Trick,
I took the bus to the libery down town. The leter you sed was comming did. I will try to do it for you here.

Dear Frank,
It's been simply ages since I heard from you and I wonder if you've changed your address. Your regular cheque has not arrived for the last couple of months, which leads me to query whether you have forgotten your actions all those years ago. There are debts to be paid, Frank. Don't think

*you can get away without paying for your sins, and your
sins are legion. You must pay Caesar, Frank, and if you
don't, Caesar will make you pay.
Elizabeth.*

*This has tooken me a hour to do and peepol want the
computer so I will get the lady to send it. Come home soon.*

Love,

Charlene.

'Hey, what's wrong?' Kitsy came up behind Patrick and
hugged him. She kissed him on the back of his neck. He'd
buried his face in the palms of his hands.

'I fucking don't fucking believe my fucking father.'

'What the fuck's he done?' she said, trying to get him to
smile.

Patrick raised his head and looked at Kitsy, his face open,
his long black eyebrows raised in disbelief. He said: 'You
know, there were times growing up when we were *so poor*
we ate spaghetti noodles with salt and pepper *plain* for
weeks. I wanted to join cross country in Junior High but I
couldn't because my hightops had holes already and they
had to last the winter. My sister wears *rags* to school and I
know all the girls laugh at her. But now I find out that we
weren't so poor after all. He was dumping our fucking
money into fucking Brune's house, for goddamn chrissakes!
Goddamn it, when I think about all the goddamn Rice-a-
roni I've eaten in my whole fucking life and we could have
been eating steak! And I thought his job was so low paid or
he gave all our money to the church, and all the time it was
HER! He fucking sent all our money to HER, Kitsy!'

'Oh my God,' said Kitsy, believing for the first time as

she looked at Patrick, truly believing without the littlest sliver of a doubt that Patrick's father had murdered his wife, had raised the knife, spilled the blood. That she was looking at a murderer's son as well as a boy, half-orphaned.

'Blood money,' she said, before she realised how well the cliché fit, that it was just that – blood money for Alice Smoke.

'Uh huh,' said Patrick.

Kitsy wanted to pull him out of the chair, to hold him. But she let him stay. She thought he needed a bubble of aloneness around him. A place to think.

'I have to go back to Wales,' he said, and his eyes were like circles of shale, bright, and black.

'Yes,' said Kitsy. 'I think you must.'

Kitsy found herself telephoning her mother to ask a favour. Could she drop Lucy around to spend the night with them? On the other end, Flo was the image of the word 'gob-smacked'. Her mouth parted in amazement and stayed there as she tried to think of replies to give the daughter who'd ignored her for weeks then suddenly turned up begging for last-minute babysitting. At last she said the only sensible thing: 'Well, of course you can. When will you be here?' and spent the next half-hour scurrying around her home bring-ing out clean linen, dusting and polishing in the spare bedroom and trying to remember what to feed a toddler.

As Flo let her daughter in the door, she had to stop herself from making tart comments like: '*I see you trust me when it suits you,*' and '*You'll let your daughter stay the night but you won't listen to my advice.*'

'What's the special occasion?' she asked instead after she'd put Lucy's overnight bag in the little bedroom upstairs and talked about what to give the child for her dinner and breakfast.

'What do you mean?' Kitsy tried to avoid the question, wondering when her mother would have another go about her pierced nose.

'It's not every day you ask me to look after my granddaughter for the night.' *My granddaughter*, thought Flo, and she felt like crying.

Kitsy searched her mother's face, looking for the dig, but there was only bewilderment there. She sighed. 'I'm helping a friend and I don't know when I'll be getting home tonight. If it's too much trouble . . .'

'No, no,' Flo hurried her words. 'Why would it be any trouble? She's my little Lucy, after all. Nothing changes that.'

'I know, Mum,' Kitsy said, steeling herself for a lecture.

'Do you?' Flo asked.

'Yes.'

'Then don't be a stranger. Your father broods about it. It isn't good for his blood pressure.'

'I know,' said Kitsy. They walked downstairs into the living room crowded with a yellow and green striped three-piece suite, a Welsh dresser, coffee table, side tables, dog toys, ashtrays and doilies. In the back garden, the poodles yapped in their kennels. Kitsy picked up a piece of Lucy's hair and twirled it around her forefinger, soft and blonde. 'It's just . . . I needed support when Michael left and you went behind my back and talked to him. I can only cope with so much, Mum. Looking after Lucy is hard enough. You should be on my side.'

'I'm on *Lucy's* side. A child needs both parents, even these days when so many people split up. It breaks my heart that my granddaughter won't have a proper father.'

'Mum, Michael *chose* not to be a proper father when he walked out! There was *no* reason for him to go.'

'I understood that you threw something heavy at him.'

'Mum, he made that up! Even if I did throw something at

him, which I didn't, is that a reason to abandon your family?'

'I suppose not,' Flo conceded. She stepped forward to Kitsy and put her arms around her daughter and gave her a hug. While she held her she said, 'I worry about you, that's all.' When she released Kitsy, both women's eyes were pink at the corners.

'I've got to go,' Kitsy said.

Flo distracted Lucy with a squeezy dog toy as Kitsy slipped out the front door and ran down the drive to her car, her senses full of the possibility of a new beginning.

The telephone rang as Patrick was getting ready for the journey. He answered it, a maroon bathtowel wrapped around his waist, his hair wet, black and spiky from the shower, the blood of his grandfathers showing itself in his height, in the muscles bunched at his shoulders, across his chest.

Christine Miles said: 'I've been doing a bit of phoning round since we talked, trying to make sense of what you said about your father and also about Lizzy.'

'Any luck?' Patrick didn't hold out much hope. To him, ten years was more than half a lifetime ago.

'A bit. I contacted an old acquaintance, Anthea. She was part of our little circle and great friends with Lizzy at first. According to her, Frank Hunter and Lizzy had been having an affair for at least three months before your mother's death. Apparently, when Lizzy saw your father it was like an electric shock to her, but it took a few months for him to come around. Anthea seemed to think your mother turned a blind eye.'

'Or was blinded by love,' said Patrick. 'Or helpless.'

'Quite. I have two children. I know how desperate you can feel to make your marriage work.'

'Did she say anything else?'

'She didn't *know* much else. She went to visit family in Australia about the time she realised Lizzy and Frank wanted to be a couple. She didn't hear about your mother's death until she came back.'

'She never went to the police?' Patrick pulled the telephone over to a chair and sat down, half-naked with his legs swung apart, the warmth of the day licking the wet from his skin.

'No.'

'The case is still open. She could go now – to Hornsey police station. The guy in charge is called Neal. DCI Peter Neal.'

'I'll tell her. We were remembering how they were together, Frank and Lizzy. Always plotting the next event. Always trying to out-do one another. Lizzy ever so dramatic, theatrical even. Of course, we couldn't remember really seeing your mother and father together. Your mother didn't attend many church functions.'

'That's because she was at home, looking after her children,' said Patrick, bitter.

'Of course she was.'

'I'm going to Wales today,' he told her.

'Whatever for?'

'Because I need to. Someone has to kick Dooley's butt, and it might as well be me. No one else has bothered to do it.'

'But Patrick . . .'

'Thanks, Ms Miles, for all your help,' he said, then ended the conversation. He didn't need obstacles. He didn't need people trying to dig ditches in his path.

Since he'd read Charlene's e-mail that morning, his thoughts had been entirely fixed on his mother's death and how it must have come about. What had Brune and Frank plotted in the months before Alice Smoke's murder? What did Brune hold over him, that his father had been paying her for ten years? What did she know? And what was *her* part in it all?

Patrick had walked through the day paralysed by questions. He'd followed Kitsy about until she'd remarked about her new shadow. While she dropped off Lucy at her mother's house, he wandered around all the rooms again, as if he would find the answer in one of them.

Upstairs he'd entered Lucy's room, the one he'd slept in as a boy. This was the room in the house which frightened him the most. There was no comfort of a child's happy memories here; in it he'd received the worst news of his life. Here he'd hidden in the days that followed, trying not to show his grief, trying to be a little man about his mother's death. In the times he couldn't stop the tears, he rolled himself under the bed and cried among dustballs and cobwebs until Charlene came to find him, asking, 'Why isn't Mommy coming back?' Patrick didn't have an answer for her and teased her instead to distract them both. Now when he thought of that little girl asking, he knew he wouldn't be able to tell her the truth: *Dad killed Mom because he was in love with someone else and Mom got in the way*.

There, he knew it now, standing in the doorway to Lucy's bedroom.

The connection had been painful to make and he felt blocked up, as if he should cry. Without thinking about it, he walked downstairs, his tennis shoes feeling as heavy as steel-capped workboots. He clunked into his room, the boxroom off the kitchen, and sat on the edge of the bed staring into the blue carpet.

This is where it happened.

The room should have felt bloodstained to him, but it didn't. He should have sensed the evil of his father's act here, but he didn't. His mother's spirit had dropped its

243

bones in this place and the only presence he felt in the room was hers. For Patrick alone there was a comforting, womanly feel to this room.

Patrick lay down with his head in a patch of sunshine, enjoying the sun's warm breath on his crown, his temple, his cheek. He tried to relax, slipping in and out of sleep, his mind making visions as it dipped and pulled. Finally he slept for fifteen minutes and woke suddenly with a very clear image. He ran upstairs to Kitsy's room, grabbed a pen and a piece of paper and wrote it down as best he could.

As they entered Wales, the *Wakinyan*, the Thunder Beings, rolled in above them from Ireland. Kitsy drove into the storm, towards tall black clouds pushed along as if by some croupier's stick, trailing grey tails of streaking rain. Thunder cracked and pebbles of rain bounced against the windscreen, drops so hugely pregnant that their splats left imperfect dark circles on the hot glass. Patrick felt comforted that the sky matched his mood; he felt that he wouldn't be entering Brune's house, his *father's* house, alone. The *Wakinyan* would be out there, flashing their eyes, clapping their wings in great roiling booms, sending down the storm.

While those drums beat in the sky, while those electric circuits fizzed and flashed sheets of light from the clouds, with the storm stiffening every little hair in its roots under his skin, Patrick wanted to stride up to that gingerbread-fronted monstrosity and bang on that hollow door. When Brune came out he'd make a fist and sink his hook into her jaw, watch her gasp, falling, to twitch unconscious on the floor.

But it wasn't that simple.

This time Patrick didn't try to pronounce the names on the signs. He saw them, but they seemed to him some kind of sick joke, mocking at his cheerfulness of before. He seemed to be seeing nothing but crows today, pecking at insects in the fields, flying overhead, hopping around road-kills, or simply standing in the rain and watching Patrick go by.

They parked in front of the B&B and unloaded the car in pouring rain. Once settled inside, Kitsy said, 'What do you want me to do? Shall I come with you or do you want to go alone?'

Patrick sat on the edge of the bed and stared at her, faraway, in another time and another house. During the car journey his mind had been jammed with questions, anger, and a newly formed longing for it all to be over, for his search to end and the ache that had dwelt in his heart and stomach since he'd woken up to the news of his mother's death to melt into taffy and slide to the floor like some green ectoplasm.

In a way, he'd been dreading Kitsy's question. Apart from his anger, he didn't have a plan. All he knew was that when he went back to visit Brune, it would be for the final time. Whatever information she held about his mother's death, he needed to get it out of her today. And he was afraid he was going to blow it, that he didn't have the experience, the skill, the cunning to do it right. He wished he was older. Maybe at twenty-five he'd be able to confront a situation like this and get it right. He had to go in there by himself and somehow come out with the ten-year-old secret that Brune had spun into her web, guarded in her cave with her son for a decade.

Patrick took a deep breath at Kitsy's question, then said: 'I have to go in there by myself.'

'So do you want me to wait for you here?'

'I guess. I don't know how long I'll be.'

'I don't mind. I've brought things to be getting on with. You take whatever time you need.'

Kitsy sensed the worry in him, his distance and pre-
occupation, and she wanted to help. But she wasn't going
to force herself into his affairs.

'Take a bottle of wine,' she suggested. 'As a present.'

'A present? Are you out of your mind? This woman was
my father's fucking mistress! His lover! For all I know, *she*
put that knife in!'

'Trust me,' Kitsy said. 'You don't want her to start getting
suspicious, do you? She'll really think she's got you eating
out of her hand if you take her some plonk.'

And so Patrick found himself, for the final time, raising
his fist to knock on Brune's door. In the other hand he held
the cheapest bottle of white Lambrusco he could find in
Safeway. His heart drummed in his throat. Rain licked flat
his hair. His mind wished it was over.

'Patrick!' Brune chirrupped at the door. 'What brings you
back to Wales again, and so soon? Is that for me? How very
thoughtful of you. Just like your father. Come in!'

Patrick scraped his muddy tennis shoes against a worn
and sodden 'welcome' mat. For a moment he wondered
what he was doing, willingly walking into the house of a
woman he'd begun to hate.

'We're in the Great Hall saying our evening prayers,' she
said as she walked quickly in front of him, tonight dressed
in white Ashram pyjamas and a wide white cotton belt.
Without the floor-length silk dresses she seemed shorter
and too skinny for her age.

'I'm going back to the US soon, and my friend was
coming here for one last time so I thought I'd say goodbye.'
Patrick said it to fill up space.

In the Great Hall they sat in a little ring of straightbacked
wooden chairs – Chloë, Sarah, Amos and John – which in
its smallness made the long room seem empty and huge.
When Chloë saw Patrick come in she smiled and went to

the wall for another chair which she placed between herself and Brune's chair, widening the circle.

'You all know Patrick,' said Brune as she put down the wine next to her chair and sat.

'Where's Hunter?' asked Patrick as he took his seat.

'He's in his room being punished. I caught him killing a little bird today,' she said.

'And so he must render unto Caesar what is Caesar's?' Patrick asked, deliberately needling her, half-hoping she'd understand and confront him on the spot.

'Noooo,' said Brune, staring at him. 'He broke a Commandment: Thou shalt not kill. Where would you get the idea about Caesar?'

'I dunno,' he said softly, backing off. 'Somewhere.'

'That's a different story,' said Chloë. 'Didn't you know? It's the one where Jesus is talking about the taxes.'

'Oh yeah. Now I remember,' Patrick said. 'I must've got confused.'

'I can find it for you if you want,' Chloë said, picking up her leather-bound *New Testament* and letting it fall open.

'No, don't worry. I remember. Honest.'

'Put it away, Chloë,' commanded Brune. 'Now, where were we before Patrick came in?'

'I was about to do my prayers,' said Sarah.

'Go ahead then,' said Brune.

Everyone bowed their heads to listen.

'Lord Jesus, help me to get strong so that I can go back to Bob. Help us to get Jamie back from the Social. Help Bob too and look after Jamie for me while I can't be there. In Your name I pray.'

'Amen,' said everyone, including Patrick.

When they looked up, Patrick said: 'I have a prayer too.'

'That's wonderful!' said Chloë.

Patrick felt conscious of Brune's stare as he bowed his

head with the others. She looked him all over, as if seeing him could eat him up, digest him, and know what was in his soul. Inside, part of him cried: *Pull back, don't do it!* but he was too angry to stop.

'Help me to find out who killed my mother. Help her to rest in peace. Help me to find out who did it and who convinced them to do it, so that justice can be done. And for my father's lover . . .'

The bottle of wine next to Brune's chair went spinning across the floor and crashed into the wall with a thud. Everyone opened their eyes.

'Did you kick that bottle, Chloë?' asked Brune, accusing.

'No, I never! Besides, I'm too far away to reach.' She demonstrated by stretching out her foot toward Brune's chair. 'See?'

John got up and grabbed the bottle from the floor. 'Not broken,' he reported and put it back next to Brune.

'I have a prayer,' said Amos, leaning forward on his chair, spreading his legs further apart to let his belly in between his thighs.

'But Patrick hasn't finished yet,' Chloë protested.

Brune stared at Patrick, her mouth tensed and hardened into a narrow line, her eyes small and unblinking. Patrick refused to look at her. He felt too nervous, too afraid that he'd blown it already.

'I . . . I've finished,' he said. 'It's Amos' turn.'

As Amos bowed his head along with the others, Patrick looked out from under his long black eyebrows and glanced at Brune. She met his eyes. Although he expected anger, he wasn't prepared for the hatred he found there. Brune had been coming onto him since they'd met, and this sudden reversal caught him unprepared. He broke the lock and bowed his head, closing his eyes to shut her out.

'Amen,' said the others, but Patrick hadn't heard a word.

After the Lord's Prayer, Brune stood up. 'If you'd like to have a chat, Patrick, maybe we should go to my room.'

'Sure,' he said.

The others stared at them as they left. Patrick walked behind Brune, looking down on her. As they climbed the stairs he had a sense of finality, as if he were climbing to the top of a big hill and was taking the final steps up to the scenic view. Soon he'd be able to see behind all the trees, all the houses, into the caves, past the mysteries. She opened the door to her room, and went in first. Patrick followed and closed it behind him.

This time she didn't sit on the edge of the bed trying to seduce him. This time she stood with her arms crossed in front of her chest and faced him, full of righteous anger. Beyond her window the sun had set, dimming the town to twilight blue.

'I want you to leave my house and I don't want you *ever* to come back. Do you understand? You're not welcome here. Now go.'

'No,' said Patrick. He felt every inch his height, over six foot and staring down on this middle-aged lady with her falling face. 'I know what you've been up to. This is as much *my* house as it is yours. We went hungry so that my father could pay for your heap of shit. I'll stay as long as I want.'

'John?' called Brune. 'John!'

'I've got your letter. I'll go to the police. You're an accomplice. You've been blackmailing him for years.'

'You do that,' she hissed. 'I wasn't there and no one can prove I was.'

'You were there, watching your lover put a knife into his wife. You probably even sharpened it for him!' For a moment he thought she looked frightened. '*He* can prove it, if there's a decent corner left in his soul!'

The fear disappeared and she smiled. 'He won't. That

money was for child support. It had nothing to do with what happened to your mother.'

'Child support? He doesn't even know Hunter is his kid!'

'He knew all right, from the moment it happened. He wanted to stay here and marry me, only I wouldn't take him on with a pair of spoilt brats like you and your runny-nosed little sister.'

'Doesn't the fact that he murdered his *wife* come into it somewhere?'

'No one will ever prove that.'

'I will,' asserted Patrick.

'You can't,' she countered. 'The police tried, and they couldn't.'

'You could prove it, if you wanted to,' said Patrick, desperate, casting around for any answer.

'Hah!' she barked at him. 'Why should I? He can't send me money from prison.'

'Is that what this is all about – money? My mother died so that you could have money?'

'Your mother died because your father was a fool.'

'So you admit it then. He killed her and *you* helped him!'

'JOHN!' shouted Brune.

'Is that the way you want to play it, bitch?' Patrick swung open the door and stepped onto the landing. He shouted: 'You commited adultery with my father and handed him the knife to murder my mother! Hunter is *my* father's child and *my* half-brother. You're fucking John although you don't want anyone to know about it because that's *fornication*!'

Hunter cracked his door open and slid his skinny body out. Chloë, who had been sitting with Sarah in her room, also emerged onto the landing. John's feet pounded up the stairs, running to the top where he grabbed Patrick's arm.

'Let *go* of me,' said Patrick, and kicked John in the shins, jerking his arm away. 'Listen to me, John, for your own good!'

'No!' said Brune.

John crossed his arms, curious.

'Do you really want her?' asked Patrick, opening his arms. 'You know what she did to my father? The demon-faced bitch got him so in love with her that he stabbed my mother *seven* times! And then when she saw that he was going to get *away* with it, she kicked him out because she wanted money off him for the rest of his goddamn life!' He jabbed his finger in Brune's direction. '*This* is a bloodsucking whore!'

'Take him out!' Brune shouted. 'Get him out of my house!'

'No!' said Chloë. 'He can walk himself! And me and Sarah are going with him, aren't we, Sar? You call yourself a *Christian*, you say prayers and quote the Bible at *us* who've never done anything in our whole lives – and you're fornicating with John? What kind of woman are you?'

Brune noticed Hunter listening and shouted at him: 'Hunter, get back inside your room!' The boy hesitated at the door, one hand on the knob.

'Are you really my brother?' he asked Patrick. Patrick nodded *yes*.

'HUNTER!' she yelled. The boy scooted inside, slammed the door behind him and wailed. Everyone standing on the landing could feel Hunter's cries.

Patrick looked around at their faces. 'Why do you think my name is Patrick *Hunter* if he isn't my brother, huh? Everything I've said here is the *truth*.'

'Your house is built on sand, Brune,' said Chloë. 'It's crumbling!'

'Oh, shut up, you pea-brained little bint,' Brune said. 'If you don't like my house, you can get out. ALL of you! GET OUT!'

She shut them off by striding inside and slamming the door to her room. John stared down Patrick for a moment, then turned and let himself into Brune's room.

'What on earth is going on?' Amos demanded, standing at the top of the steps.

'We're all leaving,' said Chloë. 'She's a hypocrite. A Jezebel.'

'How do you know this chap is telling the truth?' Amos asked. 'We can't take his word over Brune's when we've prayed with her for months.'

Patrick couldn't believe his ears. After all he'd been through, all he'd suffered as a child without a mother. He'd come here, found out the truth – and this fat-bearded jerk called him a liar!

He walked up to Amos, balled up his fist and stuck it in front of his face. '*I know*,' he gritted out, '*because I was eight years old and I was there.*'

Amos opened his mouth. Patrick was ready to slam his fist into the man's front teeth when John came out of Brune's room to say: 'She wants all of you out of the house in an hour. Pack up your things and go.'

'I can't believe you,' Sarah hissed at John. 'Chatting me up like that and all the time you're doing it with *her*.'

John ignored her, his face set against Patrick.

'As for you,' he said, pointing at him. 'Clear off right now or I'll kick your fuckin' arse down those steps myself.'

Patrick remembered the policeman's warning: *You so much as tip over a barstool and I'll have you deported.* He wanted to stay for a fight. He wanted to grapple with John, pull him to the floor and punch him senseless, to vent his rage in physical violence and beat him to a bloody piece of bone and meat. It was the most difficult thing he'd ever done, but Patrick made himself go to the top of the steps. Instead of running down he took each one slowly, deliberately. His legs wouldn't work right, jerking with each step, stilted, wanting to be going back up instead of down. Chloë followed behind Patrick even though he didn't want her there, and saw him to the door.

'Goodbye,' was all she said.

'Goodbye,' said Patrick, feeling they had a bond, that in some gentle way Chloë came close to what he loved in his mother. Her presence, the way she talked – they made him feel better.

As Chloë closed the door, she wanted to say a thousand things to Patrick: how brave she thought he'd been, how she wished him all the luck in the world, how she would re-member him and look for him in the men she met for the rest of her life.

Instead she trudged back up the stairs and began to pack.

CHAPTER 13

Walking in Sunlight

He didn't know where he was walking. Night had fallen in Abergavenny and a huge white moon sent silver shadowlight over the Welsh town. He didn't want to go back to the B&B. It felt too much like failure, like unfinished business. He'd gone in to weasel information out of Brune, and he'd nearly ended up with John's dusty bootprints on his butt. Feeling deeply inadequate he headed away from the lights, out of the town and onto a lane with a ditch for a shoulder.

He walked on the tarmac without thinking, empty of emotion for the people he'd left behind. He truly didn't care if he never saw any of them again. Chloë, the only person he'd felt connected to, would grow, change, get older and follow her own vision of how life should be. While Patrick hoped it was a good life, he didn't feel concern about it, like he felt for Hunter.

That little boy had nothing and Patrick felt responsible to him, as if he needed to steal Hunter from his mother's house and bring him on this journey.

It's impossible.

Patrick thought of his own mother, how she used to lead him and Charlene around the back yard singing. 'We'll have a parade,' she'd say, and give Charlene a saucepan and a

beater from the electric mixer to bang as a drum. Patrick
had the grey cardboard tube from the kitchen towels and
Mom would pretend to blow a trumpet, fists lined up in
front of her mouth, toot-too-looing. They'd march, high-
stepping in the grass and dandelions, singing about Humpty
Dumpty and how oats, peas, beans and barley grow.

In Kitsy's house, Charlene would stand on a chair to
reach the counter so she could help her mother stir batter
for fry bread with a long wooden spoon, before patting it
into rounds. Then Alice would stand at the gas cooker and
sizzle the bread in hot oil. When each round was golden-
brown like a doughnut, she'd drain it on a paper towel and
toss both sides in a dish of cinnamon sugar.

It was a snack before dinner – a dinner that they would
eat without Frank. Patrick remembered his father coming
indoors late and grumpy. Charlene got his only smiles and
Patrick had felt bewildered about that.

Looking back on those scenes, a discovery flashed out of
his mind's darkness by the spark of Hunter, Patrick asked
himself: *What was the Reverend doing working late? It wasn't
that kind of job.*

Elizabeth Dooley, came the answer.

In those days his mother slept in. That was part of the
comfort of England. Patrick and Charlene would wake up
early in the strange house. Alice would put them in the
double bed – where Kitsy's bed was now – while she fixed
Frank breakfast and sent him off to his daily rounds of
whatever. Then she'd go back to bed with the children,
putting herself in the middle, lying down on top of the quilt,
the children snuggled up and warm until everyone woke up
enough to play tickle fights or push off the bed. It wasn't
the kind of thing he imagined that other mothers did with
their kids. Other moms had their hair wrapped up in towels
and one hand in their make-up boxes. Other moms dove

for the coffee and cigarettes, sitting their kids in front of cartoons until they had enough energy to give orders.

I had the wonderful-est, bestest mom in the whole world and that woman had her killed so that she could sit like a tarantula in a big old house feeding on passing grasshoppers for the rest of her life.

He hated Brune. He hated his father too, but most of all he hated Brune. Sheer manipulative selfishness had made Brune plot to erase the mother who had loved him so well. At least if his parents had divorced, his mom would've had custody. He and Charlene would still have two parents, and Frank might not have sent his life's wages to England. They might have been comfortable. Brune was right: his father *had* been a fool, stupid enough to believe Brune's love-talk, stupid enough to fall for whatever marshmallow promises she'd held out on her dainty little stick. But it all burned, charcoal black. Brune was the manipulator, his father the fool, and Alice Smoke the victim.

Patrick turned around and began to walk back to town. He stepped automatically, lulled into a daze by his thoughts and the steady motion of his long legs. He thought about the night it had happened, and the corner of a memory appeared. Patrick tugged at it – hadn't he caught sight of his father's face, like a stranger's face, the face of a person who had put himself outside the law? Suddenly, he saw his father as he was on that night. Patrick himself was standing on the middle of the stairs (going up? going down?) and his father had half-turned, startled, not expecting a noise. His father wore nothing but a tank top and briefs, red paint sticking to the hair on his arms, red paint on the white tank top. Only it wasn't red paint. His father hadn't been painting, had he?

Patrick followed where the memory led: his little-boy self had known he had to go back to bed. He turned around and walked upstairs in his PJs and bare feet. He lay in bed staring at the ceiling which wasn't a ceiling any more, but people walking in clouds, standing upright and walking towards him, a whole crowd of people walking with a purpose. And then, there was only one person left – Charlene – and she was pleading with him, both her arms stretched out to him.

At the edge of the black road, Patrick stopped and sat down. The road absorbed him, dark and warm, bundled him into the night as he wrapped his arms around his knees and cried. He sobbed for the memory, and what he'd known. Tears wet the knees of his jeans and his nose ran as he hugged himself and let out the awfulness of what that little boy had seen but kept trapped inside himself through all those unbearable years.

I did wake up that night.

He *had* woken up, but didn't understand what he'd seen. Until now.

Patrick started back to town. His walk changed to a jog and then a steady, loping run. He ran down the middle of the lane until a car came, and then he'd run in the ditch until it passed. Cars slowed, their drivers alarmed at this tall young man running toward their high beams, but he didn't slow down for them. The running focused his mind, gave him a new purpose.

At Brune's house, he scaled the garden fence and swung over to an oak tree, climbing up through the darkness to straddle a broad branch outside her bedroom. He pulled a jack-knife from his back pocket and set to jimmying open the sash window. He wished he could bust through, protect his fist with a T-shirt and punch a hole in the damn glass. But that would defeat his purpose of stealth, give her a warning. Instead, he shoved the knife's shortest blade deep into the dry, crumbling wood and coaxed the window up. She'd left it unlocked. Of course – who would want to break into a house so obviously tumbling down?

Balanced on the limb and with all the skill of a gymnast, Patrick lifted his body up and over the sill. He knew which room he was in. In the moonlight he could see one body sleeping; by dawn his revenge would be complete.

Patrick stepped to the bed with the knife in his hand. He contemplated her throat; it was like the white throat of a kid goat, the white throat of a calf, of a foal. What he wanted to do was offer her a merciful way to die. It was his duty as his mother's son to take his revenge, even if that revenge came in the night.

Patrick thought about the stories he used to read, of raiding parties, of revenge for death, of stealing horses. He wondered what anger of fate had put him here, the law cuffing his hand, breathing at his back in its husky wheeze – *better not, better not, we'll getcha, better not.* He wished he were in a different time and place, in a world where the tribe defined the law and you lived and travelled and answered to the tribe, and everyone a cousin or uncle or grandfather in your band.

He unclicked the largest blade. The sound rounded the room like the stinging tick of a clock. Patrick stepped closer to the bed, moving slowly, a t'ai chi dancer. Brune breathed heavily, almost snoring, her head lolled toward him, eyes closed, her face already a death mask. Now his hand was so close to her throat that its shaking threatened to begin the job for him.

Maybe it was that he'd done too much, never shook off the jet lag, his food poisoning. Brune in her bed, her face bleached by the moonlight, retreated like a TV on a trolley. In front of his eyes a vision took over his sight and his mind.

Now he stood on a pier in Seattle, the day brighter than yellow, sun-dappled water slapping against the pilings in a small swish-swish song. Patrick stared at two sets of train tracks that veered away from each other: one toward himself, the water and the west, the others away from him – east toward the mountains.

Patrick looked to the tracks running west and saw himself, as if he watched the scene on closed circuit television, cover Brune's mouth with his hand and jab the knife through her larynx like he stabbed a pumpkin. But the cut to the throat wasn't enough. She opened her eyes and tried to breathe, tried to scream, and he had to stab her with the little blade again, again, soaking his hands and forearms with her blood. When she was dead he legged it over the window, dropped onto the tree and swung to the ground, found Kitsy and convinced her to drive him to London. Then Patrick saw DCI Neal at home on the sofa watching the news. Neal's right hand picked up a receiver, raised the telephone to his ear, and his lips moved. Patrick knew that call would get him.

He saw Charlene next, truly on her own, barely scraping through, like a goose shot in the wing, limping through life on scaly land-bound legs. He sobbed, felt the wet on his face, not for what he had done (he refused to feel guilty for acting like a man), but for Charlene left alone and his helplessness in a British jail. Over his sister's head there hung a knife, as if it dangled tied to a fishing line, and that knife twisted like a spinner on a hook.

Sloppy with tears Patrick turned his face away from the westward tracks. He looked to the east and saw the back of himself, the back of Jimmy Mac's black leather jacket. Completely covering the middle of it, like the centre of a target, swarmed a red and yellow beaded rosette of the sun. Then Patrick was driving in a black sub-compact toward the Cascade Mountains through forests of spicy evergreens, tall, proud trees lining the windy highway, driving in their shadows towards a somewhere home.

When he came to himself, saw the knife shaking across Brune's throat, he pulled it away, slowly, deliberately, as if his hand moved through mud. He snapped the blade shut, stared at the knife's brown casing, and put it back in his pocket. Instead, he took a hair from Brune's pillow and wound it around his forefinger as if to say – *I was here, I could have done it.*

He eased himself back out the window and dropped down into the garden. His heart beat hard in his chest, so loud to him he worried it might wake the house. On his hands and knees, Patrick crawled to Hunter's lilac bush and slipped into the boy's fort.

He listened. No noise, no movement from upstairs. He felt around his half-brother's small possessions, and wondered how to leave him a message. He would never be able to forget Hunter's sobs if he didn't leave a goodbye.

There was a little tin box, and in it something that felt like chalk. He held it up, the whiteness of it glowing like an oyster shell in the silver light. Praying for good weather, Patrick returned to the house and chalked onto the red bricks: *Goodbye, little bro. If you ever need me* . . . Then he wrote Kitsy's address in London.

Putting the chalk back in its tin box, Patrick knew he was saying his final goodbye to that place. He climbed over the garden fence and walked back to the B&B, wishing that he could somehow turn off his brain and not think again for the rest of the night.

At the B&B's front door Patrick dug deep in his front pockets for the key Kitsy had given him, and let himself in. Slowly he trudged up the narrow stairs to their room, unlocked and pushed the door open into darkness. Kitsy sat up in bed.

'Patrick?'

'Yeah,' he said as he closed the door.

'Are you OK?' She switched on the bedside light.

He didn't answer. Instead, he stared at her propped up on one elbow, revealing her naked and tanned shoulders, a single cotton sheet covering the lower halves of her breasts, falling to outline the cola-bottle curves of her waist and hips and the stretch of her legs. Without turning his back Patrick stripped off his shirt, his jeans, jockeys, socks and shoes. Kitsy pulled down the sheet to let him in.

He slid down beside her, facing her. As soon as she pulled his chest to hers, wrapped an arm behind his back, she could feel the tension there. His back muscles were long and hard, smooth twists of marble under his skin. The tension came to her, like a wave, and went through her, calling up the confusion that worked in her mind while she had waited for him. The evening had been long, and full of longing. She hated not knowing what was happening to him, why he was staying out until gone midnight. For most of the time she had sat in the room's wicker chair flicking TV channels, unable to settle her mind to concentrate on anything. She worried, but the worry was more of an intense desire to participate.

As they began to kiss, to explore, the tension between them came out in aggression. They didn't speak. They were almost rough, pushing at each other's mouths. Kitsy nipped at his neck with her teeth. Patrick pulled away and bent to shove her down with the top of his head, hungry with his mouth at her solar plexus, her breasts. She rolled at him, using all her weight to force him over and pull herself on top, crashing into him straddled, bringing him up and in with a silent thud. He drew his breath sharp between his teeth, and then bucked her, forcing her to an, 'Ahhhh.'

Their silent, private fight took them to the bed's edge. As they were about to fall, Patrick put one foot on the floor and sat up. Kitsy wrapped her legs around his back. He stood and she felt totally given over to him, completely carried and exhilarated, as if she existed on a single point. Carrying her in a bear hug, Patrick sat her on the edge of the vanity dresser and began a slow beat. Kitsy pressed her palms behind her, flat onto the wooden tabletop, swinging in to meet him, faster, faster until he felt the room spin under his feet. When she felt him at his edge she tightened her legs to pull him in completely, allowing herself to finally widen her pulsing into detonation.

He released, and like a toy soldier with a parachute, floated to the ground, exhausted, naked, unable to locate himself, feeling all of himself in the rush of his testicles, feeling himself gone out of himself but still in her, a bit lost to himself, gone.

Unseparated, he swung them over to the bed and crashed down on it. Wrapped together, their stomachs running with the same milky sweat, they held each other and slept, gradually separating themselves as they settled. At 3 a.m. Patrick woke her up and they made love again, Kitsy half-dreaming. Somehow, she was perched high up on a rock surrounded by water where no one could reach her. Patrick stood on the shore. Then she was writing, *Patrick, I love you*, on his chest with a blue biro. She wanted so much to say *I love you* but she knew she mustn't. She thrust it into him instead, biting it into his smooth brown skin.

Kitsy felt she would never again be Michael's. She had given to Patrick a piece of herself that Michael had never been able to shake into life. Patrick had put his mark on Kitsy, and she liked it that way.

The next morning's drive back to London enclosed the silence of contentment. Conversation stopped. Sometimes they held hands or kissed at red lights. In the night before, their bodies had spoken to each other everything they'd wanted to say.

While Kitsy fetched Lucy from her mother's, Patrick called Charlene in the US.

'Hello?' she answered.

'Char – it's me. I'm coming home soon. I want you to get ready.'

'You are?! Oh my God! You don't know what it's been like without you! Did you get the letter OK? Was it right?'

'Yep, I did. Listen, I want you to pack. Put in everything that you want to take with you. We're not going back there ever again, so make sure you got it all, understand?'

'When will you get here?'

'As soon as I can.'

'What day are you coming home?'

'In a coupla days, that's all. I got just a few more pieces of business to take care of, then it's see-ya-later time. All right?'

'Right.'

'See ya, Char.'

'Love you.'

'I know.'

After he came off the telephone with Charlene, he went into the room where his mother had died, opened the window and sat on the floor. He knew that what he was about to do might not work or be exactly right, since his mother had never had time to teach him properly about her ways. Still, he felt drawn to the act he was about to perform. He *had* to do it.

Pulling out a sheet of aluminium foil which he'd made into a circle the size of a dinner plate, Patrick rolled up the edges so it was like a big ashtray and laid it on the carpet. On the foil he placed four small piles of tobacco from a little plastic bag in his backpack, and a sprig of wrinkled-up and dried sage in the middle.

From the tight little change pocket in his jeans, Patrick fished out Brune's single hair. He struck a match and held a flame to it. The hair melted up into itself like a strip of cheap plastic, black and acrid.

'I send you away from this house, and from my family. Don't bother us any more.'

When the hair had burned into nothing, he held up the dried sprig of sage. 'Sage, you purify. Clean this room from the evil which was done here.' The sage burnt with a good two-inch flame and black smoke, sending its biting smell into every corner of the bedroom.

Then Patrick lit each pile of tobacco with matchsticks, saying: 'Grandfather, Grandmother. To the West, for guidance and protection. Please guide Mom safely, and protect her on her way. To the North for purification. Please purify Mom's spirit, and this room from the evil and murder that was done here. To the East, for new beginnings, that Mom can be free to start over where she is; that Charlene and I can start over too, and Kitsy. To the South for healing, that we all can heal.'

When Patrick finished, he took the charred bits of tobacco and sage out into the garden. He scattered them into the summer breeze and whispered: '*All My Relations.*'

'Apparently, he phones her all the time. I never knew my mother had this secret relationship with Michael. You'd think if he was that keen for us to get back together, he'd phone *me* instead of my mum! Maybe he likes her better.'

'Maybe,' said Patrick, stabbing a piece of lasagne with his fork.

'He *still* maintains that I threw that cup at him. She thinks I've got these temporary insanity blackouts. Can you believe that? He's convinced my own mother!'

'Hold on, will you?' asked Patrick. They were sitting in the kitchen eating a late supper. Earlier in the day they'd been to the police station to see DCI Neal. Patrick talked for an hour to the officer, telling him what he'd found out about his father and Dooley, promising to send a copy of Brune's letter to Neal when he got home. Patrick had asked about the crime scene as well, what the DCI remembered about that night. Neal had suspected Frank all along of the killing, but had never had enough evidence to convict him. He felt sad as he explained to Patrick how there still was not enough evidence to warrant his father's extradition, let alone a trial. But as Patrick heard the story of that night from a policeman who'd seen his mother's mutilated body, it made real what he had cached under his mind. Now that he knew the truth, that he'd dug it up, laid it out, and confronted what he'd found, there would be no more need for nightmares.

Patrick pushed back his chair from Kitsy's table, went to his room and searched for a scrap of paper, an envelope torn open and flattened out. He brought it back to the table, re-reading his scribble.

'What's that?' she asked.

'It's this really weird dream I had the day we went to Wales. I fell asleep, and . . . the images were so clear. My mom, you, Michael . . . all of you were here in the house, only it was now, like she was still alive and you all lived together.'

'So what's it say?'

'You know when a dream is like watching TV but the moment you wake up someone switches it all off and you don't remember? I got this sentence, and I wrote it down. That was all I could get. Um: "*With a cup I made a space for my son*".'

Kitsy felt herself go cold, as if Alice Hunter had stroked a chill, dead forefinger in a single mark along her neck.

'You mean *she* did it? Your *mother* threw the mug at Michael and broke up my marriage?'

Patrick frowned, not liking the idea. 'Well, when you put it that way . . .'

'It's just a dream, right? I mean, you didn't do the ouija board and she came out with this, am I right?' Kitsy said, pressing him hard, angry and anxious.

'Yeah, it's a dream, but . . .'

'Then let it drop. I don't want to hear anything more about it. As far as I'm concerned, the past is past. I like living here and I don't want to sell my home because it has man-hating ghosts prowling about the place! Don't give me the heebie-jeebies, Patrick, all right?'

'OK! OK! I won't talk about it!'

'Good. Because it's hard enough living here knowing what happened to your mum. I can't even watch the *X-Files* before I go to bed!'

In the next few days as Patrick waited for his flight home, he knew that he was finished with what had drawn him to London. He felt in a strange state of relief, as if a bucket of rocks balanced on the top of his head had finally fallen off. The relief made him focus instead on his anxiety about Charlene, about how he would confront his father, what he would do when he got home. Now all he wanted to do was to get it over.

On the day Patrick left for home, Kitsy dropped Lucy next door and they loaded up to go to the airport. As she slammed the boot on the car, Patrick said, 'Wait a minute – there's something I must do. I'll be back in a sec!' and began to run up the street. He rounded the corner to Sylvan Avenue and headed toward the park. When he returned breathlessly five minutes later, Kitsy said: 'What's going on? What did you do?'

Cynthia Rosi

'The guys squatting in the stables. I owed Ronnie a few bucks. I wanted to say goodbye.'

She drove the Cinquecento down the North Circular Road to meet the M4. On the motorway as Kitsy began to see planes stacking up in the sky waiting to land, and others angling up to nuzzle into the clouds, his leaving began to hit home. She could feel a sense of impending loss, as if it were a physical thing like the knob of the gearstick in her left palm. As usual, Patrick stared silently out of the window. She wished he would say something.

Kitsy thought, There should be more, but there isn't. I don't know why. After all, we've been through *trauma* together, we've been through *bonding*. We've made passionate love together! Maybe the whole time I knew he was a passenger, and I was the vehicle. He was a man-boy passing through. I knew he didn't belong with me. He'd always been meant to go back.

I will miss him because I love him – can I at least say that? Maybe to myself, but not to him. He doesn't need any creepers wrapped around his thoughts, he doesn't need any tie-tags trying to fasten his baggie. He needs to be like a man walking on Ben Nevis into a wind, needs his arms and his legs to be free, his thoughts concentrated, doesn't need to be towing behind him a shopping trolley or a pushchair. He will always have my address, will always know where to find me.

'What are you thinking?' she asked aloud, hoping for something in his thoughts that matched her own.

'That I won't be back here for a very long time, if ever. I'm wondering how much it matters.'

At the airport they went through the ritual of parking and unloading, checking in, a last coffee and croissant before boarding. They said nice things to each other. When it became time for him to go through passport control,

Kitsy walked him there, holding his hand. She would have put her arm around his waist if it hadn't been for his backpack.

'I'm thinking about selling the diamond nose stud. It was the stone off my engagement ring, you know,' Kitsy said. Patrick glanced at her nose and the stud he'd bought in Camden Market for her.

'Nah – don't do it. The diamond is nice on you, although that one's better. What will you do about Michael?'

'He wants to come back to live with us.'

'I guess I didn't see him at his best.' Patrick smiled. 'Still, you could've done worse. My father, for instance.'

'Point taken. But Michael bottled out of being a family man. Until he proves he's able to stick around, things won't change.' Kitsy didn't want to talk about Michael.

'What are you going to do now? Get a job or something?' he asked.

'I think I'm going to concentrate on the tattoo stuff. See if I can't get some work in somebody's shop. Maybe I'll meet someone on my course and we can set up in business together. I'm really looking forward to it, getting out of the house and meeting real people again, making new friends and all that. It'll be fun. You *will* write to me, won't you? When I see you next I'll give you a free tattoo on one of those sexy arms you've got.'

Patrick laughed. 'Yeah, right – sexy arms! Let all your gorgeous friends know that, OK?!' Then he got serious. 'As soon as I get an address I'll write you. I won't be living with the Reverend.'

'At least you've got enough money so you won't have to doss.'

'I've left some for you in an envelope under the bread-board.'

'Patrick! That's *your* money!' Kitsy told him.

'I know,' he replied. 'But I've made some calls and you've been good to me.'

'Promise me, Patrick, when you take your revenge, be careful, OK?'

He smiled. She felt helpless. They stopped at the barriers. Kitsy put her arms around Patrick's neck and he held her in a hug. She stood on tiptoe and kissed him, not a full lover's kiss, but not a friend's kiss either. Kitsy wanted to cry.

'Better go,' she said.

'Yep.'

She watched him disappear through passport control, watched his black hair above the crowd until he went behind an X-ray machine, and then she stared at the X-ray machine, willing to see through it until she understood she was being ridiculous. As Kitsy walked back to punch her ticket for the car park, she felt an emptiness knowing he was gone, that it was only herself and Lucy again. At the same time, Kitsy felt as if she was starting down a new path, heading for a future that was going to be good.

Whatever happens now, she thought, two things are certain: I am stronger for knowing Patrick, and I will *definitely* be giving him that tattoo some day.

Epilogue

On the airplane Patrick tried to get some sleep but he was too tall for coach class and couldn't get comfortable in the narrow, short seats, especially cramped in next to the window. He tried not to think about what he'd left – Kitsy's warm home, her generosity, her giving nature. To a certain extent, his mother too. He was leaving a place which had evoked strong memories of his mom, even given him some new memories of her. Sitting in this plane, going home, transported him back to the journey he'd taken ten years before with Charlene and his father when the Reverend fled. Then he had been so sad, so depressed at his mom's death, that all his little kid's excitement for flying had been drained out by a keen sense of loss at having to leave the last place where he'd hugged his mother. He felt as if he was losing her all over again as his back pressed into the seat and the plane gathered speed on the runway, tipped up to a path in the sky.

Two movies and two meals later the plane banked into SeaTac, circled around Renton, over Alki Point and part of Tacoma, the islands like green gumdrops set into a sheet of ice. It looked like ice, the way the sheer water reflected the summer sun, a flat, blank mirror to the blue sky, peppered with the teeny-tiny white flecks of sailboats and Hobycats and Bayliners.

Although he didn't have much money left, Patrick rented a car at the airport and drove to Fauntleroy Avenue in West Seattle. All the familiar sights along the route home made him understand what a jump his personality had taken. It was as if in driving past these places he saw the old Patrick – the Patrick who had tried to rob the House of Appliances, the Patrick frightened of his father – a Patrick in stasis.

He'd been. He'd done. He'd come back to do more.

Patrick parked a block away from the house, left his backpack in the trunk. He walked through the alley until he stood at the back gate of his father's rental. *I'm back and it seems like I haven't been away*. He remembered when he'd come back from the bus depot, scuffing along and full of his small-boy's adventure. How the house had looked the same and he felt completely different. *It's the same now, only this time I don't have to fit in. This time there'll be no belt, no Leviticus.*

He pushed open the gate, dropped to his hands and knees, and crawled behind a rhododendron bush, keeping low and close to the wooden fence. At the window to his room he stood to his full height and peered in, half-expecting to see his father sitting on the lower bunk waiting for him. But there was no one there. Charlene had made the beds; the floor needed vacuuming but she'd picked up the clothes. He could feel his sister's presence in the house.

He sidled up to the kitchen window, stood to one side of it and glanced in. For a moment he felt a flutter in his stomach, as if he were about to peer in at himself on the day he'd tried to commit suicide. But instead of the knife and the blood, Charlene sat at the kitchen table drinking Shasta grape and reading a trash romance. Patrick thought two things at once: *She has to be alone or else she couldn't read that book. Has Charlene always been so thin?* Her bony shoulders stuck out like apples underneath her white T-shirt, her chin pointed, her cheekbones protruded. Patrick tapped on the window with one fingernail. Charlene looked up, alert. When their eyes locked he felt so happy to see his sister again. She smiled and threw down the book and ran out of the house, the screen door banging behind her.

'Patrick!' she shouted as she flew down the stairs to hug him.

'Hey! Don't break me, all right!' he said as he hugged her too, laughing and lifting her off the ground.

'I'm all packed like you said.' She stood back from him, then stared him up and down, now all seriousness. 'You've put on weight.'

'And you've lost. Isn't there any food in the house?'

'Food? Get real. You know what *he's* like. Mostly I eat school lunches. I'm sick of pasta twizzles. God, he's been weird while you've been gone. When he's not pestering me about where you are, he's got the television on full blast on the 700 Club and the ghetto-blaster going too, always on country stations. I'm sick of country. I hate it.'

'He hasn't done anything to you?'

'He beat me up twice. It would have been three times but I locked myself in the bathroom. He kept hitting the door and I thought it would break. I climbed out the window.'

I'll kill him! thought Patrick. *Get it over and done with on the back lawn with a nice sharp knife. Ear to ear. A death smile.*

'When's he coming home?' he asked.

'Any time. Save Yourself for Jesus has almost finished now. Can you believe he wants me to do it? The whole ring shit, that marry me off to Jesus until I find a man bullshit. Can you believe that?'

'Well, it ain't happenin'. Listen up, Charlene. I've parked

a black Nissan – it's one of those real small hatchbacks –
down at the horseshoe. Here's the keys. Fetch your stuff
and go get in the car. Lock the doors and wait for me, OK?
I've put the car out of the way but I want you to lay down
on the seat.'

Charlene took the keys. Her fingers were thin and bitten
down at the tops as if she could really get nutrition from her
nails, bitten pink to the quick and ragged at the skin. Patrick
couldn't remember how they were before, but he knew they
weren't like *that*. She ran into the house and he followed
behind, looking down at her back, the vertebrae poking up
bumps through her T-shirt where it settled on her spine.
Her jeans hung loose on her hips, rode down so she always
had to be hitching them up, her bitten-down thumbs in the
beltloops, otherwise the crotch fell halfway to her knees. He
could see why she got teased, why she looked geeky, a waif.
He felt truly protective towards her, that she was somehow
precious.

'What about Mom?' Charlene called to him from the
bedroom. 'What'd you find out that you couldn't tell me on
the phone?'

Patrick wondered what he should say. Should he give
her the burden of truth? Wasn't it nicer to think Mom
had died peacefully, not to stain Charlene's memory with
the blood of what really happened? To keep from
Charlene the burden of hating the Reverend completely?
Now maybe there was a shadow of love for him in
Charlene. Maybe that shadow had to be destroyed, but
did he have the right to destroy it? Patrick looked out of
the window as he thought, as if the blue sky and trees
held some answer.

'He's coming!' shouted Patrick. His father was crossing
at the corner, walking up the sidewalk.

Charlene appeared in the hall lugging an enormous duffle

bag which looked as if it weighed twice as much as her, bulging like Santa's sack.

'What the fuck is that?!' shouted Patrick.

'You said get my stuff.' She looked at him, hurt.

'I didn't know you had so much!'

'It's my books! I can't go without them!'

'OK – look, I'll bring your shit. Just get the hell out of here, all right? *Go!*' he yelled.

Charlene turned around and ran into the bathroom. He heard her lock the door and the window slide back. Good.

When Patrick had imagined this confrontation with his father, he imagined himself waiting on the couch with a belt in his right hand, the heavy brass buckle pressed into his left palm, the shank sharp and poking white into the callus at the base of his middle finger. Instead, he stepped into the kitchen and hid behind the doorframe. He waited until Frank had come inside, yelled, 'Charlene!' and flopped down in the hairy old easy chair with the remote control in one hand. Then Patrick came out. His father looked up. The whites of his eyes had gone yellow, like an old dog's. His beard was unevenly shaven, missed entirely in patches leaving grey stubble. Like Charlene, his father had changed.

'Where you been? 'Cos you sure as heck didn't go to LA.'

'That's right. I didn't. I been to see your lover. Remember her? Elizabeth Dooley in England.'

His father lurched to his feet and threw the remote control on the chair. Patrick looked down on his father, like the Reverend was the one who had to take it now, whatever Patrick dished out.

'You know, Reverend, I don't understand what she saw in you. I can't believe she'd ever fuck such a mess.'

Frank swung a fist, shouting: 'Don't you talk to *me* like that!' Patrick caught the fist in his palm and pulled it to him, twisted his father around and forced Frank's fist up his own back. With the other hand he grabbed a hunk of hair. The sweet smell of vodka pillowed over Patrick's nose. It shocked him, to know his father had hit the bottle, but not enough to make him stop. He considered that dirty throat, considered the brown-cased jack-knife and its little weight in his back pocket, stared at his father's jugular vein pulsing to an acid-house beat.

'You know what else?' Patrick hissed as he pulled tighter on the slick hair and forced the fist up another half-inch. Frank moaned. 'I found out about your kid. Little *Hunter*.'

His father struggled to bend over, to twist out, shouting, 'Aaaah!' but Patrick wouldn't let go. He hadn't finished.

'You killed my mother, you fucking pig!'

'Did she tell you that?' shouted Frank, his head tilted back as far as it would go, his throat bare and taut.

'She didn't have to!' Patrick shouted back. 'It was so *obvious*!'

Every hair follicle on Frank's throat stood up so the sight of it was a temptation to Patrick, that he should meet violence with violence.

'I didn't!' Frank squealed.

Patrick shoved his father away, raised his foot and kicked him as hard as he could. Frank flew and sprawled spread-eagled to the floor, his head cracking against the kitchen doorframe leaving a violent message of skin, blood and hair.

From the floor Frank stared at his son. 'I should kill you,' growled Patrick. He kicked Frank, whacked him with his instep like he was sinking a soccer ball into goal from fifty yards back.

Frank doubled up into himself, groaning in pain. 'Ah ahh, you little shit! You little bastard! Son of a bitch!'

Patrick heaved Charlene's duffle bag over his shoulder and stared at the yellow eyes, the ragged stubble, the bloody spot on his father's head; he wasn't going to stand here chatting to a dog. He'd said what was said. There was no more.

He started for the door, not bothering to run. He walked out and down the steps. At the bottom he heard a crash and glanced back to see his father standing in the doorframe, a knife in his hand and a look on his face that said Frank had been here before.

The knife turned over through the air like a flying axe. Weighed down by the duffle bag stuffed with clothes and books, Patrick tried to duck. He fell over, heard the knife clatter and the rush of feet, his father bearing down on him, intent on picking up the knife sunk up to its hilt in a clump of dandelions.

They dove for it at the same time, but Charlene got there first. She unsheathed it from the dirt and stood, holding the knife stiff in front of her like a small sword.

'Unless you let me and Trick go, I'm gonna poke out your eyeballs and cut off your ears,' she told Frank.

'Give me the knife, Charlene,' said Patrick.

Her voice went hysterically high: 'Uh uhn. I'm going to cut him into a thousand teeny-tiny pieces and stuff him down the drain!' Charlene's eyes glazed hard and her voice changed. 'Go back into the house, Frank,' she said. But through Charlene, Patrick and Frank had heard Alice Smoke speak: 'You don't *have* a family any more.'

Then a sound came out of Frank they'd never heard before. He snuffled and groaned, then began to sob, covering his face with his hands. He bent over and fell to his knees rocking on the lawn, trying to give himself the comfort that his mother gave him when he was first born, rocking, rocking. '*I didn't mean it!*' he shouted into his palms. '*She tricked me! Lizzy tricked me! Can't you see? You got to believe that!*' His sobs turned into crying. Tears wet his palms, slid out between his fingers and onto the back of his hands, little wet trails of his grief. '*I've always loved your mother. I still love her goddamn it!*'

Patrick took Charlene's free hand and backed up towards the stairs. With each step they took, Patrick and Charlene wondered if Frank would stand up and rush forward, throw himself at the knife. But he stayed curled up on the lawn, crying, pouring his years of pain into the grass and summer-dry dirt.

Patrick took the knife from Charlene's hand and laid it on the bottom step. No more knives in that string of knives. This one would be the last.

Gripping each other's hands, they hurried down the block to the parked car. As they went they heard him shouting: '*Where are you going! Come back here! I'll have you arrested, Patrick! You got to believe me, I didn't do it! Come back!*

'*Charleeeeene! You got to believe meeeee . . .*'

They stopped at a gas station and bought a US Highway map, Coke, Doritos and Hostess HoHos.

Well, it's not as if Charlene's on a diet, Patrick thought as she scarfed down the HoHos and most of a bag of chips. He wondered when she'd last had a decent meal. Tonight they'd stop at a camp grounds near the Yakama Reservation and he'd buy her the works at Dennys. It might mean sleeping in the car every night, but he wanted her to fill out a little before they got to Winner.

Charlene didn't say much until they were well into the Cascade Mountains heading east on I-90. She touched the sleeve of his leather jacket.

'Where are we going exactly?' she said.

'South Dakota. First we'll try to find any of the Smoke family in Winner. If we don't have any luck I guess we'll have to go to the reservations.'

'Do you think they'll take us in?'

Patrick hadn't thought about that. He had a little bit of money left, but if he drove fast he'd get there before it ran out. Then maybe he could find a job. 'Yes, I think they will.'

'Do you think they'll let me do *hanblechia*?' she wanted to know next. 'I think vision quest is mostly for guys.'

Patrick laughed. 'Charlene, most of our lives have been one big vision quest,' he said and smiled at her. 'I don't see how anyone could stop you.'